Now I say, that the heir, as long as he is a child, differeth nothing from a servant, though he be lord of all.

St. Paul's Epistle to the Galatians 4:1

Modern Scandinavian
Literature in Translation
MSLT

Series Editor:
Robert E. Bjork,
Arizona State University

Board Members:
Evelyn Firchow,
University of Minnesota
Niels Ingwersen,
University of Wisconsin
Torborg Lundell,
University of California
at Santa Barbara
Patricia McFate,
The American-Scandinavian
Foundation
Harald S. Naess,
University of Wisconsin
Sven H. Rossel,
University of Washington
Paul Schach,
University of Nebraska–
Lincoln
George C. Schoolfield,
Yale University
Ross Shideler,
University of California
at Los Angeles

by Villy Sørensen

Tutelary Tales

Formynderfortællinger

Translated by Paula Hostrup-Jessen

Afterword by Sven H. Rossel

University of Nebraska Press

Lincoln and London

Copyright © 1988 by Paula Hostrup-Jessen
All rights reserved
Manufactured in the United States of America

Originally published as
Formynderfortællinger by Gyldendal, Copenhagen
© 1964 by Villy Sørensen

Library of Congress Cataloging in Publication Data
Sørensen, Villy, 1929–
[Formynderfortællinger. English]
Tutelary Tales = (Formynderfortællinger) /
by Villy Sørensen; translated by
Paula Hostrup-Jessen; afterword by Sven H. Rossel.
p. cm. – (Modern Scandinavian literature
in translation).
Translation of: Formynderfortællinger.
ISBN 0-8032-4185-2
I. Title. II. Title: Formynderfortællinger. III. Series.
PT 8175.S648F613   1988
839.8'1374—dc19   87-25624   CIP

"The Screamer" was previously published in *Translation* 9 (Fall 1982): 113–16.

Contents

1   A Tale of Glass
25 The Guardian's Tales
36 The History
    of a Guardianship

    Three Legends:
87 The Wicked Judas
101 Emperor and Apostle
119 The Holy Couple,
    Adrian and Natalia

122 The Screamer
127 The Boss
136 Bird in Maid's Guise
142 The Foster Daughter
155 In Strange Country
169 A Tale of the Future

231 Sources

233 Afterword

A Tale of Glass

1

Listen! Now we are going to begin. When we get to the end of the story we shall know no more than we do now, for it was the work of a dear old optician who was sitting at his melting-pot. He was in a really foul temper and, as ill luck would have it, he came to make a pair of glasses which had this peculiarity: when you peered through them anything evil and ugly immediately looked as good as anything of real value. Seen through the glasses, even boiled spinach looked like beautiful green landscapes, and people who had lost a leg in the war or had been born with three instantly looked delightfully normal. The old optician at once took a brighter view of things and began to make glasses with a will. That was the beginning of the end.

2

In the big city, which is so overcrowded that there is hardly room enough for all the houses and people, a young man and a young woman were living in one shabby little room. This was forbidden, of course, for it is not healthy for two different people to live in one and the same room; but they had moved in in secret just the same, because living in the open air was not permitted either. The young man, whose name was Gert and who was away at work all day, enjoyed coming home to his wife in the evening. But his wife, whose name was Kaja and who didn't go away to work, began to feel bored in the depressing room and to take walks in the daytime; and the walks became longer and longer and so did the journey home. What she liked best was to stroll among the finest houses in the town. It was these that lay farthest away, and she often wished she were living in one of them together with Gert. One day a young man came out of one of the houses and, when he glanced at her, she noticed that his eyes looked just like Gert's—even though the man was wearing glasses. She couldn't take her eyes off his, and, after they had been walking silently together for a while, she begged him to remove his glasses so that she could take a better look. But no sooner had he gallantly removed his glasses than they could no longer look into each other's eyes, and, affronted, they went their separate ways.

Kaja hurried home to her husband, but the nearer she got the uglier she thought the houses looked, and the next day she walked among the fine houses once again. There she met more and more young men, all wearing glasses and making glad eyes at her. One ugly day, when it was raining and blowing hard and she was soaked through and numb with cold, she was about to hurry home when a young man wearing glasses came up to her and said:

"What a beautiful day it is today. Just the right weather for a stroll!"

Kaja was about to make some angry retort, but his eyes seemed so friendly that she couldn't say a word.

"Do you like my new glasses?" he asked, since she couldn't take her eyes off them. "Here, try them yourself! Really! Try them!"

For a moment he seemed to her abominably insistent, but the glasses had such pretty lenses that she put them on and looked through them.

"Why, what beautiful eyes you have," he said, and she thought well of him too. So she didn't notice that Gert was biking past at that very moment with a windowpane under his arm (he was a glazier's mate, you see). Not until Gert dropped the pane—not exactly quietly—did she notice him, and then she rushed away from the strange man and after her own.

"Stop the spectacle thief!" Kaja heard behind her, as, with pounding heart, she ran toward home, trailing far behind her bicycling husband. She realized that she had been treading forbidden paths, and not until she reached the narrow streets did she feel at home. The old houses stood hiding her, like old friends, from her pursuers, and when she saw her own house her eyes brimmed with joyful tears of recognition. Even greater became her joy of recognition and tears of remorse when she saw her husband and flung her arms around him. But he pushed her away roughly, and she sat on the floor thinking how handsome he was when he was angry. That he had lost his job for dropping a valuable windowpane by no means detracted from her joy:

"That was because you loved me, and when the pane shattered it was as if something inside me shattered too, something hard," she said. But Gert shouted:

"Why are you wearing his glasses?"

She had forgotten about the spectacles. Gert snatched them off her—and now she thought that he had gone too far: here she was, full of love and remorse, even though he was poor and out of work! She saw his distorted mouth and screwed-up eyes and felt his rough hands nearly twisting her arms off, and began screaming "I hate you!" until he withdrew his hands in order to shield his face.

Kaja refused to be appeased. Defiantly, she gathered up the glasses and set them crookedly on her nose. Then she felt sorry for him—after all, he was out of work—and she gently took hold of his hands so that his face became visible; she could see his tears through her own. But Gert snatched his hands away in order to dry his eyes, shouting:

"Why are you wearing his glasses again?"

"Something has been the matter with my eyes," she lied, glancing down, "that's why I got these glasses. Wearing glasses is good for the eyes."

"Was he an optometrist, then?" asked Gert, who was naturally reluctant to think the worst. "Just like that, in the middle of the sidewalk?"

"Yes," she continued. "And I've been afraid to say anything, for many people say that girls don't look nice wearing glasses. But now I can see you clearly."

"Let me try," he said, stretching out his hand. She handed him the glasses—annoyed with her suspicious husband, who sat there wearing her glasses, saying:

"But they don't magnify at all, they're just ordinary window glass. I hope he hasn't cheated you."

She was about to say "I hope *you* haven't cheated me"—but in the same instant she met his troubled gaze behind the glasses.

"Why, what beautiful eyes you have," she said.

3

For quite some time now Science had controlled the experiments with the new glass, and the State had controlled the manufacture of it. Almost everyone wore glasses, and almost everyone could see that everything was good—which only God had been able to see in the beginning. Patriotism knew no bounds other than those between nations, and eventually even they faded. Glasses were exported to all progressive countries, which consequently all began to seem equally progressive.

But there were some backward countries whose inhabitants were unable to see how idyllic their conditions were—as all enlightened people could see in the films; and so, to give them a brighter view of life, glasses were exported to these too. The underdeveloped people, who were obliged to live on a few grains of corn a day, put on the glasses, and the grains looked like God's plenty. Once in their mouths the grains no longer seemed so abundant, but the world around them was more beautiful than a technicolor film. Even the sun, the destroyer of all living things, looked like the great life-giver, and so they praised life while dying of hunger.

In the progressive countries the glasses created greater problems, though on closer inspection they turned out not to be problems at all. Through the new glasses everything looked equally wonderful: couples who had previously been particularly fond of one another suddenly began to like all the others just as much. There was no longer any difference between beautiful and ugly, or between clever and stupid; equality was introduced and fraternity too. Marriages dissolved like sugar in tea: why should people stay together two by two when everyone was together with everybody else? As for the children, everybody knew that all misbehavior was simply caused by discontent, and that the coming generation had no reason to be discontent—for they wore glasses from birth.

4

Soon Gert and Kaja also had a child in their room, which was strictly forbidden; but the local health committee came, all wearing glasses, and said: "This is a fine room for three people," and went away again. Gert protested: married couples had previously been entitled to proper flats, but Kaja was pleased that the health committee had become more humane; she lay in bed wearing her glasses, thinking her tiny wrinkled child the most wonderful on earth.

"Gert," she said, "Be a love and go buy me some little glasses for little Gerda?"

"No," he said.

"Please, be a dear," she said.

"I won't," said Gert.

But Kaja just laughed and fell asleep, still exhausted from the birth.

As he had done so often before, Gert removed the glasses from his sleeping wife. He had let her keep them for the sake of peace and quiet, and from sheer gratitude she was always content and no longer complained about the small room and his meager pay. She had heard there was going to be a labor shortage in the glazing trade, for the new glass was already being used for windowpanes, and Gert, who was an experienced glazier's mate, could expect a promotion. He had told her that he didn't want to have anything to do with the new glass, but she had merely smiled, saying:

"How funny you are!"

Once again, with trembling hands, Gert put on his wife's glasses, but they still refused to augment the room. When Kaja began to stir he hurriedly replaced them on her nose, but so clumsily that she woke up, saying:

"Gert, I came to think that when you start working with the new glass you could make us some new windowpanes. The view is not very nice."

"I won't work with the new glass," he said.

"You are a dear," she said, falling asleep again.

Gert couldn't sleep. There wasn't any room for him in the bed, but he was more concerned with the fact that there wasn't enough space in the room for the child to grow. If he was to have a luxury flat—and in those times they were the only type being built—he would have to work with the new luxury glass. But everyone was blinded by the new glass—even the health committee and his own wife, who never tired of saying she was living in paradise.

And yet, how could it be a delusion when the State and Science promoted the glass and appointed the old optician Public Benefactor? In the end, Gert became so confused that he began to attend popular lectures on the epistemology of glass. Except for Gert, everyone listening wore glasses and gazed enthusiastically at the bespectacled academic, who regarded his audience with equal enthusiasm. A quantum leap in understanding had taken place, he said. Previously it had been impossible to discuss questions of taste, and so it had been foolish of certain philosophers to speculate about what might be of greater value than anything else. If it was impossible to discuss questions of taste, then questions of inherent value were only empty speculation. But now it *was* possible to discuss questions of taste, for everyone had the same taste, and the same things seemed tasteful to all. Now it was clear to everyone (and it wasn't the glasses in themselves that had made people so clear-sighted, it would be truer to say that they had cleared their sight) that everything was of equal value and so the word "value" was meaningless. And this was not only an advance in understanding but also in society. For wasn't it true, before the glass, that the élite had lost the people's unreflective view of life, professing that "the valuable" (if we are to use that expression) was what they alone saw—or rather, determined by way of reflection! But now every Tom, Dick and Harry could see that the things that everyone could see—those were the things of value!

When Gert was unable to sleep the lecturer's words kept on ringing in his ears together with the cries of his child and his wife's comforting words: that little Gerda would soon get a really sweet pair of glasses. He had always considered himself to be one of the people, and he had never realized that it was the people who could see what "the valuable" was (it was with trepidation that he thought that term). He had thought that to the people the world had always seemed so wretched that they had imagined that—oh well, that "the valuable" lay beyond this wretched world. And if the people had always had that unreflective view of life, why were they now wearing glasses? And why did everything seem so wretched to him even when he put on his wife's glasses?

Was it he whose sight was defective—so seriously defective that he was the only one who suffered like that?

Perhaps it was due to lack of sleep. He went to work in the morning not having slept a wink all night—and everything he saw made his eyes smart so that the tears ran down his cheeks. Plaster sprinkled down from the old houses, bricks fell out of their walls and killed people (much to other people's amusement), and nobody thought of repairing the houses because they looked so picturesque. Only the windowpanes had to be renewed—even before they were broken.

"Happy days!" said the glazier when Gert arrived at work one day. "Happy prospects! Here is the first batch of new panes, though I don't understand why people want them. If they're to have any benefit from seeing through them they'll have to remove their spectacles. Now, you're not wearing any—take a look at the stuff and you'll be sure to think differently of the glass!"

Gert stood with his eyes closed.

"Well, you can't very well glaze without looking, can you? Open your peepers, buddy!"

Gert was naturally thinking of his newborn child who

would never get out of their squalid room if he refused to touch the new glass. But if he took on the work he might lose sight of what was best for the child, of what was to the benefit of everyone.

"You are throwing away your own happiness! You're my best man, you could earn a fortune. You are throwing away your family's happiness. You're an egoist."

Then Gert glared furiously at his master. But the latter stood shielding himself behind a window pane, and Gert saw what he had never seen before—that the glazier wasn't an old money-grubber at all, but a kind old man who was thinking of Gert's happiness and wanted his customers to have the best. And the glass in the workshop sparkled like diamonds, and the street, which he knew so well that he never paid any attention to it, became suddenly so brimful of sheer familiarity that he had to shut his eyes in order to stand the sight of it.

"Well?" said the glazier, putting down the pane. And when Gert cautiously opened his eyes, he found the sight of the glazier disgusting, and picked up the glass and went on his way. Everywhere he went to install the panes people flocked around him shouting "hurrah," and Gert had to hold the glass right up in front of him so he could ignore how stupid they were; there was no end to their enthusiasm. When he finally got home after work the room was such a pitiful sight that he declared:

"We'll soon be moving."

"Away from our dear little room!" exclaimed Kaja. "Here where our happiness knows no bounds!"

"I've started with the new junk. We'll buy a luxury flat."

"Haven't we got everything we need? What are wealth and luxury so long as we are together? Though perhaps you should put some new panes in. It would surely improve the view."

Gert didn't answer. He thought his wife was beginning to look sick. Was it fatigue after the birth? As soon as she fell asleep, he again removed her glasses with trembling hand—and lo and behold! In her slumber she was as plump and pink as the very first time he'd seen her asleep. Tenderly, he was about to replace the glasses on her nose—when see! The tip of her nose looked as pointed as an awl, and her face pinched and pale; he threw the glasses to the side, and they smashed. Kaja woke with a cry and the child with another one. All night long they screamed, mother and child, though Kaja was the loudest—not another day would she go on living in that place.

"Tomorrow I'll fetch the new panes," said Gert. This calmed Kaja down so much that in the morning when Gert had to leave she stopped screaming. Her voice was full of tenderness or sleepiness when, bidding him goodbye, she said:

"Why, how ill you look."

5

Gert was not the only one not wearing glasses. Certainly, on his trips through town he met fewer and fewer people not wearing glasses, but the fewer there were the more customary it became for them to nod to one another. When there were almost no non-eyeglass-wearers left he occasionally met a whole band of them, and he realized that they were starting to join forces. One afternoon, on his way home, he was surrounded by such a band.

"Why do you, who are not wearing glasses yourself," said one leader, "help spread the delusion by putting in windowpanes that are of no benefit to those wearing glasses, but which are harmful to yourself and to the rest of us? Every time we see you rushing through the town with your shining glass we catch ourselves believing that it is not us but the glass that is right. Once you have passed by, and our eyes are once more filled with all this emptiness, we realize that it is you who are working the hardest against us. Think how many non-eyeglass-wearers there have been whose vision you have blurred, forcing them to buy glasses. We have discussed your case a great deal, and there are still those among us who maintain that we can continue our work only if we liquidate you."

With shaking legs, Gert walked surrounded by so many non-eyeglass-wearers that he could scarcely have fallen. All the people they met wore glasses and indulgently poked fun at the non-eyeglass-wearers, as if they had been children. The children were more malicious—they pointed at them, screaming "They haven't got any glasses on!"

But, unaffected by the surroundings which the darkness had now begun to hide, the non-eyeglass-wearers went on accusing the glazier's mate. One of them thought he could speed the process by frequently giving the accused a good push in the back.

"But perhaps it is only the weakest among us who think that," continued their spokesman. "Or maybe we others have a weakness for you because we have seen you so often through your own glass. One thing we can say in your defense, however: to judge from how our own eyes swim when we see your glass and the new panes all the houses will soon be glazed with, always compelling us to lower our gaze—then you, who have to face all this vanity every day, must have a strong character not to be wearing glasses yet. So we will let you choose: do you want to be liquidated, or will you give up your work and start on ours?"

Gert almost felt it was cowardly not to let himself be liquidated; however, he also found it much too heroic to die for the sake of other people's point of view.

"I have a wife and child," he said, letting it rest at that.

The non-eyeglass-wearers smiled among themselves: "Without glasses you don't keep a wife and child very long. Wives and children can't resist the temptation of wearing glasses, and no sooner do they put them on than they can no longer see that their husband and father is a better husband and father than all other men."

"My wife isn't like that," said Gert, and the non-eyeglass-wearers, a few of whom were young women, laughed at his words. He himself was unable to laugh; he knew they were right, though he knew he was too. Kaja was not like that; it wasn't as if she considered other men just as good as he was when she put her glasses on—no, only when she had them on did she think him good enough. What he had experienced of married strife since he had snatched her glasses off exceeded anything of that nature he had ever experienced. It had helped a little when he put in the new windowpanes, but now Kaja hung around the window all day long, turning her back on the room which they were, after all, living in. And to little Gerda, who was also in the room, she no longer paid any attention.

"Well?" asked the non-eyeglass-wearers.

"But I need a new apartment," confessed Gert. "Mine is so wretched that my child doesn't thrive. When my wife is wearing her glasses she says that it is growing healthy and strong, and when she isn't wearing them she can't stand the sight of it. If we moved to a better place, she wouldn't need glasses!"

When the non-eyeglass-wearers didn't answer Gert looked so desperate that the passers-by could see it in the dark through their glasses. They laughed loudly at the non-eyeglass-wearers, saying "Look, they're playing!"

Gert turned and walked homewards. The non-eyeglass-wearers made no attempt to stop him, but followed him like a bodyguard—or, thought Gert, like a funeral procession.

"He's thinking," they said, shushing each other.

At length they arrived at his door. Gert walked slowly up the stairs, the conspirators following behind him with such heavy steps that the old staircase writhed beneath them. As always, the sound of a child crying came from inside the room, though louder than usual. Gerda was alone in the room, standing beside the window-sill and beating on the dark panes. Gert seized the child, but the conspirators came in backwards, smashing their elbows through the panes. As they shattered and tinkled down into the yard, Gert thought of the day when it had all started—when he dropped the windowpane and was fired for the first time. This time it was merely repetition.

"Are you with us?" said the spokesman for the non-eyeglass-wearers. Gert stood with head bowed so low that there was no need to nod.

6

People gradually began to realize that the non-eyeglass-wearers wanted to be taken seriously, and they found this even more amusing. A small group of them assembled in front of the monument to the old optician in the main city square in order to make speeches. The square was soon full of spectators who laughed loudly at the speakers, who despite their youth seemed like relics from a far-distant past. But whereas the Revivalists of the past (whom the oldest among them still remembered) preached that people had to suffer on earth in order to be blessed in heaven, the non-eyeglass-wearers only said that people had to suffer on earth. Some of them even said that people *did* suffer on earth, and they said this to an audience who felt better than ever before. And who were these speakers? Were they philosophy graduates? No, one of them was a former glazier's mate, and he was saying:

"Were you satisfied with life before you started wearing glasses? No, you were not—not if you think it over. Well, has anything changed? Yes it has, but not for the better. Have houses become better houses because you think they look better? Are children raised better now because their mothers leave them? Have you yourselves become better because you have a better opinion of yourselves? Why do you like things that are bad? Because you won't recognize that they're bad, because you are wearing glasses!"

"Hear! Hear!" roared the crowd, launching into such prolonged clapping that the glazier had time to stop and think, though he couldn't think of anything else to say anyway. Staring into the twinkling glasses of his audience had made him confused, and he got down from the platform shaking his head. But when the audience went on clapping as if they wanted to hear more, yet another non-eyeglass-wearer jumped up on the foot of the monument:

"Then take off your glasses so that you can see we are right!" he cried. And now the laughter knew no bounds—surely, if people wore glasses, it was in order to see better!

Nevertheless, quite a few of the listeners found the young people so touching that they smilingly followed their suggestion and removed their glasses. But standing with them in their hands they soon forgot to smile. There were those ranters, trying to be so clever, although you could see at once what sort of shabby customers they were!

"Down with them!" came the cry from more and more

places in the crowd. But the majority, who had wisely kept their glasses on, found the furious listeners just as funny as the furious speakers: first the listeners had been foolish enough to do what the speakers said and now they were shouting "Down with the speakers!" Then the angry listeners grew ashamed of what they had been talked into doing, replaced their glasses and smiled sheepishly. And the non-eyeglass-wearers withdrew as a body, while an even greater body followed after them, hoping they would oblige with yet another speech.

For a while the non-eyeglass-wearers were not far from being the idols of the nation. Everybody recognized them because they were not wearing glasses, and were almost saddened as fewer and fewer appeared. Even the non-eyeglass-wearers saw reason and started wearing them, or proved that they had been crazy the whole time by being crazy enough to commit suicide. But when the non-eyeglass-wearers stopped making funny speeches and their madness began to take a more serious turn, they lost their popularity. At night, in the murky streets (along which the eyeglass-wearers walked confidently even at night, seeming no murkier than any other streets) they would sometimes jump out of the entrance-ways and snatch off the law-abiding citizens' glasses, or they would throw stones at other peoples' windows so that the streets were made almost impassable by broken glass. Nobody thought of sweeping it away because the fragments sparkled like diamonds both in sunshine and moonshine.

However, they who had so shamefully been deprived of their glasses could see that something was wrong—at least until they acquired new ones and admitted that the assaults had only been a manifestation of youthful playfulness. The authorities thought likewise, for they had gotten used to everything running smoothly by itself. But suddenly—possibly because more and more people had had their glasses and windows broken—one could detect a feeling of discontent. Even the authorities began to feel discontented with society's malcontents. For the first time in a long and hitherto happy period they received stacks of complaints about the lack of windowpanes in the houses, about the streets being full of broken glass and homeless children not wearing glasses, and about the fact that nobody was safe from the attack of non-eyeglass-wearers who ought not to be allowed to walk about freely. The authorities read and read these letters until their eyes smarted so much that they had to take off their glasses to rub them. And suddenly, there they were, none of them wearing glasses, and all looking at one another as if they were traitors. And when they nervously replaced them again they viewed one another no more kindly.

At that point it became clear to them as never before that something had to be done. First of all they had to make sure that people's glasses couldn't be snatched off: the glasses would have to be replaced by law with contact lenses. But since the glasses had apparently lost their effect (because people's eyes had grown accustomed to them) the glass had to be made stronger immediately. So the scientists and the authorities worked until they dropped and the glassblowers blew themselves out of breath. A critical point in the development of society had been reached, and during this period the non-eyeglass-wearers had not so little influence, although they were in the minority. So these dangerous persons would have to be detained in custody now, while they could still be distinguished from the others by not wearing glasses. But when the non-eyeglass-wearers protested that they were not living in a free society (how absurd that was, for they were not only alive but society was not putting any obstacles in their way!) it was no good making them appear to be in the right by arresting them. After all, they were not criminals—well, actually they were, but people had grown accustomed to viewing them simply as ignorant. But their ignorance was a disease, of course—presumably an eye disease, and it would be necessary to investigate whether their mental condition might not improve if they were to wear glasses for a while (or the new contact lenses). They were not to be coerced, however; merely sent to a hospital for observation. After they were discharged they would be free to choose whether they would wear glasses or not. In the meantime it would be possible for the authorities to introduce contact lenses so that the non-

eyeglass-wearers—or whatever they should now be called—
would not be able to snatch people's glasses off.

Meanwhile the non-eyeglass-wearers had lost sight of one
another. They dared not appear in public lest they were
snared and taken to the hospital eye departments. But though
they had to cease their visible activities, their cause pros-
pered: more and more people began to think as they did, and
to throw away the glasses that no longer did them any good.
Broken glass lay everywhere, and people trampled on it until
the blood flowed. The houses had no windowpanes and became unhealthy to live in; most people lived in the streets, and
so there was street-rioting around the clock. The authorities
did everything they could to remove the broken glass and to
provide the malcontents with new contact lenses—and gradually the population began to take the brighter view of things
again: most of the broken glass had already been removed,
and what was left even looked quite pretty. It was proclaimed
that malcontents were henceforth to report, not to the authorities, but to the eye departments, for all discontent was
caused by illness and could be cured. It could be foreseen
from bitter experience that the contact lenses too would
sooner or later have to be made stronger. But for the time
being the danger had been averted, the authorities could once
again look contentedly at one another through the new contact lenses, and the country earned untold wealth by export-
ing them to other countries—those that were almost as progressive but where catastrophe was brewing. Even the fashion
of letting brilliant pieces of glass lie about on the streets spread
to many progressive countries.

7

Now we shall look at how Gert has been getting on in the
meantime. He dared not go out during the daytime. Not because he was afraid of being put in hospital (for now no one
wore glasses) but because he was afraid of the wonderful
windowpanes and the inviting show-windows that adorned
all the shops. Only in the evening did he venture out, always

bent double to avoid seeing the fronts of the houses or the eyes of his fellow beings. He knew none of the people he met, but one evening one of them obviously knew him, for he shouted:

"Gert, old friend! Old comrade-in-arms! How wonderful to see you again, you haven't changed a bit!"

Gert submitted to the other's handshake, and eventually he recognized the non-eyeglass-wearers' old spokesman, although he was hidden behind both extra flesh and fine clothes.

"How marvellous," said the spokesman, "to be able to meet as free men. I've often thought about you, Gert, often wished I could have a good chat about old times. You were made of the right stuff—one could say you were high glass, ha ha! Can you remember when we used to make speeches down on Optician Square—the monument was blown up during the revolution, of course, but now it is being set up again on a grander scale. Not that I sympathize with the old fogey—but everything for continuity! Though it's really you they should have erected the monument for. . . . ."

"Me?" said Gert.

"Yes, you, damn it! Why, you were the inspiration for us all, when you came carrying your glass without wearing glasses! You were a pioneer. I suppose now you must be earning vast sums of money in the glazier's trade—you certainly look as if you're alive and kicking!"

Gert felt as if he were about to die.

"And then your speeches, all those words of wisdom! Why, it was we who started that incredibly peaceful revolution. If we had never existed, everybody would still be wearing glasses, and what kind of a world would that be! Where are you living, by the way? Still in the old place? A bit sentimental, aren't you. Well, continuity, that's what I always say—connections, and not forgetting one's old friends. Well, now I must be off to the ministry. Look me up one day, won't you, and take care, though I can see you're doing that, no grounds for complaint, ha, ha! Good-bye!"

Once again Gert went up to his room, which still lacked windowpanes. Despite the eternal draftiness little Gerda was still living there—though with difficulty. Her father could not go looking for work, for he would immediately reveal his lack of glass and be taken to an eye department. And who was then to look after the child?

One day Kaja returned.

"Gert," she cried, "you're looking just the same as ever! And everything here is just as it used to be—why, isn't it simply the most wonderful place on earth?"

Gert didn't answer, but when she embraced him, he embraced her so violently it was as if they should never be separated again. All the tender scenes of the past sprang so forcibly to Gert's mind that he noticed at once that Kaja no longer shut her eyes when they kissed; they were open and full of love as never before, and not until he shut his own eyes in abandon did it dawn on him that if she were to shut hers she would immediately stop loving him. So he slipped out of her embrace and turned his back on her.

"How straight your back is!" Kaja exclaimed behind him, joyfully. "And what a beautiful child you have—all children are so sweet. Gracious me, if it isn't Gerda! Mummy's own Gerda. . . ."

Now it was Gerda who was embraced more tenderly than ever, and the child gazed into the eyes of the strange woman and stopped crying, which she had just begun to do.

"Gert," said Kaja, whose motherly eyes noticed everything, "you don't mean to say that she's not wearing lenses! Look into my eyes—no, I can see you aren't. Gert, you old misery! How I love you, you're still the same, and I don't know whether to laugh or cry about you. Perhaps I'll laugh, for crying's so uncomfortable with contacts in your eyes. But you *are* different from all the others, that's why I haven't forgotten you. Have you forgotten me?"

"Have you come to stay?" asked Gert, without looking at her. She looked at him, however, in astonishment.

"Just because I said it was lovely here? For it is indeed lovelier here than any other place on earth, or at any rate just *as* lovely—but there isn't enough room for so many people, and there aren't any windowpanes either, I see. No, I've come to take you, and the child—since you've kept her after all—to a great big house," she said, turning towards Gerda, "with great big windows."

"And men with great big glassed eyes, eh?"

"Gert, what's the matter with you? No one lives alone any more, except you, poor Gert. And Mummy's poor Gerda. Is it all my fault, my pet, because I left you? But it was really your fault, because I loved you more than all the others. Yes I did, strangely enough, until you took away my glasses, and that I couldn't stand. But now I've forgiven you. Who thinks of wearing old-fashioned glasses now!"

"How many men are you living with?" asked Gert, turning one side towards her.

"How many men are you *better* than!" answered Kaja. "You, who don't even dare look me in the eyes!"

Gert stared furiously into her glassed eyes. But although he went on staring, he stopped being furious. Could two lensed eyes be more attractive than the two eyes that had once attracted him? When the others became blinded by the new glass he had already been blinded by her for some time, and was happy in his blindness. He didn't *want* to see others in the same light! What is love when it's only the love of a woman, and what is humanity when it's only the love of human beings? Was it this they had found out—found out with the help of the glass, because they cannot find out anything for themselves? That no one is worth loving, that all are equally lovable! He had fought so selfishly against "development" that his own child had not been able to develop; he had snatched away people's glasses—while they were still wearing such things—in order to let them see the undisguised truth. And all from vanity, for what business of his was the truth? He had dreamed that she, Kaja, would return and say: it is *only* you I love—as she used to say in the beginning when she was still blinded by him. Was it not she who took an impartial view of things, and he who was still blind? Wouldn't she be bound to prefer all other men to him—all those who loved her no more than they loved anyone else and thus made no demands on her?

"Gert," said Kaja.

"Kaja" said Gert.

"Are you coming?" she asked.

"Yes," he replied.

"Gert," she went on, "then you must promise me to wear lenses, otherwise I don't dare take you with me!"

"Mummy's eyes," said Gerda, who couldn't take her eyes off them.

"She seems to remember me, doesn't she?" asked Kaja.

"Very likely," said Gert, turning his other side towards her. And suddenly he shouted, so loudly that both Kaja and Gerda put their hands up to their ears:

"Wear lenses! So that all women appear to me equally wonderful. Then why should I go with you! Wouldn't it be better to wear lenses and be rid of you at last!"

"Gert," said Kaja, "didn't I come back to you despite the fact that I'm wearing glass in my eyes, even though I know nicer men than you? Goodbye, I say."

But Gert didn't feel like saying goodbye, and remained silent as Kaja departed. Gerda, on the other hand, began to bawl as childishly as in her infancy, but it was for her mother she was bawling and for her mother she suddenly made a dash.

"Gerda," shouted her stern father, but she took no notice of him. Gert stood trying to think that people are strongest when standing alone, but he felt so faint that he had to clutch hold of the table, and he didn't think the thought to its logical conclusion.

In the course of time Gert began to look like a tramp and people thought he looked funny. In their glass-eyes he was both a romantic reminder of the past and a proof of how progressive their own times were. They returned his scowls kindly, and many people gave him alms in fun, saying "It's just like in the old days." He liked best to wander in the shabby parts of the city where the chance of meeting shabby characters like himself was greatest—people who had not profited from the present state of affairs and were therefore able to see things impartially. If, during his dismal wanderings, he encountered a dismal look from anyone less well-dressed than most of the others, he tried to bring up the subject of revolution. He dared not come straight to the point lest he should be sent to an eye department: he had become such a great liar that he said the same as all the rest:

"Life is wonderful," he said. And when anyone thus addressed waved his arm, saying "Wonderful!," there was nothing else to be said.

One dark evening, when the moon was shining so brilliantly that the reflection from the windowpanes made him screw up his eyes angrily in pain, he bumped into another person, though was at once cunning enough to say "Oh, my good sir. . . ."

"I do apologize," said the other, who turned out to be an old man with a stick, "I'm so sorry I couldn't see you!"

"My fault," said Gert.

"Don't mention it!" said the blind man, "the forgiveness is mutual! You take it very well when we bump into you, but I suppose it's because you don't yourselves try to avoid us. Years ago the blind used to attract the attention of the seeing—you could tell from their whispers—and I've even heard that people with one leg attracted the attention of those walking on two. Now you've become more civilized, now no one notices that a one-legged man has only one leg and that a blind man cannot see—and that is why we are always being knocked over. Well, you didn't succeed in knocking me over, but then you don't seem to have much flesh on your body. And I can hear your heart pounding away right through it—what's wrong with you?"

"I don't know whether it's me there is something wrong with," whispered Gert, as if he were afraid of giving himself away by speaking loudly.

"Aha! You are pondering about things. I thought that was only necessary if one couldn't see them."

"I don't see things like other people," whispered Gert, "and I don't know who is seeing right."

"If things are what they seem to the seeing," said the old man, "then I, at least, am wrong. Once we used to say that things we could see and feel were real, but we no longer say that. We are knocked down by a seeing person who doesn't notice we are blind because that would upset his view on life. We fall and cut our hands to bits on the broken glass lying about on the ground, we ask a seeing person whether he wouldn't mind removing the glass splinters, and he says 'Whatever for? The glass splinters look so pretty against the red background. . . .' And when I say it hurts—for I am not one to extol suffering—they listen carefully to what I say, and say 'Hurts? It doesn't appear to hurt you, you're feeling very well, and besides, there are no other evils apart from eye diseases.' But tell me, surely you must have a bad heart?"

"It's a long time," whispered Gert, grasping the old man's arm, "since anyone has said anything to make my heart pound."

"That's because my speech is so edifying. But how is it possible that you can hear? Oughtn't you to go to an eye department?"

"You musn't report me to the eye specialists!"

"A hole-in-the-corner existence. I thought as much! I can tell by the voice. We've got them in the Blind Institute."

"Yes, blind people," said Gert appreciatively.

"Yes, and seeing people too. They are there in order to preserve their sight. In our place the doctors don't wear lenses, for if they did they wouldn't be able to see the blind people. You have no lenses either? I can tell from your whisper. Come with me, then. Our doctors will give you asylum; they will be able to see at once that you risk becoming blind."

"Me?"

"You are all in danger of becoming blind. The Blind Institute is growing bigger and bigger, for many people have already become blind from using stronger and stronger lenses."

"Then things are progressing," said Gert.

The blind man laughed:

"Don't forget that it can never be an advantage to be blind."

"Isn't it the disadvantaged people who are right?"

"A bit sweeping, aren't you? What if the situation turned to your advantage?"

"What a hope!" exclaimed Gert without answering.

"At any rate, you've got ears to hear with," reprimanded the old man. "So listen! We who live in the eternally invisible world cannot trust those who only know things that are—for a time—visible. That they are wrong, even seeing people will come to see—if not before, then after they have become blind. But people don't see things correctly just because they can't see."

"The truth," said Gert, groping in the dark.

"What do you mean?" asked the blind man. "People always mean well, and that lies at the bottom of all their wickedness. Once I had a twin brother—inseparable we were, and opticians we both became. Because we were always dealing with strong lenses, I lost my sight and he his temper. He wanted to restore my sight so that we could see the same things again. Being an optician, he thought it would be sufficient to invent a strong enough pair of glasses. He is now an oversized monument in the centre of the city. The blind didn't regain their sight by looking through his glass, but seeing people who saw nothing saw what they'd never seen before. Perhaps they saw things more clearly. Who knows? But when the glass began to see for them they stopped seeing things for themselves. When the glass made history, their own history came to a standstill."

"Now we've arrived at the Blind Institute," said Gert.

"Already? No matter how far away we get there are always shorter ways home again. Come with me, if you hold your sight dear."

"Ought one not to fight for one's sight?"

"How have you been fighting, other than by shutting your eyes? There's no need to do that here. Besides, the front-line is here, and it's getting pushed farther and farther forwards. So long as men are not masters of their own history it proceeds from necessity; only the free man follows voluntarily."

The blind man walked into his Institute and Gert followed after him.

8

And history takes the necessary number of years in which to proceed from necessity: the Blind Institute expands to a bursting-point, stronger and stronger lenses replace one another at shorter and shorter intervals, and discontent increases because nothing lasts forever. No one is able to see things in the radiant light of the old days; the strong glass just awakens a sickly memory. The free people have to choose between wandering in the dark without lenses or furnishing their eyes with glass that instantly deprives them of their sight. Who should believe these are the same people who liked each other equally well in their youth? Now no one thinks of the others any more; everyone bumps into everyone else and complains about the others' thoughtlessness; everyone goes around colliding and bleeding and no one sees the others colliding and no one sees the blood flowing everywhere. The authorities, in their blindness, cannot see any way out of the situation. Everyone wanders about in the dark, the Blind Institute takes over the whole country, and the few people who can see—the Institute's old eye specialists, and those ancients who have been non-eyeglass-wearers in their time and still are—lead the blind single-handed. When they leave the Institute they lack resistance to the blinding glass that blazes in the eyes of the newly blinded, and when they see them staggering about, beseeching the aid of an invisible heaven, they can hardly stand the sight of them: now the dreams of their youth have come true, now justice had been done! Only the blind old-timers can see what is needed, only they know how to cope with the wonderful glass from which destruction emanates; it is up to them to destroy what is destructive.

Since there is no longer any stronger glass to export, nor anyone to export it, the catastrophe spreads to other equally progressive countries. But from the less progressive, optically underdeveloped countries, where glass is still a luxury article everyone fights over, come great forces, unnoticed, to the glass countries. The foreign soldiers do not see the misery around them, for they are accustomed to seeing misery and are glad to be rid of it. They arrest the new authorities as well as the old, accusing them of shattering the glass the whole world is lacking. All the seeing people are hanged—among the first is an old man, a former glazier, who managed nevertheless to be appointed Minister of Glass before his death.

And since only the blind are left, no one can prevent the foreign forces from occupying all the glass factories and glass depots. No sooner do their primitive eyes catch sight of the magnificent glass than they lose sight of everything else—lose their sight and dance blindly on the glass, trampling one another until the blood flows, while their exotic cries of joy drown out the cries of the natives.

The Guardian's Tales

1

Following the death of both his parents in a single air crash, I learned to my astonishment that I had been appointed guardian to the son. I was not old enough to have been his father, and if he had been my son he would not have been called Louis and would hardly have been the owner of the amusement park that lay in the center of the city and was therefore called the Center. His deceased parents had been the richest couple in the city, and so the son, who strictly speaking was under age, naturally needed a guardian to administer the vast property willed to him. But I knew nothing about horses, and after all the horses had disappeared from the streets of the city they turned up in the Center in greater and greater numbers, and the son—who was all but born on a horse—had developed into a circus rider of almost world renown. I, on the other hand, walked on two legs at most, and had been enticed onto a horse's back only once, to be tossed off immediately. Naturally my primary job as guardian was to keep the accounts and hire people and fire them again, but I was also supposed to attend to the purely human aspects of the son's upbringing, and how was I to make him respect me? Until then I had been living with my only stepbrother; now I had to move in with the orphan, who had so much room that he would surely be able to ignore me. But sometimes we met anyway, and never without his making faces at me behind my back.

The ridingmaster was an expert—so clever that he had been called in from abroad long ago. He spoke exclusively Hungarian—a language the horses understood as well as any other language, and which the son in his official capacity as circus rider had understood and spoken from earliest childhood. The only Hungarian I knew was that the ridingmaster was called Hunyadi. As a rule I didn't know what to do with myself, so I frequently used to stay in the Center, where I almost as frequently met the ridingmaster. Bowing politely, I would say "Hunyadi," and he would say "Frederick" brokenly in my language, and in that way we got along very well. But scarcely had his parents died than the son wanted to introduce new acts into his program. He wanted to have even more horses and to make these walk only on their forelegs with their tails waving in the breeze, since for years the others had been walking only on their hindlegs in order to look human. I was afraid that horses that walked only on their forelegs might easily break them, or even lose their balance. So I considered it sufficient to hire a couple of new horses, and I was pleased that Hunyadi sided with me and seemed more and more worried every day. Now when we met we no longer bowed to one another but shook our heads instead, while the son grew more and more uncooperative and finally refused to appear in the ring with the horses at all. And now it appeared that all the other amusements were only of passing interest; people came to see the horses, and if there were no horses to see, they didn't come. Naturally, there were other circus-riders than the son; despite his age Hunyadi himself was an experienced horseman, but perhaps it was due to his parents' death that the son had become everyone's favorite. I went as far as to hire the best female circus-riders I could find from far and wide, but however attractive they were, not even the young men were interested in seeing them—they demanded to see the son, who would consent to perform only with horses that walked on their forelegs. All day long he lay on a comfortable sofa with his riding breeches in the air, and even though

Hunyadi went on his knees every day and spoke Hungarian to him, he did nothing but whistle.

I would have liked to consult Hunyadi, but when I had spoken to him on the odd occasion in the olden days, the son, who was then smaller, had acted as interpreter. All the other circus-riders seemed to be hostile, all of them demonstrating their sympathy for the son by not appearing in the Center, and eventually I walked alone among the multicolored fountains that had lost their color and stopped playing, among the complicated rollercoasters that no longer uttered wild female shrieks, among the merry-go-rounds that had stopped turning round and the swings that no longer swung. The son's great fortune, for which I had been honored by being appointed administrator (although I had never had any understanding of money) decreased every day, and my despair increased accordingly. So did the general dissatisfaction; since there were no horses to be seen anywhere else but in the Center, people's longing to see horses increased, but nobody wanted to see horses that were not accompanied by the son, who just whistled or slept.

"Hm!" I said. And not knowing what else to say, I said:

"I wonder what your father would have said had he been alive?"

Louis either couldn't answer, or wouldn't. I went away in anger but returned in sorrow:

"What a strange idea—for horses to walk on their forelegs!"

"That's what people want to see," said Louis, to my astonishment.

"It's you people want to see. And it's you who want the horses to walk on their forelegs."

Louis didn't even bother to open his eyes.

"But horses can't learn to walk on their forelegs. Hunyadi can't teach them."

"No!"

"No living creatures can walk on their forelegs alone—if they have both forelegs and hindlegs. Not even monkeys, who are the most closely related to human beings. The special thing about animals is that they do indeed walk on four legs—if, unlike monkeys and people, they do in fact have four legs. Even monkeys occasionally walk on four legs or else on their hindlegs alone. Of course human beings can walk on their hands, even though it may not be practical. But horses! That's against nature."

At that he opened his eyes and said:

"Amusements are against nature."

I had never thought of that, and it had never occurred to me that Louis could say anything worth thinking about.

"Louis," I said—but I discovered that I was addressing him for the first time by his Christian name, and held my tongue.

"Hunyadi," he said, "that's the old school."

"But who is going to teach the horses to walk on their hands?" I asked, deciding at the same time to consult a doctor, even though he wouldn't of course be able to solve the problems of the Center. But Louis said:

"Hasenkleber is."

"Who?"

"Hasenkleber."

"I see."

With these words I departed. On the stairs I met a man who was younger than I and not much older than Louis, whom he seemed to resemble.

"Mr. Frederick," he said, bowing. "Hasenkleber."

I realized of course that this was Hasenkleber.

"Louis," he said. "Parents' death—understandable."

"Yes," said I—understanding nothing. But Hasenkleber followed me into the Center, right into the stifling stables, and all the horses who had room enough knelt before Hasenkleber. Hunyadi stood in a corner weeping, muttering something in Hungarian I didn't understand.

"Hasenkleber," he whispered and walked slowly away, while the kneeling horses slowly rocked their hindquarters in the air and waved their tails.

"That's a start," said Hasenkleber.

"Yes," I said. I knew what was expected of me and hired Hasenkleber as ridingmaster, even though I didn't like the look of him. Almost at once Louis stood smiling in the ring and the horses gathered around him and the audience streamed in in such crowds that there was no room for me as guardian. But I heard the rounds of applause, and the fountains played in almost every color, the rollercoasters shrieked, and the merry-go-rounds and swingboats turned a full circle. At sunrise I stole into the ring. It was full of horses with broken legs. In the middle lay Louis, his head covered with blood. I had never much cared for his head, but his body was shapely even in death.

I never saw Hasenkleber again. I stood alone in the middle of the ring, while around me the amusements paused. Would this pause ever come to an end? I didn't know. What business of mine was the Center? For whom was I to be guardian now?

Suddenly I began to speak Hungarian. I muttered what Hunyadi had muttered.

2

My ward had been everyone's favorite, and when he died such a dreadful death it became generally known that I had been his guardian. Previously I had been able to walk around unnoticed. But now I could no longer do that; everyone noticed me and said: "Look, there's the guardian!" I was afraid they might mean mischief and blame me for his death, even though I for my part had tried to prevent it. But no charge was forthcoming. On the contrary. I was treated with great courtesy—almost with deference; everyone asked whether they might disturb me for a moment, and I was continually engrossed in conversation with children who wanted me to be their guardian so that they could be rid of their parents, or with parents who wanted me to be guardian for their children. I even received proposals of marriage; a guardian who wished to give his ward a proper home must be married, for what is a home without a mother? Soon so many people wanted me for a husband or a guardian that I refused them all, and they all lost interest in me.

But gradually, as I was once more allowed to walk about alone, I began to be plagued by loneliness, for it is not good for a single person to be single. I had never asked to become a guardian, I had always asked to not become one, and yet as a guardian I had had a task. At that time I had been able to stroll in the city's amusement park; I couldn't do so now, for it was closed. People probably still amused themselves in smaller circles, but I was not amused. I began to ask stray children whether I might become their guardian, but accosting minors can become dangerous, and the gaze of the police followed me wherever I went. So I began to accost women who could no longer be said to be minors; they always turned out to be the same as those who had previously wanted to marry me, but when I now wished to marry them, they all laughed at me; even the police laughed.

Not until I was accosted by an old woman who was as red and wrinkled as a rotten apple did the police turn their backs. Her eyes were not as old as her head—they were full of tears as she said:

"My mother is dead."

I was deeply moved: it is always moving to hear of mothers dying. And I was seized with righteous anger when I learned that her mother had not died a natural death, but that her daughter had been the death of her. The deceased had in fact had two daughters, of whom the old woman was the elder, the murderess being half a century younger.

"How can it be," said the older sister, "that wicked people are always younger and prettier? Everyone cares for my sister and believes what she says, but nobody cares for me."

I felt the remark go home. Of those I would have married but who no longer wanted to marry me, her little sister had been the youngest and the prettiest.

"Wickedness is diabolical," I said.

"And now she wants to have me made a ward. So now I've a mind to ask you—who are, after all, a well-known guardian—whether it would be something you'd do? My name is Alice."

Alice was old enough to have been my mother, and it seemed somewhat against nature to have one's mother as ward. But I needed a cause to fight for—especially a just cause—and I dared not refuse.

"Yes," I said, to Alice's great delight. She smiled so broadly that the wrinkles on her face made her look quite sinister. I gave no thought to the fact that I might simply be driven by the wish to revenge myself on her little sister, and yet I really ought to have thought of that, for, sure enough, I asked:

"What is you sister's name?"

"Why, her name is Elisa."

"That makes a difference," I said.

I felt obliged, as guardian, to go and live with Alice, who lived in a wretched little room so devoid of furniture that there was certainly room enough for two.

"I have not inherited anything from my mother," she said. "Elisa persuaded my mother to leave everything to her in her will before murdering her."

I was indignant about this grievous wrong. I wanted to have a talk with Elisa immediately.

"No!" screamed Alice. "She always gets her own way."

"Am I a guardian, or am I not a guardian? Either your sister transfers her inheritance to you or I shall accuse her of matricide. She cannot be both rich and free."

"But Elisa murdered my mother in order to become rich."

"Feminine logic!" I said. I stalked off disdainfully in order to speak to Elisa, but Alice uttered wild screams when I left her, and up came the police who informed me that she was too dangerous, or at any rate too noisy, for her surroundings, and that she must not be left alone.

"But I am used to going about on my own."

"We realize that," said the police. "But now that must stop. You must not leave home without taking your ward with you, and her mental state is such that we think it advisable for you to take her on a leash."

"On a leash?"

"It is considered advisable for you to take her on a leash."

"But her mother is dead," I objected.

"Miss Elisa's mother is also dead. It cannot be worse for one than for the other."

"It is precisely Miss Elisa—as you say—who ought to be put in chains. She was the death of her mother."

"That may well be. But she keeps quiet about it. Your ward is too loud-voiced."

Her loud screams could be heard. I had to go back in order to silence her with a gag and put her on a leash.

Tied together and in silence, we succeeded in reaching the deceased's estate where young Miss Elisa was already living. When the two sisters stood face to face once more, it was in fact the youngest who screamed.

Guilty conscience, I noted immediately. The younger sister went on screaming, though I managed eventually to distinguish proper words among her screams.

"Mother," she shouted.

"Is it 'murder' you're screaming?" I asked.

"No," she screamed, "mother, mother. She looks like my mother! She looks dreadful!"

True enough, Alice looked a sight. Her hair was wispy and a pale sickly red, and her eyes looked like red lumps in their sockets. Her skin has already been described, but now it was stretched to breaking-point, so that all the wrinkles were quite smoothed out. If I had not had her on the leash she would presumably have fallen down dead with a crash; now she sank comparatively gently to the ground to commence her death-struggle there. It was my task as her guardian to close her eyes, but they had bulged so far out of their sockets that it was quite impossible.

"You must take the body with you," gasped Elisa.

"No!" I cried. "It's your own flesh and blood!"

At that Elisa burst into tears. To my astonishment she threw both arms around my neck:

"Frederick! Is it a sin to live?"

I realized now that Elisa was innocent, and yet there was blood in us and between us. And I answered:

"If life was as it should be, it would know nothing of guardians."

3

It had been decreed that all those without dependents should make themselves available as guardians. I referred to the fact that my previous guardianships had all come to an unhappy end, but the authorities answered unreasonably: "Yes, the first step is always the hardest." I was informed that I could expect my ward at any moment, and that was indeed the case—I never got a moment's peace. I eventually succeeded in making myself comfortable; I used to go for a morning walk every morning before dawn and an evening walk every evening when it grew dark, accompanied by my two sticks, which had become so used to my company in my protracted old age that they could almost walk by themselves; and I used to spend most of the day making use of my guardian's pension in private. And now life's wild dance was to start all over again. This time my ward was unlikely to be older than myself (for I was approaching 550), but almost certainly would be so much younger than me that the generation gap would become tremendously big. Not for centuries had my heart beaten so violently as now, when, together with my sticks, I stood at the peephole in my door, anxiously expecting to see my ward standing behind it. But all the twisted figures emerging from the staircase and straightening out as they passed by continued up the stairs; for the time being the danger was over, although my heart was still beating wildly.

The fact that I had become aware in this way of human life unfolding itself on the stairs was enough to change my entire life. Whereas during the first few days (for time went by and my ward failed to appear) I wished that everyone would pass on, eventually I caught myself wishing to retain one of the passers-by of my peephole. Not only had my legs grown tired of standing for days on end, but I realized that people were still different; some of them seemed more suitable as wards than others. It had never fallen to my lot to choose; in my day I had been born a prince and been Emperor of the Holy Roman Empire, but the historians had long ago pointed out that no Christian prince had been less influential than I. By virtue of my position I had been guardian several times, but had never chosen the wards myself, just as I had not chosen my Uncle Frederick to be my guardian in my own distant childhood—he had been allotted to me. A prince, and still less an emperor, is never granted the right to choose—a prince is born and an emperor elected. And yet the Emperor is supposed to be the mightiest man in the world.

As I stood waiting behind the door, so many recollections

of my time as Emperor sprang to my mind that I was afraid that for many years I had been suffering from loss of memory. Perhaps that was why I couldn't remember how I, as Emperor, had come to be deposed. Or perhaps my memory was fine, and I was still Emperor. I found that standing behind the peephole in my door was beneath my imperial dignity; I bade my sticks accompany me, and for the first time within living memory I went out into the world in the full light of day.

My imperial bearing aroused attention everywhere. People stood still and bowed, and even children who were apparently not very good at history became so interested in the subject that they asked: "Which Frederick are you?" But I merely replied:

"It is a matter of dispute."

Naturally my errand was to seek out the History Faculty in order to learn what the position was regarding my dethronement. The professor recognized me at first glance and said:

"Gracious me! If it isn't Emperor Frederick! To what do we owe the honor?"

Surrounded by a circle of students, I said that I didn't feel I was being treated with due respect. For centuries I had been minding my own business, but lately I had felt that the authorities had been taking liberties. After all, it was I who had authorized the authorities in the first place, and it seemed only reasonable that they should remember me as the greatest guardian in history. That is why I could not consider myself obliged to be a guardian for just anyone. In reality I was *everyone's* guardian, and it was a favor on my part, if not due to purely political reasons, that I in my time had adopted specially selected princes and princesses as my wards.

Of course I could not reveal the fact that I was not quite sure whether I was still Emperor, and merely pretended not to be. It pained me deeply and even made me feel ridiculous that I felt at a loss as regards this particular point, and a few of the students, who were well hidden behind the other students' backs, even seemed to be laughing at me; but that may have been because they were not sufficiently conversant with the subject. I made no attempt to stop my voice from sounding threatening as I was wily enough to say:

"Naturally it is many years since I have asserted my power."

At that the professor bowed and said:

"That shows your true greatness, Emperor Frederick. No one can elect himself Emperor, but to stop being Emperor is a truly imperial decision."

The students broke out into applause, and although it was naturally intended for me as former Emperor, the words of the professor had deserved it too. Suddenly I remembered that I at my great age had abdicated many years ago in favor of my son, for otherwise he would still not have come to the throne—so many years after his death. Without demanding any outward ceremony I had borne my imperial dignity throughout five centuries, and my sticks stood to attention by my side.

"If one has retired, one has retired," I said. "I now live in an ordinary two-room apartment. But the demand that I should become a guardian yet again in my old age has awoken so many grievous memories. And I have decided that if I am to be a guardian again, I must also become Emperor again."

"There must be some misunderstanding," said the professor, politely. And some of the students repeated politely in chorus: "There must be some misunderstanding."

Then I had to lean on my two sticks, Caspar and Aeneas. My heart was full of grief—or was it joy—I can't remember the difference. Was I sad because I was not to be a guardian any more, or was I pleased because I was not to be Emperor any more? I have been thinking about it ever since, and it still sometimes happens that I stand behind my peephole, watching my wards walk up and down the stairs.

The History of a Guardianship

"He seldom held great banquets unless he wished to display his wealth or felt obliged, as Emperor, to invite some princes, when he would entertain them most royally and with the choicest of dishes. Then he would warm to the occasion and become communicative, relating without exaggeration of his youth and changing fortunes; he could even relate whole chronicles about his own family."

JOSEPH GRÜNPECK: The History of Frederick III

When I was young the world was very troubled, and I too was troubled, for it was I who was supposed to create world peace. On Our Lady's Candlemas Day, I in my twenty-fifth year was by the grace of God and the seven Electoral Princes elected King of the Holy Roman Empire, and the message reached me in Neustadt only eight days afterwards at Shrovetide on St. Apollonias' Day. Only two years previously my second-cousin Albert, King of Hungary and Bohemia, Dalmatia, Croatia, Margrave of Moravia and Duke of Austria, etc., had also been elected King of the Romans, but he had died a sudden hero's death in perilous battle with the infidel sons of Mohammed, and I thought twice before treading in his footsteps. Albert too had thought twice before taking upon himself the world's heaviest though most glorious burden, and I, as his nearest second-cousin, had ridden to Vienna at the time in order to persuade him. But when I arrived in Vienna his wife Elizabeth had already persuaded him, which she, as Albert's consort and the only daughter of the late Emperor Sigismund, was in the nearest position to do.

I had no one to persuade me. Indeed, my brother Albert came riding to dissuade me from becoming King. He said that the Crown was no blessing for our house, for Albert had died in the war, and the previous King Albert of our house, our great-grandfather, had been murdered by his own brother's son and three barons, while Albert's son, Frederick the Fair, had been put in prison in disgrace when he wanted to be King. But I realized that Albert wanted to be King himself, for he was always thinking selfishly and never of our house as a whole.

I always thought in sorrow about our house as a whole, for a house that is divided against itself cannot stand, and so long as the faithful oppose the faithful they cannot win over the infidels, for the infidels cannot do anything on their own but are God's mode of punishing those of little faith. When I was elected King, Duke Amadeus of Savoy was elected Pope by the General Council of Basel, even though Eugenius was already Pope in Florence, being banished from Rome at that time, and how can one pope gather all the Christian princes for a Crusade when there are two popes? When pope opposes pope, then the King must stand united and create peace, but how can he create peace in the world when he cannot maintain domestic peace in his own house? That is what I asked my brother Albert, and he replied: "Well spoken. He who stretches out his neck for the Crown risks losing his head." I said that if we could only stand united no one would be able to stand in my way. But Albert went away in order to oppose me.

All the misfortunes that have befallen our family were due to lack of family feeling. After our house had already become the world's mightiest and my great-grandfather Albert had succeeded my great-great-grandfather Rudolph as King of the Holy Empire, it was his own brother's son, John the Murderer, who destroyed its might by murdering his uncle,

King Albert, although he himself was scarcely of age. Since then all the uncles and cousins in our family have been afraid of their nephews and cousins, and whenever fathers died, cousins and brothers fought each other in order to become the guardians of the fatherless sons and make them their wards. Ought not sons to be a blessing? Ought not a family to become mightier the bigger it grows? Alas, the bigger our family, the bigger the family quarrels. Whenever I look back on the history of my own family—and now in my old age I am quite interested in family history—I am terrified to think what might have happened had not so many died at so grievously young an age.

Thus, my murdered great-grandfather had five sons, Rudolph and Frederick and Albert and Leopold and Otto, and only Rudolph died in peace. Leopold and Otto fought as brothers against Frederick (the Fair) because he had lost both the Crown and our Swiss domains; he could not have won them because his own brothers opposed him. But, as punishment, they all died, and Albert was the only survivor; he had been lamed by poison and could not go to war, and he did not want a brother-war to break out between his own sons. From olden times it had been decreed that our domains should never be divided between brothers, but in order to leave no doubt, Albert decreed in a house rule that his four sons, Rudolph and Frederick and Albert and my grandfather Leopold, should live together in a heartfelt, seemly and brotherly union, and that the eldest should be as the youngest and the youngest as the eldest, and that there should be no dissension, strife and enmity between them, but each and every one should honor all the others. Rudolph and Frederick died before their father did, and Albert and Leopold lived long enough to divide the domains between themselves because they could not agree about the whole, and Albert was given Inner Austria to rule over, and Leopold, Outer Austria. But in this way the two domains became only half as big, and Leopold fell in the war against the Confederacy, and that was not the first time my forefathers lost against the enemy because they could not stand together and because the Austrian standard is not always victorious.

But Leopold had left four sons: William and Leopold and Ernest, my father, and Frederick, my uncle and guardian. William and Leopold wanted to divide their father's domains before they were old enough to rule over them. My grandfather's brother was their guardian and forbade them to divide up the outer domains any further, but they said it was because he wanted to rule over all of it himself. So the lords of the realm had to impress upon my young uncles that division would cause the ruin of both themselves and our domains and subjects, for when princes quarrel the nobility has more say in the matter.

So long as Albert was alive he kept everything under control and was everyone's guardian. But he died and left not only four nephews but also a son named Albert. His last will and testament stated that all five should rule in unity and concord according to the rule of our house, but now it was Uncle William who was the eldest of our house, and he too wished to rule alone and be guardian to all his brothers and cousins, and they all took sides against one another. True enough, Albert's son Albert was poisoned, but he left a little son, Albert, King of the Romans, and so William wanted to be his guardian. Then he himself died, and Leopold too wanted to be little Albert's guardian, so that my own father Ernest and his brother Frederick, my guardian, had to oppose this, and the Estates intervened in the dispute and liberated Albert from Leopold; and Leopold died in wrath, for the Estates ought not to control those in control. But now Frederick wanted to be Albert's guardian, so my pious father had to oppose this, and Albert became old enough to oppose it too. For the sake of peace in our house, though contrary to our house rule, they divided the domains into three parts, so that Albert, like his father and grandfather, received the innermost part, Upper and Lower Austria, while my father Ernest was to rule over the middlemost, and Uncle Frederick over the outermost domains together with Tyrol.

When my father Ernest the Ironhard died, I was only nine years old and my brother was six. Then Uncle Frederick, who was generally called Frederick the Elder after I was born because he was older than I was, became guardian to us both;

for Albert, who was often called Albert the Elder after my brother was born, because he was older than Albert, was too wise to fight with Frederick about our guardianship. When I was twelve, Uncle Frederick and his wife, Anne of Brunswick, had a little son who was called Sigismund, after the Sigismund who was Albert's father-in-law and Roman Emperor, and I often used to go down on all fours and play horsie with my cousin Sigismund, having no idea that he would later become my ward and cause me great political trouble. I myself did not cause my guardian great trouble. But when I was sixteen and to come of age according to our house rule, he prolonged the guardianship, for he said that he was both my brother Albert's guardian and mine in one and that Albert was only thirteen and not yet of age.

When Albert turned sixteen and I a full nineteen Uncle Frederick of Austria prolonged his guardianship of both of us, for he said that he himself had not come of age either until he was older. I said nothing, but Albert was not as peaceable as I was, so he never gave me any peace, and I as the eldest had to demand that Frederick the Elder instantly make us free ruling dukes. But Uncle Frederick summoned us and said that we were old enough to understand that if he divided the middlemost domains between us, each of the two middlemost domains would become only half as big as the whole of the middlemost domains, so it would be best if he as the oldest cousin were to rule over all the domains according to our old house rule so that they should not become smaller. I said nothing—already at that time I could see that the realm was the more whole the more undivided it was, but Albert was never able to grasp that and said he was being unfairly treated. So I as the eldest had to write to our second-cousin Albert the Elder of Hungary and Bohemia, etc., and bid him mediate between us dukes before it came to strife. And Albert made known that for the present Frederick the Elder and the Younger together with Albert the Younger should rule in concord and undivided for six years from that day; Albert and Frederick the Younger, Duke Ernest's sons, however, should administer the middlemost domains together as their father Ernest had done, while Frederick the Elder should continue to administer the outermost domains he was already administering. But when the six years came to an end, Frederick the Elder, as the eldest, should choose that part of the domains he wanted to rule divided, and that was probably why he still would not hand over to Albert and me the letters, documents and books, firearms and gunpowder that belonged to us. He even kept my pious father's silver in his custody; I had to write him many letters before he sent me six old goblets, eight spoons and a little studded belt, for which I acknowledged receipt. Albert said that we were being unfairly treated and wanted me to declare war on Uncle Frederick, but how was I to wage war against him when he kept all the gunpowder in Tyrol. Instead, I set out for the Holy Land with fifty high-standing barons whose names it would take too long to list, in order, like my pious father, to be created Knight of the Holy Grave. I wanted to take Albert with me so as to keep an eye on him, but he said scoffingly that the Holy Grave was sufficiently protected whereas Austria was not. I was created Knight of the Grave in my twenty-first year on the Sunday evening after the Birth of Our Lady. I swore loud and piously to protect all widows and fatherless children, to do justice to rich and poor alike, and to reconquer the Holy Grave from the heathens and infidels. I was also in Venice and bought beautiful cloth and jewels for two thousand seven hundred and ninety-nine golden guilders, and I bought some green and silver cloth for my little brother Albert for six and a half guilders. But when I returned home with the cloth, Albert slashed it to pieces and said that if I was a Holy Knight, bound by duty to protect the fatherless, it was my duty to protect him against injustice.

Then Uncle Frederick died, and so our domains were not divided. His son, my cousin Sigismund, now became fatherless too, and it was my duty to protect him, for he was only twelve. Albert the Elder was the obvious one to be made Sigismund's guardian, but he was to be King of the Romans and had no time, and he was only Sigismund's second cousin. So I, as his nearest and eldest first-cousin, had to become Sigismund's guardian although I had only recently come of age. But my brother Albert said that since Sigismund's father

Frederick had been his guardian as well as mine, he as well as I should become Frederick's little son Sigismund's guardian, and when I set out for Tyrol with one hundred and fourteen horse to take over the guardianship together with the documents, firearms and treasures which Frederick had not wanted to hand over to me while he was alive, Albert too set out for Tyrol on the same errand. I thought we could have travelled along the perilous path over the high mountains together, since we would be going the same way anyway, but Albert was impatient and went ahead.

I had nothing against being guardian together with Albert, if only Albert could agree with me about the guardianship. But the Tyrolese, who after all were our subjects, did not want to have two guardians for Sigismund, whom they called their own Duke of Tyrol, although Tyrol is a countship and Sigismund was the undivided Duke of all Austria. This was the outcome of the unfortunate and unbrotherly family quarrels. It was indeed humiliating to a Duke like Albert for the Tyrolean Estates to forbid him to enter Innsbruck, which was his own native town, before he had reconciled himself with us. They also forbade me to enter my native town of Innsbruck before I had reconciled myself with Albert, but that was in order not to insult Albert more than me, for they had no reason to fear that I would enter Innsbruck. With my one hundred and fourteen horse I entered Hall near the rich silver mines, and Albert entered too with one hundred and fourteen knights who were no friends of our house. I summoned the town's most cool-headed men and told them that if fire were to break out either by accident or intent they would be in great danger, for Albert would make use of the slightest disturbance as a pretext for attacking me. Therefore I had summoned my courtiers to assemble in front of my lodgings, and I called upon the citizens of the town to do likewise, and even the cool-headed men took up position outside the door. But behind the door I was bargaining with the Tyrolean noblemen and squires about the guardianship. I declared that for four years from St. Jacob's Day I was myself willing to treat Sigismund lovingly, to take care of his upbringing and health as a father would, and to provide him with an able man as steward so that he could learn discipline and good conduct, and with a learned man as tutor so that he could learn Latin. I also promised to place horses and other things at his disposal and to let him grow up in the air he had breathed and been brought up in, in a healthy and convenient castle in the part of Tyrol most suitable for the season. I declared, however, that in the case of dire need I was to be allowed to remove Sigismund from Tyrol so that no one else could abduct him. I could not tell the Tyrolese straight out that they had no right to retain Sigismund, for then they might make Albert guardian. Nor could I say that they had no right to regard the treasure Frederick the Elder had left as Tyrolean property, for much of it had been left by my own father. But I had to promise the Tyrolese not to separate Sigismund from the treasure.

While Albert rode away in anger to make friends with the enemies of the Tyrolese, I rode happily to my native town with all my horses in order to keep an eye on Sigismund and the treasure. It is in the nature of our family to have big noses and chins, and Sigismund's chin and nose were still too small and insignificant; even as a boy he had the habit of walking around with mouth open and lower lip drooping so that his chin showed up to greater advantage. But he had large eyes, and they were full of childish tears when he saw me—possibly because his father had died recently, whereas his amiable mother, Anne of Brunswick, had long since lain in her grave like my own pious mother, Mistress Cimburgis, who died on the Eve of St. Michael in my fourteenth year. "Well, Sigismund," I said in a fatherly manner, but it was not exactly filial of him to answer "Well, Frederick." We entered the treasury, and although in his younger days Frederick the Elder had been called Frederick with the Empty Pockets, the treasury he left was filled with buckets of uncoined gold and silver, of necklaces, belts, armlets, rings, goblets and jugs of the same precious metals, of pearls and precious stones of every kind—sapphires, rubies, emeralds, amethysts, diamonds, cornelians, sardonyx, turquoise and coral—as well as coined gold and silver; and so as to leave no doubt I had it all counted and noted down, and there were four thousand six hundred and fifty-five gold ducats and one thousand two hundred and seventy-two silver marks. Sigismund yawned while it was being counted and noted down, so in order to encourage him and stimulate his interest in economy I said: "From now on I think you should be known as Sigismund Full-bags." But Sigismund wrinkled up his insignificant nose and said: "And you, as Frederick the Warder."

I did not take Sigismund's small, ward-like impertinances seriously, but I had no intention of neglecting his upbringing. It was then autumn, and I regarded Castle Taur, close to the rich silver mines, as being the healthiest and most comfortable abode for Sigismund at that time of the year, and I myself took up residence in Taur and distributed great favors and collected great taxes. There I received the grievous message that my second-cousin Albert, King of the Romans and husband of Elizabeth, had breathed his last on the Eve of Simon and Judas, and suddenly there I was—the eldest and senior Duke of the Austrian House. At that time there were fewer Austrian dukes than usual, for there were only myself, my ward Sigismund and my full but hot-tempered brother, and it ought to be more practicable to unite the whole realm now than ever before. I could not remain in such an outlying province as Tyrol, but had at least to move to the central domains, and I thought there was good reason to take Sigismund with me, for Albert was riding around in the neighborhood of Tyrol with evil in mind. But I had promised not to separate Sigismund from the treasure I had had counted, so I took that with me too. At this time the Tyroleans had begun to speak evil of me because they had evil in mind; and yet I had saved Tyrol from Albert, for no sooner had I fallen out with the Tyroleans than Albert made peace with them and set out for Vienna.

I had made a holy vow to protect widows and fatherless children, and the late Albert's widow Elizabeth had two little fatherless daughters, Anne and Elizabeth. Of course fatherless daughters need no guardian while their mother is still alive, and little Anne, moreover, was betrothed to William of Saxony; but Queen Elizabeth was exceedingly great with child, which all the world knew, for were she to give birth to a son it would be an important world event—he would be the lawful heir to Bohemia, Hungary, Dalmatia and Croatia, etc.; he would be the fourth undivided Duke of Austria. But the Estates in all these domains would not be pleased at the idea of having a prince who was able to unite them all, and although sons ought to be a blessing, I almost wished that Elizabeth would give birth to another daughter, so that much bloodshed could be avoided. I hoped just the same that she would bear a son who could inherit his father's inherited domains, for if we four Austrian dukes could agree, we might be able to unite all the Christian domains into one peaceful realm and win for Christendom that peace for which it so bloodily thirsted. And while I was thinking these peaceful thoughts at Shrovetide, when everyone was wearing big noses, I received the glorious though solemn message that I had been elected King of the Holy Roman Empire, and was most ceremoniously invited to Aix-la-Chapelle, King Charlemagne's old royal city, to be crowned with the Royal Crown.

No man is worthy of being King, for Christian kings must do what God wills, not what man wills. Even as a little boy I could not understand how my guardian Frederick could speak evil of the Christian king and emperor who had put him under the ban of the realm, for all that a king does must be good. But I received a letter from Duke Amadeus of Savoy; he congratulated me on the great appointment and wrote that he himself had been appointed Pope and wished to be recognized by me immediately, and I thought that if even a pope is a man, then a man can also be a king.

I used to pray a great deal at that time, and so as not to have to make my way over to the cathedral or to the Dominicans and Capuchins every time, in my own castle I founded the Chapel of St. George, which Master Peter is still building. When I was not praying, I used to walk, deep in thought, up and down the garden paths of the deer park. I cultivated pear trees and eagerly followed their growth. I myself placed birdcages in the great trees, and these always had bars on three sides, while the fourth side was open to enable the birds to fly in and replenish themselves with food and drink in plenty. But no sooner had they flown inside than the fourth side fell down and the bird was caged. From childhood I had been a little short-sighted, and so I had to cage the birds in order to view them at close range, and the garden was soon full of birdcages and strange birdsong. Every day I used to walk in the garden with Sigismund, paying fatherly attention to his upbringing. I taught him the names of the tiny birds—the little nightingale and the merry starling and the gray sparrow—but he showed very little interest in bird-life and thought it a pity for them to be in cages. I explained that, quite apart from my being short-sighted, the bars protected them against birds of prey, so he asked me whether it wouldn't be easier to shut up the birds of prey instead. I replied that while falcons were caged so that they could be tamed for falconry, hawks and eagles were too big and proud to be put in cages, for our own family was named after the hawk, and the two-headed eagle fluttered on the standard of the Holy Empire. I knew that Sigismund called me Frederick the Hawk- or Eagle-nosed behind my back.

I had promised the Tyroleans to provide Sigismund with an able man as tutor and steward, and I let him keep the tutor the Tyrolese themselves had given him; he was a Doctor of all the free arts, and it was not until later that I realized how unable he was. But I was already surprised that Sigismund had so much free time. I placed horses and other things at his disposal, but I forbade him to ride outside the moats, for there might be Tyrolese lying in wait for him anywhere. For company he had common boys of the same age, so that he could become acquainted with them, and they climbed in my pear trees and ate my pears and hid from one another. I often used to see Sigismund lying at the bottom of a scuffling group—a position already unworthy of a coming ruler. I taught him that it was unseemly for a duke to be beaten in battle, and if he was unable to hold his own it would be better to keep clear of all fights, but Sigismund replied childishly: "A duke has surely to show that he is the strongest." They slung stones with slings and shot arrows with bows and marbles through hollow tubes, so it could be dangerous to take a peaceful stroll in the deer park, and on some days I had to forbid them to charge so ferociously at one another. Then they caught a peacock and tied it to a tree and slung stones at it, and they laughed like children when the bird spread out its tail as a shield.

In that difficult period of respite my brother Albert came to try to dissuade me from becoming King. His embrace was as brotherly as if there had never been any brotherly strife between us, and I embraced him too, for I could not stand being on bad terms with my own brother. Then I said: "It is written that you should love your enemy, so you shouldn't fight against your brother." "I also love having enemies," answered Albert, profanely, "and it is written that you should hate your fathers and mothers, wives and children, sisters and brothers. But it is not written that one should hate one's cousins, and I was fighting to take loving care of my cousin Sigismund. Where is he?" I tried to hide Sigismund from him, but they found each other at once, and because I had forbidden Sigismund to ride outside the moats, Albert offered to take him for a ride through the streets of Vienna personally, so that no misfortune should befall him. I said that Sigismund might catch cold at that time of the year, and I had promised to consider his health. "So you forbid me to ride to Vienna with my own flesh and blood!" said Albert. "I do not forbid *you* to ride to Vienna," I said. "Then I shall not ride to Vienna," said Albert. "I shall ride to Hungary and take over the guardianship of Elizabeth's son; then we can share our cousins like brothers, and if he's a daughter, I'll return to the matter and to you." I thought of detaining Albert, but I had the drawbridge lowered just the same, and the herald blew a fanfare in farewell. But Sigismund went around sulking because he wasn't going to Vienna.

On the Feast of St. Peter's Throne, Elizabeth bore a son who received in holy baptism the name of Ladislas after the Holy King of Hungary of that name. I have been told that she was scarcely given any peace to give birth—the door kept opening and closing and the Hungarian dignitaries going in and out to see if it was a king or a princess. I almost think my brother Albert must have been the only one to rejoice over the birth of a king's son, for the Hungarian Palatinates and Warvodes had already secretly elected another king. They said that a baby in swaddling-clothes was not sufficient to protect the exposed Hungarian kingdom from the Turks. They wished to have a king who could go to war at once, and so they elected King Vladislas of Poland. They knew they were acting contrary to law and justice, for Ladislas was the rightful master of Hungary even as a newborn babe; only the King of the Romans is elected by the Electors, who are born electors, all other kings being just born; and to make their unlawful election lawful they wished Elizabeth to marry Vladislas who was only half as old as she was, and I wondered how best I could protect a widow like her. For Ladislas was also heir to Bohemia, and the Bohemians behaved just as treacherously as their Hungarian neighbors. Bohemia was a kingdom divided against itself, where heretics fought against the orthodox and one another, for that is what heretics are; it was not only Hussites we heard of then, but Taborites and Calixtines as well as Adamites, who used to walk around most shamefully naked as if sin had not come into the world. How would all these dissenting peoples be able to assent to having one king! The heretics also thought of electing Vladislas of Poland, but they were afraid of his becoming king over too many countries and so they elected his little brother Casimir instead; and the orthodox, who ought surely to know about law and justice, elected Duke Albert of Bavaria, but my brother Albert felt insulted because nobody elected him and went to war with the Bohemians, and as long as it lasted I was left in peace. But Elizabeth thought it was Ladislas he was fighting for and not himself, and in gratitude she transferred to Albert the guardianship over Ladislas and his big sister together with the administration of Inner Austria above and below the Enns until Ladislas became sixteen according to our House rule. But at that time the Austrian Estates were law-abiding enough to confirm my guardianship over Ladislas, for a newborn fatherless duke is the eldest duke's ward—a good old house rule—and I and Albert could not both be guardians.

But I had no wish to be Albert's and Elizabeth's enemy, and I had heard that they had formed a league against everyone except the Pope and the Holy Roman Empire, and if I were King of the Romans they could do nothing against me. I also had a strange dream: I saw Elizabeth sitting in a stable rocking the royal child on her lap, and I was standing behind the door with a donkey in order to protect the widow and the fatherless child. But three kings came along in a row, so there was nothing I could do; and they entered and each took a crown from the sleeping child's head, and when Elizabeth tried to snatch it away they made as if to embrace her or do her injury, and I was standing outside and could do nothing. But when the three kings had departed, each with his crown, Ladislas lay with an even bigger crown on his head. Then I entered the stable and put the crown on my head and Elizabeth tried to snatch it away, but I woke up and realized that I ought to accept election as King in order to protect Ladislas. The royal crown lends luster to the head that wears it, and gives it greater authority. But I could not journey to Aix-la-Chapelle to be crowned just then, for while I was away Albert might take possession of both Sigismund and Austria. Besides, I am not very keen on the irregular life of the road; I had always fulfilled my religious duties with ardent devotion and at appointed hours, especially when my health permitted it, but that is not possible when traveling. True enough, Pope Eugenius had permitted me to take a transportable altar with me, but that is not quite the same thing.

Since the word of the King is law, I wrote as King to Albert of Bavaria, my liegeman, forbidding him to become King of Bohemia because it was unlawful. I wrote to Elizabeth and, in the name of my ward and her own son, King Ladislas, I bade her not to wed King Vladislas and deprive King Ladislas of the Holy Hungarian Crown with the crooked cross. Before I managed to write to Vladislas, he wrote and congratulated me on my new rank as King of the Romans and bade me stop the robbers in my ward's domains from pillaging his Hungarian kingdom. The Austrian Estates sent envoys bidding me place one thousand knights in readiness as defense against Hungarian pillage, and even though they were reluctant to mix themselves up in family affairs they begged me to reconcile myself with my brother, Duke Albert, for he was constantly begging the Estates for money to wage war on me, and they thought that our dispute would cause our joint domains and the entire Austrian House more harm than all external warring and unrest. The Bohemians too sent emissaries to me to complain about the Austrian and Hungarian robbers who were pillaging their country. I realized that he who is blinded by frontiers acquires a limited outlook; the Christian King knows no frontiers except for the frontier with the infidels, and if I were to place one thousand knights on either side of the common frontier between Austria and Hungary and Bohemia, how many knights would then be left to protect Christendom from the Crescent Moon? My late second-cousin, King Ladislas's father, had protected all these countries in one, but these countries' great men had not been of great help—they were fighting selfishly against one another while Albert was fighting in vain for them all. Because they had not placed any knights at his disposal, which they should as liegemen have done, he had had to hire soldiers and pledge his own castles to the nobles, and now masterless mercenaries were pillaging all the frontiers of the countries whose frontiers they were paid to protect, for no one paid them any longer. I had never cared for the bad practice of hiring soldiers, for soldiers should fight from holy conviction, not from money, and if I myself had hired soldiers to fight mercenaries they would only have fought one another, and nothing would have been gained but much money lost. I hastened as King to call for a diet in Nuremberg in order to create peace in the entire kingdom, but because of the unsettled conditions the diet did not take place. I promptly called for a new diet in Mainz, but because of the same conditions I myself could not attend, and the princes of the realm thought they ought to follow my royal example and did not attend either, so that the diet could not form a quorum; only some bishops attended in great numbers, and they discussed the lack of unity in the Council of Basel, which had deposed Pope Eugenius, and in Eugenius's Council of Ferrara, which had disbanded the Council of Basel, and they proposed that I invite them to a new council which could mediate between them, for the Council of Basel had already come to terms with the heretics in Bohemia, and the Council of Ferrara had united with the Patriarch of Constantinople in declaring that the Holy Spirit issued from both the Father and the Son, and if the Councils could also come to terms, the entire Christian world would be reconciled. I bade my chancellor Caspar convene a Council, but he laughed and said that a temporal prince had never yet gone in for arranging church meetings, that I should instead rejoice that the spiritual powers were disunited, and go to Aix-la-Chapelle to be crowned, holding a diet on the way.

Sigismund pestered me daily for permission to ride outside the castle, and I thought that riding all the way to Aix-la-Chapelle might satisfy his eagerness for a while. But I had to take Albert with me too in order to keep an eye on him. I could no longer stand his traveling around in Hungary with Elizabeth and her infant children whose rightful guardian I was, for I was worried lest he should also be thinking of marrying Elizabeth in order to force his paternal authority on her royal son and all his domains. During my first period as King I often had many reasons for lying awake, and during these sleepless nights I pondered whether I ought not to offer Elizabeth my royal hand so as to forestall Vladislas and possibly Albert too, and become stepfather in the flesh and not only guardian to Ladislas. It reassured and pleased me that Elizabeth wrote and poured out her troubles to me in answer to my letter. I still have the letter. It starts: "Most Illustrious Prince and Dear Cousin. May it please you to learn that some Lords and countrymen from our Kingdom of Hungary came to us before Almighty God had joyfully accomplished our childbirth and travail, desiring that we should take the King of Poland as consort, but that at the time, though it had never been our good will, we dared not decline for reason of much worry and travail, but kindly desired postponement until after our royal childbirth, whereafter, when we had given birth to the Illustrious Prince Lassla as heir to our Kingdom of Hungary, the same Lords and countrymen came to us anew, desiring heartily and sorely that we should take the said consort from Poland, but that they did this against our will, and that we could not sanction any other heir to our lands and people and especially to our Kingdom of Hungary than the rightful and natural heir, our dear son, King Lassla." Of Albert she wrote nothing, but she mentioned how much money she lacked to feed and clothe her children and defend their domains, so I realized that Albert was not a good guardian. Then Albert too wrote to me, begging for money with which to discharge his duties as guardian to Ladislas and his sister. I laughed slyly to myself and invited them both to Neustadt.

Elizabeth came to me with her royal son and her royal daughters and Duke Albert and their great train of men—though especially of women to take care of the children—and they were received heartily and festively by me and Sigismund at the eastern gate of the town. I myself accompanied Elizabeth to the castle, saying: "Our dear cousin, we are pleased to know you in safety from wicked attack and offense." Elizabeth answered: "We should also be pleased to know us in safety." This answer grieved me, and it vexed me that Sigismund and Albert rode behind me, laughing noisily. The two dukes were together a great deal during that visit, for each time Albert left me in anger he went down to the deer park to shoot marbles with Sigismund. I did not forbid them to speak together, but I was afraid of what they might be speaking about, for Sigismund stopped pestering me about going outside the castle as long as Albert was in it. In a way it was a happy time that winter, when we four undivided and fatherless dukes were all together. I sent for a master painter in order to paint us as a family group, but he was used to painting altarpieces and said that it was impious to paint temporal kings and princes—he had never heard of such a thing. He said he would paint Elizabeth and Ladislas as our beloved Virgin Mary with Child, and I and Albert and Sigismund could be the Holy Three Kings even though Sigismund was really too young to be a king, but one of the kings had to be a Moor with a black face and Albert did not want to be a Moor. So the painter said he would paint Elizabeth and Ladislas as the Virgin Mary and Child, and I could be there too as Joseph, with Sigismund and Anne and Elizabeth as angels of various sizes. When Sigismund heard this he broke out into plainsong, waving his arms as if they had already turned into wings, and so I had to tell him to be quiet. But Albert was offended because he was too big to be an angel on the altarpiece and departed in anger; and so it all came to nothing, even though it would amuse me to have that painting today, when so many of us are dead. Ladislas was a beautiful fair-haired child; he looked like his mother and maybe also his father, but Albert had buck teeth and Ladislas no teeth at all, and it was too early to pronounce upon the true size of his nose and chin. But he had a loud voice, and even during his holy baptism he had screamed as terribly as if he were already four, and even his sister Elizabeth, who was five years old, could not scream as loudly as Ladislas. But she was not envious and always used to call Ladislas her King Little Brother, while she called me Uncle King and often sat on my lap. But their poor mother could not sit still for very long at a time; she used to walk up and down the room sighing, which made me sigh too—I don't know why.

We deliberately negotiated in the room next to Ladislas's chambers, so that his wails could be heard and soften Elizabeth's motherly heart, and sometimes she shed tears too, so that even I nearly became softhearted. But Albert was always hard and said: "There is nothing to negotiate about. You will share with us your fixed and liquid assets so that we can discharge our duties as guardian to King Ladislas; in return you may keep the infant Elizabeth." I replied: "We will share with you from our liquid assets and give you two-fifths" (for I had also to take care of my pious sister Katharine, who was Albert's sister too, and always deep in prayer). "In return we will take charge not only of Elizabeth but of King Ladislas, since we are the rightful guardian to them both." But Albert raised his voice and said that I was not to be guardian to both Sigismund and Ladislas—that was unfair. I answered: "Have you enough money to be guardian to anyone?" But Elizabeth wept and said: "We are speaking of my children and you are speaking of money"—but that of course was no fault of mine. Then Albert kicked up a fuss and said that I was always speaking of money. I was a money-grubber, he said, and it was neither princely not knightly but bourgeois and mercenary, and if I had been worthy of being a guardian to King Ladislas, Elizabeth's son, I would have gone to war against his enemies long ago. I replied that if I had gone to war, Ladislas would not have been with me in peace and safety, and if I were to throw my fighting forces into the war, still more people would be slain. Having to fight wars makes people poor, and poor people have to humiliate themselves and beg for money like Albert was doing now. When princes and knights are not princely and knightly enough to provide the King with knights, so that the King has to hire his soldiers, what is he to hire them with if not with money? "Again he's speaking of money," said Albert to Elizabeth. "So you must pledge the royal crown so that we can get away from here." For Elizabeth, in her distress, had carried off the Holy Hungarian Crown of St. Stephen so that Ladislas could be crowned with it, and she had not put it back again lest anyone should be crowned unlawfully with it, so Vladislas had been crowned with a different crown. She wanted thirty thousand guilders for it, but I was not sure she had the right to pledge the crown; only Ladislas had the right to pledge it, and he was my ward, but I was nevertheless willing to give her two thousand five hundred guilders for it. "Two thousand five hundred guilders for a royal crown which cannot be bought for money!" cried Elizabeth. "I'm not buying it for money but accepting it as security," I said, and Elizabeth had to go and attend to the King who was crying loudly. But Albert said: "You Jew!" and went down to shoot marbles with Sigismund.

I felt sorry for Elizabeth, for everyone failed her in her hour of need, but a king must never show his feelings, and preferably not feel them, if he wishes to keep calm. I was prepared to go a long way in order to prevent Elizabeth from marrying anyone else but me, for such a match could be a disadvantage both for me and for the realm, but I reckoned that Albert would soon realize that it was no advantage for him to bind himself in matrimony to her cause, for he only thought of himself. But if I had no political reasons for marrying Elizabeth, I could not marry her solely because she was an unhappy woman. Every morning she looked worn out from lack of sleep, and I too was sleepless, and in a long sleepless night I wrote a poem:

With no sweetheart to caress,
I am free from great distress,
Be it short or be it long,
Courtship turns to woeful song.
He who loves but grief and pain
Is in truth a happy swain.

Our negotiations were interrupted and speeded up by eighty orthodox Bohemian knights who suddenly came riding to offer me the Bohemian crown, for Albert of Bavaria had refused it when I had written forbidding him to wear it. But I took the envoys to task, saying that I had Bohemia's King under my roof—if they were to keep quiet for a moment they would be sure to hear his royal voice—and I was also prepared as guardian to govern Bohemia too in his name, but to steal a crown from an infant king was beneath my royal dignity. I had begged Elizabeth to witness that conversation in secret, however, and when the Bohemians saw their rightful and former Queen they were ashamed and fell on their knees; and I had King Ladislas brought in, even though he had teething pains, and they had never seen such a beautiful royal child. They excused themselves on the plea of the troubled state of their homeland; their heretical countrymen had elected a half-grown Polish prince as King, and they felt obliged to set up a fully grown king in opposition, all the more so because their country was constantly being pillaged by robbers from my and my ward's domains. I thanked them for the honor they had done me, I was willing to permit my noble brother, Duke Albert, to wage war against the robbers if they in return would fulfill their duties towards their infant king.

When the Bohemians had ridden away with this message Elizabeth fell on my neck, addressing me by name: "Frederick," she said, "I have misjudged you. After my husband's death I thought I would never find a man I could rest my head against. You are not like Albert, but you shall be guardian to King Lassla." I let her rest her head against me, and said: "Elizabeth, it would be best for you all if you all stayed with me." But Elizabeth withdrew her restless head and said: "We must go to our Kingdom of Hungary to vanquish the nobles," and I could not restrain her, but felt uneasy at heart, for how can a single woman vanquish faithless nobles. I promised I would not do anything extraordinary with her children, and she bade them farewell with many a motherly tear, receiving two thousand five hundred guilders for the crown of St. Stephen.

I shared my assets with Albert in as brotherly a fashion as I had promised, and helped him to hire the vagrant mercenaries in order to fight the Hungarian and Bohemian and Austrian robbers. But I did not disclose all our assets, for I knew that he would come and share with me again when he had squandered his liquid assets and pledged his fixed castles. So I made him sign that he had no further claims. But when the contract was signed he said in a friendly way: "Now Sigismund and I will ride to Vienna and celebrate the reconciliation." But I said: "Now we are getting everything under control, perhaps we can permit ourselves to ride to Aix-la-Chapelle and be crowned. Would you like to come too, Sigismund?" And Sigismund grew red in the face with joy, or else a bit ashamed in front of Albert, though he had no cause to be. He did not speak in reply, but I winked at him secretly, and he winked back. So Albert went to war in a fury and, needless to say, he also went to war against me. It is no good trusting a reconciled foe forever. But the weakness of my foes was that they were also foes of one another, while my strength lay in my being no one's immediate foe; the war against me did not reach me until several years later.

A few days after Elizabeth had left me I was informed that she stood weeping beyond the outer gate of the castle. I went joyfully to meet her, for I was unhappy to think of her among Hungarian nobles. "Elizabeth," I said, "so you've come back after all." "You must give me back my children," she said, "for otherwise I shall have no peace for missing them." Those words grieved me, and I had to speak sternly to her in the name of her own son, King Ladislas, whom she called Lassla. He was in safe keeping with me, but would not be on unsafe Hungarian roads. She was heartily welcome to take motherly care of her children in my castle, and I would let her take care of the whole of the inner castle, but I had promised not to do anything extraordinary with her children, and it would be extraordinary if I were to hand them over instantly. Then she fell on her knees and wept so bitterly that I could not bear to see her and had to look aside, and she begged and prayed to see her children. I said that she had already taken leave of her children and that one should not exaggerate the pain of parting. Then she flung terrible accusations and curses at me—I had enticed her children away from her, she said, and I could not stand hearing such unreasonable words from Elizabeth's mouth and ordered the castle gate to be closed upon her. I never saw her again; naturally, I climbed up into the gate tower to see her ride away, but she rode so fast that she had already gone by the time I got to the top. She rode to Vienna and placed her accusations before the Austrian Estates, and her accusations won them over and they demanded that Ladislas should grow up in the Inner, Upper or Lower Austria over which his father had ruled; I replied immediately that the country was undivided and that Ladislas felt comfortable in Neustadt. Elizabeth sent me many letters, first bidding me bear with an unhappy woman, and then upbraiding me for taking advantage of her womanly misfortunes. I never answered her letters, still hoping that she would return to her children. Ladislas had begun to walk, though he preferred riding, and once again I went down on all fours and played horsie in my spare time. But most of the time I sat in council, for the problems were many.

Most of the councilors were noblemen who always wanted to go to war, but they could not agree as to which of my foes I should wage war against, and some of them wanted me to subjugate the whole of Italy, for the small states in that country had suffered so greatly from internal fighting that it would be easy to conquer them all at once. But I saw no need to subjugate Italy, since it was already under the power of the King. Most of the others were bishops who wanted me to side with one pope against the other, but they were unable to agree as to which of the popes I should side with. I seldom said anything in council myself, for it was I who had to make the great decisions, and I often used to pretend I was asleep, all the better to hear their honest opinions; but in case they thought I was merely pretending to be asleep, sometimes I really did fall asleep and did not wake up until the meeting was over. But I had heard the councilors say that it would be a pity if I were not to attend my third diet in Frankfurt, for the princes demanded this and would not come unless I myself came. But it is not for princes to demand something of their king, and I replied that if they had held a diet before without achieving anything, then it would be a pity if His Grace were to set out and not achieve anything. The diet was not held, the conditions being too bad, and I was anxious about the good relations between Elizabeth and the Austrians, especially if Albert too had some relation to them. If I were to go to Frankfurt I could not avoid Bavaria, where Ludwig the Hunchbacked was at war with his old father, Ludwig the Bearded, and Ludwig begged and implored me to intervene with my armed forces since I was going that way anyway. But I replied that I would under no circumstances travel that way before the dispute was settled, for it did not befit a king to tolerate or sanction such an unjust and quarrelsome dispute, and a quarrel of that kind between father and son was both unseemly and unnatural and almost unheard of in our time. But I permitted the unhappy father to found charitable foundations in his towns with the large sums of money he had acquired by less than honest means, and sanctioned the appointment of sixteen choristers and one organist to perform masses for his soul both day and night. For I wanted religion to regain its power over people's minds, and nothing lay nearer to my heart than settling the dispute between the holy fathers and popes who ought to be the light of the world. Furthermore, I thought that as long as there were two popes, I could not be crowned by only one of them.

Sigismund was more filial at that time than usual—he talked a great deal about the coronation journey and the route we should take and whether we should visit Tyrol. He pestered me frequently for a suit of armour, and I would have liked to have given him one as a surprise, but it is not possible to surprise anyone with a suit of armor because it has to be measured, and princes who are not fully grown would outgrow their measurements before the armor was completed. Instead, I decided to surprise Sigismund by showing him greater confidence. A king has councilors but no confidants, for too much confidence leads to contempt, and yet a king would like to be a man and a cousin and not always a king. I would have liked to speak confidentially to Sigismund about all the problems of Christendom, for his sake as well, but he was too young to understand them. For the time being I considered speaking Latin to him, for it is important for a ruler to gain command of that tongue in time to be able to read his own letters, and in Latin we should not be able to express ourselves well enough to overdo the confidence, unless Sigismund was already more learned than I. I entered Sigismund's schoolroom in secret in order to hear how far he had come. Teacher and pupil alike were speaking eagerly, but not in Latin—it was honest German they were speaking, though what they were speaking about, so loudly and incautiously that they drowned out my cautious steps, was not so honest. They were speaking about the coronation journey and the route we should take and how Sigismund could best allow himself to be attacked and carried off by Tyrolean knights. This was rebellion. I had already had to stand much from my own flesh and blood, but that my fourteen-year-old ward should already be tired of my guardianship worried me also as guardian. I said "Et tu, fili mi, Sigismunde," but I had my suspicions as to how much Latin the free Tyrolean had taught Sigismund, for Sigismund seemed not to understand. That was the first occasion on which I saw Sigismund lie as if dead, as only dogs and animals usually do when their masters get the upper hand; he lay down on the floor without saying a word, his mouth pursed, not even deigning to look at me. I must confess, I was angry enough to shake him, but I had vowed to protect the fatherless, and Sigismund was only a child. I said as punishment: "Then I shall ride alone to Aix-la-Chapelle with a thousand horse, and you shall not have your suit of armor." He should, of course, have been childish enough to weep and beg for mercy, for then no more would have been said, but he continued to lie as if dead, without even wincing. The free doctor winced all over and begged for mercy, but he was too old for that sort of thing, and I had him confined to the dungeon, for Senika has said that justice without mercy is severity, while mercy without justice is weakness.

Now there was no way out—I had said I would ride to Aix-la-Chapelle and I had given my word. In a way I regretted my own severity, for what might not take place in my absence! I gave orders that the willow hedge around the deer park should be replaced with a twelve foot high wall in order to protect my wards. I requested safe conduct and lodging in all my domains and let it be known that on St. Kilian's Day in Frankfurt I would attend my fourth diet in person and would be at full strength on my way home from the coronation city. I set off, without saying good-by to Sigismund, with about one thousand knights and squires whose names I shall not mention. It grieved me to think I was causing him grief. But I soon had other things to think about. Everywhere I went the roads were so bad that we could only make our way with difficulty, and in all our beautiful towns—Augsburg, Nuremberg, Würzburg, etc.—the citizens came to me complaining that they could not travel in peace along the roads; not only did they fall and tumble into the ruts, but they were attacked by thieves and rogues. It pained me to hear that our domains were in such a poor state, and although I saw nothing of the war between father and son in Bavaria, I heard of much other discord and injury. I scarcely slept a wink in any of the large towns, for everywhere my faithful subjects stood in long rows, complaining of pillage and murder and damage and bringing me their sick and their aged for me to heal and make young again. I promised them all to do my best with God's help.

Two days after St. Vitus' Day I was crowned King of the Romans in the Church of Our Lady in Aix-la-Chapelle by Bishop Didrik of Cologne, and was acclaimed by all as the mighty, peace-loving, God-crowned King—it was the greatest moment of my life. There was a roast ox for all and a well of wine outside the church, and I had rejoiced in bringing my family silver and plate with me for the coronation banquet in the City Hall; but all my noble guests took their spoons and forks and knives and silver platters away with them, so that my trusty men had to fight with them until far into the night. When the struggle was at its peak Elector Ludwig of the Palatinate came to me, saying: "Gracious Lord, there are strange rumors going round the town that I am setting myself up against you, but they are quite unfounded—I would gladly die and be resurrected with you at any time. But at coronation banquets it is an old custom to take away the coronation service when one leaves the table." I thanked him for these words, but still thought it an unchristian custom, and I had to buy back my family silver with the money the city was obliged to lend me.

For everyone only thinks of his own, and I departed in speed so that—as my first act as crowned king—I could reform everything at the diet in Frankfurt. I made a speech saying that in the Holy Roman Empire, and especially in the German nation through which I had recently passed with difficulty, too many violent and otherwise unseemly and dishonest attacks and pillagings had taken place, and that much plunder and murder and arson were still taking place which ought not to take place in an empire that was called holy, because it caused this empire's subjects and persons spiritual as well as temporal debasement, harm and great hardship, about which a great wave of complaint was spreading throughout my domains. I forbade all civil wars and skirmishes and reformed the laws of pledge so that it should become possible to redeem feeding pledges like live animals and horses after three days and dead pledges after three weeks, all under the vigilance and jurisdiction of the High Court; and I commanded that all holes in the road should be filled in so that all might journey in peace upon the roads, whether they be sick or in labor, pilgrims or priests, merchants or carriers transporting perishable or unperishable goods, and that all those who violated these laws and regulations were to be outlawed and pay a fine of one hundred gold marks to the King, for I also decreed that gold coins should be fixed at nineteen carat. While I was arranging these matters I noticed some princes laughing in the hall. It was beneath my royal dignity to ask them what they were laughing at, but I realized later on that they were laughing because they had no intention of putting these orders into practice. I decided never again to attend a diet in my own illustrious person, and set out forthwith for my Swiss domains, which had been in a state of unrest ever since the Confederacy broke away from our empire and had Leopold, my and Sigismund's grandfather, killed.

The confederates greeted me politely enough as king of the realm, though did not acclaim me as lord of their country, and so I lavished no favors upon them. Only in our faithful town of Zürich was everyone pleased to see me, for Zürich had remained faithful to our house: they were afraid of being attacked by the Confederacy and hoped I would support them. I promised the town all the support I could give, but I had other matters to attend to. I had been obliged to leave the diet without solving the question of the papal Schism, and the two popes' most distinguished cardinals had attached themselves to my train in order to persuade me to recognize each of their popes as the only one. I permitted first one and then the other red-clad cardinal to approach and ride beside me, and I let them say what they liked, reserving my own opinion. Every time I and the Cardinal from Arles rode alone through the Swiss countryside he spoke to me of holy matrimony. My councilors too had counseled me to take a wife before I was too old, so that I would have a son in time to inherit the kingdom, but sons are not always a blessing, and I could not see that my private life was any concern of a cardinal. Then he gave me to understand that no marriage could be holier than a marriage with a holy father's daughter, and it occurred to me that Pope Felix of Basel had led a wordly life while he was Duke of Savoy, and still had grown-up children. Strictly speaking, a pope cannot have a daughter, but if he had a daughter before he became pope, it is reasonable that he should continue to think of her future. She was called Marguerite, like a flower, said the cardinal, painting her beauty for me, and her hair was black and her lips were red. My own sister, who had been married to Saxony, was also called Marguerite, and I rode along the long, blue lake to Geneva in order to see her for myself, and all her brothers of Savoy rode heartily forth to meet me.

The King's power is great. It was within my power to make Pope Felix my father-in-law and thereby the rightful pope, but Pope Eugenius had already permitted me the use of a transportable altar, which I sorely needed on that long and arduous journey; he had also graciously permitted me to choose a confessor who could absolve me from sin, once during my lifetime and again at my death. I also considered that if I were to wed Marguerite of Savoy I would not be able to wed Elizabeth and steal a march on Albert if he were still nourishing such plans. So I tarried several days in Geneva before visiting Marguerite, and while I was tarrying there a message came from home to say that Elizabeth had drunk the cup of reconciliation with her enemy, Vladislas of Poland, and had thereupon fallen down dead. It would have been better for Elizabeth to have stayed with me, but she had an uneasy heart, and my heart too was uneasy. Mournfully, I clad myself in mourning and paid Marguerite a visit. She too was clad in a high-necked black gown; she was a widow and no longer quite young, but her hair was black and her lips fairly red, and we spoke at length about life and death and related matters. I spoke also of the responsibility of being King, of which I never usually spoke, and Marguerite said it was also a responsibility to be a pope—her father and I would be sure to understand one another. I promised to visit her holy father in Basel and kissed her white hand in farewell.

In Basel a host of cardinals and bishops were waiting at the gate to receive me and lead me to both Council and Pope. But I waited outside until they grew weary of waiting inside, for I considered it unfitting to permit myself to be received as King when I came on a secret and private errand. Escorted only by the most necessary men and horses, I rode at night to Pope Felix of Savoy. He had not expected me so late and had sent his cardinals home, so I was received by a mere confidential secretary—the Aeneas who later became Pope—and he welcomed me with so lengthy a speech in Latin that Felix found time to attire himself papally. I understood only little of the speech, but I thought he might make a suitable Latin tutor for Sigismund. I bade my chancellor Casper negotiate secretly with Aeneas about becoming my secretary, while I secretly negotiated with the Pope.

I knelt respectfully before the Holy Father, though noticed that he had a beard, which no pope ought to have, and although I was in the act of bending to kiss his toe, I stopped on my way and kissed his hand instead; I could not bow to him entirely, since he was, after all, a former duke and only half a pope. So I could not address him as Your Holiness, but addressed him instead as Your Benevolence. He did in fact treat me benevolently, and he permitted me to choose a confessor who could absolve me from my sins once during my lifetime and yet again after my death. I thanked him for that favor, but said that Pope Eugenius had granted me the same favor before he was dethroned by the Holy Council. Then Felix took off his papal crown and offered me his daughter Marguerite as lawful wife and a dowry of two hundred thousand ducats. This was not much for a queen and a pope's daughter, but Amadeus had spent a lot of money in order to become a pope, and to make him as powerful as Eugenius his court had bought just as many benefices as Eugenius's court sold, and thus Amadeus was the poorer of the two. He said that the Pope entrusts the rule of the world to the Emperor, and as a symbol he would entrust his daughter to me to rule over, and he would crown me as Emperor at the wedding. I replied that this would doubtless be the greatest moment in my life, the hitherto greatest one having been that of my coronation as King. But I had considered for such a long time whether I should accept the royal crown that I would have to consider even longer still whether I should accept the Emperor's crown and his daughter Marguerite. Felix blessed me and said: "Consider well, my son, but not too long, for Count Ludwig of the Palatinate has already asked for Marguerite's hand. But to you I make no secret of the fact that I would prefer you as my son-in-law. Ought not the whole of Christendom to be as one big family? So ought not its mightiest men to be as father and son?" I thought that sounded so right and proper that I kissed the Pope's toe in farewell after all. His secretary Aeneas accompanied me as my secretary, and I rejoiced that Sigismund could now learn proper Latin.

If I avoided Tyrol the Tyrolese would say I was afraid to ride through, so I rode through Tyrol, though with a heavy heart. For nowhere was there anyone to give me a royal welcome; the countryside was deserted, and only in the distance did I perceive many heads peeping out from among the mountains. On Christmas Eve I arrived at my native town, and to demonstrate my peaceful disposition I sang in the Church of St. Jacob dressed up as an ordinary deacon; with loud voice I sang "Exiit edictum a Caesare Augusto, etc.," and the church was crammed; after Holy Mass was over, and I was attiring myself once more as King, all the churchgoers speedily left the church, and when I rode to my inn in the silent night all the streets were empty. But I summoned the lords and bishops whom I had set to administer the country in my and Sigismund's name, so I could complain to them about the impoliteness of the Tyrolese, and they all came to me to complain about the lower Estates, who were constantly holding assemblies and demanding that Duke Sigismund be handed over. They could only just manage to keep peace in the land until Duke Sigismund was sixteen years old, and he was already fifteen. I realized it was high time I returned home.

Sigismund received me at the western gate of the town with the beautiful words, "Welcome home, King Frederick!" and bowed so deeply that I grew suspicious. "I have a Latin tutor for you," I answered, and Sigismund became red in the face and dropped his chin. He had grown much bigger in my absence, but his nose and chin were still too insignificant. King Ladislas, on the other hand, already had a beautiful nose although he was only two, and I lifted him up on to my horse, thinking sorrowfully that we undivided dukes were all both fatherless and motherless. Duke Albert had not come to receive me, but I was told that he had allied himself with King Vladislas of Poland and was attacking my borders with Hungarian troops, and since I had ordered him to stop the Hungarian and Bohemian raids on Austria, there was now no one to stop them, and emissaries from Hungary and Austria were waiting impatiently to ask me to stop the raids on these three countries from the two others immediately. I ordered diets to be held forthwith in all my domains with the object of creating peace, but after my homecoming I had so much to do that I could not attend any of them in person, and without my presence nothing could be accomplished. A king has to be everywhere at once.

Sigismund was always going around with his mouth open, but in a manner reminiscent of foxes and other sly animals, and I suspected mischief. I bade Aeneas take him strictly to task, and while Sigismund was at his tasks I entered his innermost chambers. His servants, all of whom had already been replaced so that I could better trust them, said that their master was not at home. I said that I was their master and I was at home. They were walking around with some papers in such a suspicious manner that my suspicions were aroused. They were illegal dispatches to knights and town in Tyrol. They were not written by Sigismund, but sent to him by some Tyrolese so that he could send them to Tyrol and urge the Tyrolese in town and province to support his fight for majority. I was upset about their attempts to treat my ward as an irresponsible minor by dictating him such letters. In order to justify their nasty project, a certain Hans of Knöringen, who was unknown to me, wrote that I as the eldest duke was thinking of seizing all the power myself, but that we were all undivided, and therefore Sigismund ought to receive his share too. He also wrote that I myself had revolted against Sigismund's own father of Tyrol when he had prolonged his guardianship over me, so Duke Sigismund should not put up with my prolonging the guardianship over him. He failed to mention that at that time I was nineteen and my brother Albert only sixteen, whereas Sigismund was not yet even sixteen and I had not prolonged any guardianship. I comforted myself with the thought that Sigismund had not dispatched the letters the Tyrolese had wanted him to dispatch, and that he had not thrown away the letter Hans of Knöringen had written and asked him to throw away for safety's sake, and I almost began to think that Sigismund had seen through the Tyrolean schemes. But then, with trembling hand, I discovered a letter from Sigismund to Hans of Knöringen which he had not dispatched either, and I could only interpret as carelessness and negligence the fact that he had neither dispatched nor thrown away any letters, and this only supported my conviction that such a careless and negligent duke was by no means fit to rule. I read Sigismund's letter with horror, and I shall never forget it. "We are so watched over," he wrote, "and so sat on that we can neither attend to our own nor our subjects' well-being. On St. Jacob's Day we shall seek with God's help and the assistance of you all to come into possession of our father's inheritance, for neither suffering nor love will be able to persuade or force us into a postponement of our coming of age. We shall also expect you to commiserate with the great wretchedness and ignominy we are obliged to suffer and to endeavor to help us out of that ignominy and wretchedness. Otherwise, let it thus be known that with the help of Almighty God in this and all our other matters we and all our trusty men will continue to be fearless and bold. Sigismund, Duke of Austria, Styria, Carinthis, Carniola, Count of Tyrol, etc."

So that was gratitude! I was shaken, and had to sit down. What were all the other matters Sigismund had written about—as if one were not enough? Who were the trusty men of whom he spoke? Could I not trust anyone in my own castle? Sigismund came rushing in. I would have almost preferred him to have lain dead than make such a fuss. He was red in the face, though unfortunately not from shame but from unrighteous wrath, and his eyes were full of tears, though unfortunately not from repentance but from fury. "You are sitting on me!" he shouted—an expression that had confused me when I read it in his letter. I replied that I had recently been on a long and perilous coronation journey, and had not been sitting on anything other than my horse, and that he should not tell such tales. Then he shouted, "You are spying on me!" I asked him if I had ever spied on him before, and he replied that that was what I had just been doing. I asked him whether I didn't have the right to read his letters if those were the sort of letters he wrote. He replied that if I didn't read his letters he wouldn't have written such letters.

I asked when I had wanted to prolong the guardianship. "Isn't that what you want to do now?" he asked. "Yes, you can be sure it is," I said, "when this is the way you behave." And he said, "Have I been telling lies, then?" for he could twist and turn things just like Albert. I said that he ought to consider himself above being a plaything for some lower Estate in Tyrol. He said he considered himself above being a plaything for me. I had promised, he said, to let him live in the air he had breathed as a child in a healthy and convenient castle. Living with me was not only unhealthy but inconvenient, and the air was not fit to breathe. I said that his own father had kept me under guardianship until I was nineteen. He said that that was my own fault for putting up with it. I asked him whether he was speaking ill of his own late father, my guardian. He roared: "I am speaking ill of all guardians." That was the most terrible thing I had ever experienced.

I was so angry that I wanted to send the unruly Sigismund to Tyrol forthwith in order to teach him a lesson. But I had vowed to protect the fatherless and parentless and couldn't be angry with him for long. But I could justly punish him by keeping him under guardianship and preserving our house undivided. For I knew that if Sigismund became a divided duke and was recognized as the sole ruler of Tyrol, then Albert would feel slighted if he did not receive his share too, and then our joint realm would be broken up and might never be joined together again. Nor could I justify my sending a disobedient child down to the angry Tyrolese, for the Swiss were also angry and already attacking our faithful town of Zürich, and they would be sure to attack Tyrol too if its ruler were not yet of age. So I was content to sentence Sigismund to house arrest; only his Latin tutor was permitted to visit him and take him even more strictly to task. I promised Aeneas that if Sigismund made progress both in learning and good conduct I would grant him a vacant benefice in gratitude.

I wrote to Ludwig the Hunchback of Bavaria and promised to forgive him his disobedience to his old father if he would declare war on the Swiss immediately. But I myself never got any peace to prepare for war. A continual stream of Austrian envoys came wanting me to hand Duke Ladislas over so that he could grow up in Vienna, and Hungarian envoys wanting me to hand King Ladislas over so that he could grow up in Pressburg, and Bohemian envoys wanting me to hand King Ladislas over so that he could grow up in Prague. And if I were to placate them all, I would have to chop the child into three parts like the wise King Solomon. But I wished to retain Ladislas undivided. The Bohemians wanted to solve the problem by gathering all Ladislas's domains under the kingdom of Bohemia, for they had no understanding of the overall situation. Those who only have to manage a part of the world have an easier time than those who have to manage the whole, and I suppose that is how those unhappy partitions and frontiers behind which people fortify themselves have come about. Even the Hungarians who were honorable enough to regard Ladislas as King reproached me for having taken not only the King but also the royal crown out of the country, even though I had accepted the crown as security in an honest way. They also reproached me for not having fought for my noble ward against King Vladislas, for whom I would certainly be a match since he was hard-pressed by the Turks. But I found it unseemly to conquer the kingdom behind his back. Even my own councilors wanted me to go to war to punish my enemies. But the Austrian standard has not always been triumphant, and I could not in any case punish them all at once. Revenge is a task for time and God, if justice is to be done.

When spring came I went walking in the deer park, whose walls were now almost high enough to protect me from curious glances from without. I listened wistfully to the birdsong of the tiny birds and to the cooing of the turtledoves while thinking of what lay nearest to my heart. I could resolve the great Schism and abolish my royal loneliness by wedding Marguerite, and I ought not to take too long considering, my possible father-in-law had said, but I never had any peace in which to think of Marguerite. It was soon St. Jacob's Day and I had to be prepared for an armed rising in Tyrol. I would let Sigismund feel that he was still in disgrace by refusing to see him, and I had no time at all to see anyone. Impatiently, I waited to hear his tutor's report, and in the end

I had to send for him. "Why do I see you so seldom?" I asked, and Aeneas replied that he had incessantly tried to see me, but the doorkeeper would not let him enter even though he spoke German to him. He saw cupbearer, cook, birdkeeper, chamberlain, head groom and master of hounds going in and out, yet he himself, my confidential secretary, had to remain outside. Alas, yes, I sighed, we never have an hour to spare. Treasurers and physicians come and attend to the external matters, confessors and curates to the internal ones. Councilors, chancellors, notaries, knights, nobles and barons come at appointed hours, but our secretaries may come at any time providing there is no one else with us, for to judge from the multitude of letters we need them all day long. But Aeneas thought I preferred to grant Germans audience with the King because I would rather speak German than Latin. I said he had no reason for complaint, for I had already spoken more Latin to him than to anyone else for a whole month. Then I ought to speak more to him that to anyone else, said Aeneas: the King of the Romans ought to speak Roman just like Julius, Augustus, Tiberius, Gaius, Claudius, etc. "My kingdom is German," I said. "The kingdom should not be of any tongue," said Aeneas. "Do we ever speak of the Holy Catholic Church of a particular tongue? Latin is the language of languages just as the King is the king of kings. So you, who rightly surpass all others in goodness, piety, religiosity and justice, ought not to be worse at Latin than anyone else." I was a bit offended, for I spoke just as good Latin then as I do now, but Aeneas said that a king ought to be able to make long speeches in Latin, for he does not rule with weapons alone but with every word of wisdom that comes from his mouth, and that was what he was trying to teach Duke Sigismund of Austria. And then he handed me an exceedingly thick manuscript that had been written for the purpose of Sigismund's instruction. I said that I would read it when I had time, but Aeneas wanted to read the whole manuscript aloud, and before I managed to stop him he had already begun. Despite his young age, Duke Sigismund was not only handsome but clever enough to realize that he was still too young to rule before he became still cleverer. For the deeds of a prince are the most difficult deeds of all, and since a priest and a pope always have to be twenty-three and thirty before they become priest and pope, a prince ought to be just as old before becoming a prince. No matter how many councilors he has—and the younger he is the greater the number—they counsel him to do what they think is most pleasing to himself in order to win his favor and obtain great favors and offices. But is what is most pleasing always the wisest thing to do? And even if he were to possess all the wisest councilors it is nevertheless the prince who must make the decisions as prince, and is he experienced enough to make them so long as he has no experience? Thus Duke Sigismund would be wise to follow Aeneas's advice and let his illustrious cousin (that is to say, me) rule until he had gained enough experience under my illustrious guidance. Tyrol could rightly do with a wise ruler during those difficult times, but only the power and glory of the royal majesty would be awe-inspiring enough to inspire its foes with sufficient awe. In the meantime, however, Sigismund should endeavor to acquire wisdom and foreign tongues so that when the time came he would not be a prince like all the others but a prince whom all the others would want to be like, and just as the Queen of Sheba and many other beautiful princesses had come to Jerusalem to admire the wisdom of Solomon, they would come likewise from all over the world to admire Sigismund. Never had I heard anything written so much after my own heart, and even though I had to stop Aeneas in the end, I promised him that if I kept Tyrol within my power I would give him the first vacant deanery in Tyrol and crown him as poet, and I bade him compose Sigismund's declaration that he had asked me to prolong my guardianship for three years. But Aeneas immediately prolonged that by another three years, because priests do not become priests until they are twenty-three and Sigismund was still only sixteen. I rejoiced at having obtained such a learned man in my service and rejoiced that Sigismund too would become learned if he remained under his guidance for yet another six years.

Whereupon Aeneas composed yet another epistle in which Sigismund authoritively entrusted me to rule Tyrol in my and his name, with the power to instate or dismiss captains, burgraves, stewards, tax collectors and other officials; to appoint all the officials in all large and small towns, villages and hamlets; to collect all taxes, rents and dues, and to nominate all the deans whom the secular powers were authorized to nominate for six years from St. Jacob's Day in the present year of Our Lord Jesus Christ; for he would still be too young to rule our domains during these so serious times for yet another six years. In addition Sigismund thanked me for my loving guardianship according to our praiseworthy house rule and exempted me from accounting to anyone for my administration of the country, including the salt and silver mines. I was satisfied with this wording, and said: "Then just ask Sigismund to set his seal on it." But Aeneas looked at me in astonishment, intimating that such a solemn act of jurisdiction could only be performed in my own presence. I decided to restore Sigismund to favor again and sent for him.

He did not appear to have a guilty conscience. "Our King and cousin!" he said, with a fitting bow. "Sigismund," I said, "you are soon sixteen years of age and clever enough to understand what is best for our house and thereby for you. If you understand that, then set your seal on this declaration and I shall issue your coming of age certificate on St. Jacob's Day." But Sigismund became both red and white in the face while he read it, and he had not even read to the end before he shouted "This is a breach of contract!" I sat down in order to explain to him why it was not a breach of contract. It was not for the Estates in Tyrol or in any other part of our domains to dictate conditions to us dukes, and if we were to stand together we could disregard the contract of Hall. For it was not the high-born nobles who wanted me to hand Sigismund over, for they were faithful to me and to our house. But it was the provincial estates and towns who were exploiting him, Sigismund, as a pretext for rising against the nobles and the highest authority in the land: it was the Tyrolese nation which was rising high-handedly and selfishly against us cousins by the grace of God. Duke Sigismund started crying. I cannot stand seeing children cry when they are no longer infants in arms, so I said: "Is it seemly for a prince who is of age to shed tears? Tyrol can still be saved if you just set your seal." But Sigismund screamed "I shall not set any seal." "Well and good," I said, "then we shall issue no declaration and you shall not come of age." Then Sigismund behaved quite like a child, begging and praying me to become a free ruling duke. So I felt sorry for him as a duke and said: "Alas, Sigismund, you don't understand that the more power you acquire, the less freedom you obtain." But he didn't understand that and said: "But I have no freedom." "You are a child," I said, "and the happy days of childhood never come again." "But I'm not happy," Sigismund shouted, and thus we got no further.

I would not force Sigismund to sign, and St. Jacob's Day came and went without any declarations. My councilors advised me to prepare for war against the Tyrolese, and I unfortunately took their advice. I had heard that my colleagues, King Charles of France and King Henry of England, were at the moment making a pause in their Hundred Years' War, so that King Charles's mercenaries, the "Poor Fools," had nothing to do. So I wrote and asked him if I might hire five thousand soldiers to protect Sigismund's and my domains, and I reminded him of the special reasons why he had to support my ward Sigismund. Of course I couldn't yet write and say that I also expected trouble in Tyrol and needed troops to create peace. But I had already learned that the Tyrolese estates had held a diet and sent deputations to me as well as to my provincial captain, Master Ulrich, and all my stewards in Tyrol. They were to regard themselves as dismissed if they failed to make common cause with the rebel Estates, and I was not to be regarded as Sigismund's guardian unless I handed him over to them. As soon as he entered Tyrol he would be free to choose whether he still wanted to be under my guardianship or not, but it was plain to everyone how much freedom of choice he would have once he entered Tyrol. The Tyrolese only thought of their own gain, and they did not expect Sigismund, as free ruling duke, to introduce anything new regarding taxes and duties beyond what his father, Duke Frederick, had already introduced. They failed to mention what I had introduced. I was angry on Sigismund's and my behalf and waited for King Charles to reply. And I did not have to wait long: he promised me as many Poor Fools as I liked and at a reasonable price, and for love of Duke Sigismund he would even place his own son, Louis the Dauphin, in command of them. I was surprised at his wanting to send his own son into foreign military service, but I thought Charles might be finding it difficult to control him and wanted to be rid of him for a while, for Louis had only recently come of age. I was used to the relations between fathers and sons not being of the best. Alas, I did not realize at that time that the relations between them were all too good. I was content to rejoice over the many soldiers who were already advancing upon the Confederacy.

Nevertheless I felt a growing uneasiness as the deputation from Tyrol approached. I would be unable to deny them audience with Sigismund without wicked rumors being spread that I was keeping him concealed; and should he not declare himself in agreement with me, wicked rumors would doubtless be spread that I was keeping Sigismund captive against his will. I made yet another attempt to talk sense to Sigismund and Sigismund into sense, but he lay as if dead. It pained me to think that Sigismund had become so badly brought up, and I didn't speak to his upbringer for several days. The Tyrolese were already in the country with forty-three horse. I consulted my councilors, who reassured me that whatever Duke Sigismund said to the Tyrolese had no political significance, as long as he was not yet declared of age. The Tyrolese were already waiting when Aeneas came to me. I had no time to talk to him just then, though he managed to slip in that I could safely allow Duke Sigismund to be present. I demanded an explanation, but the Tyrolese were already standing at the door. They were in a great hurry; they said that the Hall agreement had long since expired, and asked whether I would hand over their gracious Duke Sigismund of Tyrol according to the expired agreement, yes or no. "No," I said, for I had no wish to enter into a discussion with rebels. They said they wished to hear those words from Sigismund's own mouth. I bade Sigismund enter. He smiled so enigmatically that I suddenly suspected a conspiracy between him and Aeneas: if Sigismund were to become Duke of Tyrol, it was he who would appoint the deans. When they saw Sigismund they fell on their knees and had the effrontery to present him with a suit of armor before my very eyes, and I wondered anxiously how they had taken his measurements. "Illustrious Duke," they said, "we have come to accompany you home to your mighty inheritance." Sigismund thanked them most graciously, and with an authority and skill with which I had never credited him he said: "Non sum adhuc adeo maturus ut gubernare patriam possim," and when the Tyrolese rose up on their knees, looking at each other as if they couldn't understand Latin, Sigismund said in German: "I am not yet of so mature an age that I feel able to rule our land." Then the Tyrolese got to their feet and Sigismund nodded to them, saying "Pax vobiscum!" and the Tyrolese rode away in haste.

Aeneas came to me and praised Sigismund's words as princely words that would pass from mouth to mouth for ever after. But I had a feeling that Aeneas himself had put those words into his mouth, for if Sigismund were able to pronounce such words on his own, he needed neither guardian nor Latin tutor. Aeneas drew forth a manuscript. I said I would read it when I had time. But Aeneas had already stepped back a couple of paces to make a sweeping gesture, and he read out the following letter with raised voice:

Hannibal, Duke of Numidia, sends with his own hand most honorable greetings to the sole ruler of his heart, the virtuous maid Lucretia, daughter of the King of the Epirots.

I have always wished to speak to you and confess my love. But at my age I am still too shy to express my feelings. Scarcely do I start to speak than I am concealed with blushes and fear makes my voice catch in my throat. I fear that your virtues will find fault with me, that your ladies will laugh at me and that I will begin to stammer. What I wish to confide in you I shall therefore confide in this letter, for a letter does not blush, fear or stammer. Perhaps you think I am making unreasonable demands, but what I am asking of you is only reasonable. If you permit it, I shall treat you with great respect. For I, O virtuous maid, must confess that your light has so inflamed my love that day and night I cannot think of anyoneelse but you. When my eyes find you they are filled with joy, but when they do not find you they are filled with tears. The poets praise Helen, but I cannot believe that she was your equal, and still less Deianeira, dearly beloved of Hercules himself. Like another Philomena, you conquer all others from the highest to the lowest with your beauty and virtue. For were I able to regard you as closely as I wished, I would discover no blemish. The shine of your hair surpasses that of gold, your brow is as broad as it is high, your eyebrows arch at a passing distance from one another, your eyes are like stars that send forth arrows to wound young men: whomsoever they gaze upon they slay, and whomsoever they gaze upon they bring to life. Your nose most beautifully adorns your face and harmonizes so delightfully with the other parts of your snow-white face, snow-white all excepting your blushing cheeks. I extol your coral lips and likewise your crystal teeth, and the whole of your mouth from which stream both honeyed words and ofttimes the laughter that makes my heart bleed. Oh happy the man who will one day bite those lips and kiss those cheeks and caress that chin and embrace that throat: I extol everything about you except your breast and the apples it bears, for those I cannot extol without losing my last shred of peace. You are indeed so beautiful both inside and out that you are more easily worshiped than described. You have made a servant of a duke, and that is what was said of Phoebus, son of the Jupiter who was worshiped as a god in ancient times—he who turned himself into a shepherd for love of Admetus's daughter even though he feared the herd. That is how I would serve you, and I beg for nothing other than permission to love you.

I know that even greater and better men would be unworthy of you, for scarcely either Paris or Hippolytus is worthy of your love. But you will not demand good looks of me, for those who are good-looking are also wanton and inconstant in love. In me the love that has sprung from the flower of my youth will last forever; it will grow with my years and endure into my old age, if only you do not despise me. For the gods have bestowed on me both average looks and riches far above average, all of which shall be yours if only you will give me your love in return. What am I saying? I am not begging you to love me, but to permit me to love you. If you will grant me that of your grace, my happiness will be as great as my love.

Fare thee well, thou my soul, thou my delight, thou my heart! Write soon!

HANNIBAL

Aeneas bowed deeply when he had read the letter, and I realized that he wished to remind me about my crowning him as poet. However, I considered the subject ill-chosen and felt somewhat embarrassed. But I asked him for a copy just the same, for I had been thinking of writing to Marguerite for a long time, and although this letter was quite unsuitable, I could make use of a word here and there. Only then did it occur to me that I had received no explanation of Sigismund's conduct and asked him for one. Aeneas banged his rolled-up letter on the table, saying that was the explanation. "How?" I asked. And then Aeneas told me that the Duke had apparently become inflamed with passion for one of the maidens in the castle, exactly as the letter described. That was why he suddenly no longer wished to go to Tyrol. "Did Sigismund write this letter, then?" I asked, greatly alarmed. "No," said Aeneas, bowing, "I did." But I was not at all reassured, for I realized that Aeneas had written it for Sigismund. "But Hannibal," I said, "and Lucretia, daughter of the King of the Epirots . . ." "That is more poetic," said Aeneas. "Naturally there is no king's daughter in the castle." "But Sigismund is betrothed," I said in great distress. "He is betrothed?" said Aeneas. "He has never said so. To whom?" "To Radegundis, daughter of King Charles of France. They were betrothed when he was three and she, almost newborn. And that is why I have asked King Charles to help me against Tyrol, for he is Sigismund's father-in-law." "Alas," was all Aeneas said, "in matters of love not even princes are happy, for they must always marry for the sake of the kingdom and not for their own sakes—and that is why there are so many bastard princes, particularly in Italy, my native land." I did not care for that conversation. But I had to find out. "But a maiden here in the castle—that must surely be one of the castle maids. And such a maid is not of noble birth." Aeneas shrugged his shoulders, and I positively shouted: "This is immoral!" "By no means," said Aeneas, "by no means. He who does not make love in his youth does so at an age less fitting for love; an aged lover makes himself ridiculous and the object of gossip. Is not love the most beautiful thing on earth? Is it not in the habit of awakening the lax morals of young men? It calls one to arms, another to books. Is it not virtue that gives a man a good name? And will not he who loves his beloved engender countless virtues in order to be praised in the beloved's presence? Youths must not be treated too strictly: if their heart is not stirred while it is young, how can it grow while in the growing-stage, and what is greater on earth than a great heart? It was sinful of Adam to get to know the difference between good and evil, but since the world has now become evil after Adam's sin, it is a good thing to know the difference between evil and good, for how else is one to avoid evil?" "How you chatter!" I said. "It's awful." "Very well," said Aeneas, "then banish him for immorality and all your problems will be solved. There will be no rebellion, and you won't need any help from Master Sigismund's father-in-law." "Who is the maiden?" I asked. "How should I know? I don't mix myself up in my pupil's private life. Perhaps there is no maiden. Perhaps she is only the figment of a young man's imagination." But I could not believe that Sigismund at his age could conjure up those kinds of fancies and fantasies on his own. I had a suspicion that Aeneas himself had put the idea into his head so as to be able to influence him and become a dean in Tyrol. I sensed that he was not a man of pure morals and habits after all, but as lecherous as Italians usually are, and so would I be able to appoint him a dean with a clear conscience? I dismissed Aeneas, but later that day he brought me a copy of the letter, and I read it by day and night with a troubled heart. It might indeed be better for Sigismund to stay with me, but it was no good if those kinds of tricks were necessary.

I decided to write to Marguerite. I had discovered that Pope Eugenius had recognized King Vladislas of Poland as King of Hungary, and I could not lawfully recognize a pope who recognized so unlawful a king. What was then more natural than to recognize Pope Felix as my father-in-law? But I soon had something else to think about. No sooner had the Tyrolean envoys reached Tyrol with Duke Sigismund's memorable reply than rebellion broke out. Both towns and Estates were besieging all my trusty men in their castles and collecting all the taxes that belonged to me as guardian. I sent an express message to the Dauphin, asking him to invade

Tyrol and support his brother-in-law. But an express message returned stating that the Dauphin had already made peace with the Confederacy so that they could conquer Zürich, our faithful town, in peace, and he had been appointed Eugenius's papal captain so that he could conquer Basel and depose Pope Felix, my father-in-law. I sent envoys to King Charles to ask why the Dauphin was behaving in this manner, but King Charles was not at home; he had advanced far into Alsace together with the faithless Duke of Lorraine and was moving his frontier forwards to the Rhine, for he said that it made a very natural frontier. Alas, when—on my councilors' advice and against my principles—I had begged for five thousand Poor Fools, he realized that I was short of soldiers, and now fifty thousand Poor Fools were invading our realm, and wherever they went they behaved as if they were among infidels, murderers and heretics. Every day I had to hear of their outrages—they spared no one, but cut off people's noses and ears and robbed them of their belongings; they even deprived maidens of their maidenhood, and those who would not lie still during all this mischief had their hands and feet tied together behind their backs so that they could better get at them, one Poor Fool after another—so that I couldn't stand hearing about it any longer, not to mention how they polished their boots with holy, consecrated oil. Once again I suffered sleepless nights and had to remain in bed all day long. I called for a diet in Nuremberg forthwith, but in order to give all the electors and princes of the realm a chance to attend in those dangerous times, I could only fix the date for half a year hence. And just then I heard that Vladislas of Poland was negotiating for peace with the Crescent Moon, most probably so that he could conquer the whole of Hungary and advance into Austria.

Then all my councilors counseled me to hand Sigismund over to the Tyrolese, though on condition that they instantly turn their forces against the French in order to defend Sigismund's domains. With sorrow in my heart I had to send for Sigismund. I thanked him for his responsible behavior towards the Tyrolese and declared him to be of age from that very moment; he could set out for Tyrol at once as a free ruling duke. But I could see almost at once that Sigismund had changed his mind. The longer I spoke, the paler he grew, and when I stopped speaking he said: "Mighty cousin, I am no longer childish enough to believe myself capable of controlling a country which you with your experience cannot control. I am old enough now to realize that they are not revolting against you, but against us, for we are both undivided dukes of Tyrol. And since we have extended our contract for six years, it would be a breach of contract if I were to break it now." I was obliged to agree with him and to explain why it was better for the whole of our house if he were to go to Tyrol and defend the country against the French; as soon as he was in the country they would be sure not to attack it, for he was the French King's son-in-law. Then Sigismund shouted: "I will not be the son-in-law of a man who advances so shamelessly against us!" But I said that he had been betrothed to Radegundis for nearly fourteen years now, and so lengthy a betrothal could not just be broken off like that. But Sigismund said: "Do you not understand that King Charles has only wanted me as son-in-law in order to gain control over Tyrol?" Sigismund's political acumen astonished me. "If you understand so much," I said, "you are wise enough to rule." But then Sigismund behaved quite childishly; embracing one of my knees, he said: "You must not send me away. My own father Frederick did not send you away when you were my age either, and the country was not even at war then."

I could not justify sending Sigismund away merely because my councilors and the good of the kingdom demanded it, for Sigismund was of my own flesh and blood. But could I as his upbringer, before God and his late parents, justify allowing him to remain, if he truly was leading an immoral life? I suggested he ought to have a castle of his own, now that he had come of age, and he said: "If I am parted from you, I shall not learn how to rule." Alas, if it were only me he had no wish to be parted from! But it was the virtuous maiden Lucretia as well, whose name was not Lucretia and who was not virtuous and who was probably not even a maiden. I had begun to keep an eye on the castle maids; I entered the kitchens and the women's quarters, which I had never entered before, and wherever I went the maids blushed so much that I suspected them all. For according to Aeneas's description, the maiden Lucretia did indeed have red cheeks, but otherwise I didn't think any of the maids I saw fit the description. Not one of the maids had hair more shiny than gold. There was a fair-haired sewing-maid whom I inspected more closely, but she laughed straight in my face and I could see that she lacked crystal teeth. There was a white-toothed kitchen maid with coral lips, and even though she had dark hair I looked at her frequently, and she too blushed a rosy red. But that was no proof, and it seemed to me as if all the maids knew of something I knew nothing about—I always heard them giggling behind my back. At night I stayed awake wondering how to surprise Sigismund in the act so that I could assert my authority. But I had declared Sigismund to be of age and had no political power over him. Every day I visited the neighboring monastery, for the castle chapel was not yet fully built, and I knelt for hours in front of the Almighty's altar, bidding Him help me.

My brother Albert came to me in need, for in need shalt thou know thine enemies. He laughed and said that God was punishing me now for behaving in such an unbrotherly fashion towards my own brother. Because I had wanted to keep the whole inheritance myself, it had all been spread to the winds. Now, for the last time, he was demanding his share together with the guardianship of King Ladislas, for I had more than enough with Sigismund's domains. He happened to be on his way to form an alliance with King Vladislas of Poland, who had already made peace with the Turks for the coming ten years, so I had better watch my step. This was not brotherly talk, but nevertheless I had no wish to stand on martial footing with my own brother. "Fine," I said, "you shall be allowed to rule the outermost domains, including the Swiss, together with Alsace and Lorraine, in Sigismund's name and mine." Albert was dumbfounded, and wantedto set off immediately to take possession of his domains, but he was quite an inexperienced ruler and had forgotten that he lacked soldiers. I advised him to attend the diet in Nuremberg in order to muster an army to fight the enemies of the realm in my name. I found it inadvisable to travel to Nuremberg myself, since I had to be prepared for Polish and Hungarian attacks and possibly also for Turkish ones, but my councilors counseled me to do so just the same, because otherwise the princes of the realm would not attend. Much against my will and with a heavy heart I set out, taking Sigismund with me so that I could keep an eye on him. He begged to be allowed to stay at home, still on the plea of his youthful age, but I said firmly: "If you are parted from me, you will not learn how to rule."

It was the first time I journeyed together with my brother Albert, and on the way I heard him praying several times in a loud voice, so that I could not help noticing that he too was making use of a portable altar, which I supposed one of the popes had allowed him to transport. I found it undignified for popes to compete for the favor of princes by lavishing undeserved favors upon them, and was of a mind to resolve the Schism; and naturally I could not recognize a pope like Eugenius, who had supported the Poor Fools and their unchristian war. I thought a lot about Marguerite on the way, since I now had time to think about her, and it grieved me that I could not travel straight to Geneva from Nuremberg because the countries in between them were at war. It was summer when we rode to Nuremberg; the roses were blooming on the rose trees, Albert whistled because he was going to rule, and Sigismund kept on singing a song which began "My heart, it is a rose tree, and always bathed in dew. . . ." but I wouldn't let him get any further. It was a happy journey nevertheless—until we reached Nuremberg.

For I began to speak about the undignified Schism which now had to be resolved, but the princes interrupted me and said that it was the safety of the realm that was at stake. Although it was unseemly to let myself be interrupted, I complied, saying that in order to safeguard the safety and the frontiers of the realm I was prepared to raise the Imperial standard and appoint my noble brother, Duke Albert, Captain of the Realm, providing the princes of the realm would instantly provide him with knights and horses in plenty. I had scarcely finished speaking before the princes shouted out that since I had enlisted the aid of the Poor Fools to defend my house, it must be my own private concern to beat them off again. They had nothing against Duke Albert's beating them off, but they could not provide him with knights and horses, for he was not a true prince of the realm but only Duke of Austria. I replied in righteous anger that I had not summoned fifty thousand Poor Fools, but I had entered into negotiations with my colleague of France with regard to hiring five thousand. But before any agreement had been reached, he had sent all his infidel hordes into the realm. I had long since sent envoys to King Charles to ask what the meaning was, but the envoys had returned without an answer.

However, some French envoys were secretly attending the German diet—two foppish liars with exceedingly high hats and exceedingly pointed shoes. They sent greetings from His Grace, King Charles, and his son, the Dauphin, and said that, magnanimously and with great danger to their own country, they had granted me even more soldiers than I had asked for, but I had provided no winter quarters or provisions for them in the middle of the cold winter—they had had to find those for themselves. Now King Charles was demanding payment for fifty thousand brave soldiers, many of whom had fallen with honor, as well as the late Duke Frederik's treasure, which I had unlawfully carried out of Tyrol; and to his great sorrow, King Charles had learned that his beloved son-in-law, Duke Sigismund of Tyrol, was still being detained, and Louis the Dauphin viewed it as his holy task to liberate his brother-in-law and escort him to the beautiful city of Paris so that he could be wedded to Princess Radegundis. For France by no means considered herself at war with the German Empire, but only with me as unlawful guardian to Duke Sigismund. Moreover, his Highness the Dauphin could not sanction the existence of a pope in Basel when there was already one in Rome, nor the unseemly relationship between father and son in Bavaria; he demanded that I should resolve the Schism immediately and make peace between father and son, otherwise he would have to settle the dispute and remove the unlawful pope by force of arms. And the German princes did not interrupt that shameful speech, but greeted it with applause. Only one person spoke up manfully against it, and that was Duke Sigismund, my faithful ward. He read out a declaration, which he must have written himself, for I had not ordered Aeneas to write it. He thanked me for all the love he had received in my castle, and said that he was not heir to Tyrol, for it belonged equally to King Frederick, Duke Albert and himself, who were all undivided dukes, but he and Albert were under obligation to obey me as the eldest and senior duke. He, on the other hand, was under obligation not to do anything unexpected, or to marry without my consent and knowledge, and he knew nothing of any match between himself and a French King's daughter.

After Sigismund had spoken there was a great hush in the diet. But then one after another they began to shout out that the Duke was clearly not allowed to speak freely. "Why don't you answer them?" whispered Sigismund, who stood at my side. "Alas, Sigismund," I said, "do you think they will believe me when they will not even believe you? Everyone here stands united against us, for they are only thinking of themselves and have no overall view of things." And without deigning to look at the princes, I left the diet, resolving never again to set foot in it, for a king should not enter into discussions.

Nor should a king act in anger. In my anger I had contemplated allying myself with Burgundy—which had been at war with France for nearly a hundred years—and finding a Burgundian consort for my pious sister Katharine, who was always deep in prayer. I had also decided to recognize Felix as father-in-law and Pope, and to take Marguerite to wife. But while I was preparing for my departure, Elector Ludwig of the Palatinate came to me. Even during the fight about my family silver in Aix-la-Chapelle he had been prepared to die and be resurrected with me, and once again he did not fail me. He was prepared to defend the realm against the Poor Fools, and especially Basel, for Pope Felix was his father-in-law and Marguerite of Savoy, his bride. I thanked him for those words, betraying no grief about having to rule the world alone, without a faithful wife at my side.

But the will of the Lord was for the best. Even the Almighty, like the King, His faithful regent, has to sanction much evil for the sake of good. Under cover of darkness, the cardinal legates of Pope Eugenius came and thanked me for my good intention to resolve the unfortunate Schism. They had been unable to get a word in at the meeting on account of the loud-voiced princes, but in confidence they promised me two hundred and twenty-one thousand golden ducats, which included economic support for a journey to Rome with the prospects of becoming crowned as Emperor, if I would acknowledge Pope Eugenius as sole Pope. Hereafter His Holiness would command the Dauphin to withdraw his troops from the realm and send the Poor Fools against the Turks, for he was highly displeased with King Vladislas for having made peace with the foes of Christendom, and was prepared to recognize King Ladislas as sole King of Hungary. For my ward's sake I agreed to the papal proposals.

The same night I secretly left Nuremberg as victor. I bade Caspar and Aeneas attend to Sigismund's lawful transfer to the Tyrolese Estates. As soon as Sigismund was in Tyrol, neither the Tyrolese nor the French were likely to make war on me, for they had officially declared that they were only making war on me for the sake of Duke Sigismund. Sigismund cut such a princely and dignified figure that I could certainly let him stand on his own feet, all the more so because he would be able to depend on Duke Albert, and as soon as he was wedded to his betrothed, Princess Radegundis of France, I need not let his way of life trouble my conscience.

It was a happy journey home, and the roses were still blooming on the rose trees. Even before I reached home the message reached me that Vladislas of Poland had broken his ten-year treaty with the Turks in order not to incur the wrath of Pope Eugenius, and he had fallen heroically in the war. Now Ladislas was sole King of Hungary. A legation of both orthodox and heretic Bohemians was waiting to acknowledge me as Ladislas's guardian over Bohemia, and I spurred on my horse. Joyfully, I saw the many towers of my faithful town in the distance, now drawing nearer and nearer, and King Ladislas received me at the western gate of the city. "Where is Sigimund?" he asked, for he could already speak properly. I rejoiced over his undivided family feeling and lifted him up onto my horse. I held the fatherless and motherless king firmly, so that he would not fall down and hurt himself. Now I could attend to his royal upbringing in peace, so that one day he might be able to carry on my undertaking and make Austria extend all over the globe.

For *Austriae est imperare orbi universo.*

Three Legends:
The Wicked Judas

*O felix culpa quae tantum
meruit redemptorum.*

ST. THOMAS

1

It came to pass some days after a decree had gone out from Caesar Augustus that all the world should be counted and taxed. Simon too had to be counted and went up from Cariot to Jerusalem to be registered there with Cyborea his wife, who was great with child. And as they lay lay in the inn after having been counted, Simon was awoken by his wife's weeping, and he said: "Be silent, wife." But when she heard that her husband was awake anyway, she wept even louder, for she had had a bad dream, where a black angel had spoken to her and said that she would bear a son who in this city would commit a greater sin than any other would ever be guilty of. When Simon heard that he said: "Since it was a black angel, it must be a lie. It is the Wicked Fiend who has put that idea into your head." But Cyborea said: "You must know that you yourself have made me with child, so the Wicked Fiend has not put anything into my head." Then Simon became frightened nevertheless, and said: "Let's get away from here before an accident happens," and they went home to Cariot.

As soon as they got home Simon said to his wife: "You must not tell anyone," and he himself said very little during those months. Cyborea hoped for a daughter, but when the time came she gave birth to a son and was so terrified that she told all the neighboring women of her dream, and they were amazed to discover that the child was no uglier than any other newborn babe, except that it had a black mark on its forehead. When Simon came home from work he chased the neighbors out, and said: "You stupid woman! Had you not said anything, our child might never have come to know it. Now everyone will talk about it, and we shall have to be sure that the child doesn't hear anything and never goes to Jerusalem." And he took the child from its mother and rode away with it on his donkey through the Wilderness of Judah to the Dead Sea. There he laid it in a chest of bulrushes, which he daubed with slime and with pitch and set out in the sea. The child's mother thought it had been killed, and so did the neighbors; they kept on talking about the child that had made its father a murderer, and Simon and Cyborea fled from Cariot to Jerusalem where there were many people, and Simon became a gardener.

There was so little wind that the chest floated straight across the Dead Sea to the land of the Moabites. Now the King of the Moabites had a Queen who used to walk to and fro along the seashore, wringing her hands, because she was unable to bear the King a son. When she saw the child in the chest she considered it a gift from God, for the child was lovely, except for a black mark on its forehead; and she bore it home under her skirts and told her husband that she was with child. Soon all the Moabites were commanded to rejoice that a King had been born to them, and it was not long before the Moabites had to rejoice once more, for the Queen gave birth again. Her first-born she named Judas, probably because he had come floating from Judaea, but the second one they called Lot, for he was of the Moabites' own race. When the boys were old enough they began to tease each other like boys of that age generally do, but Lot in particular teased Judas because he had a mark on his forehead, and Judas called him a "stinker," so Lot ran to tell his mother, who scolded Judas. Then Judas called Lot a "tattletale," and Lot ran to tell his mother, who boxed Judas's ears, and then Judas boxed Lot's ears in order to get even with him. But the older Judas became, the harder he could hit Lot and the angrier his mother became, until finally she said: "You are not even a King's son for you came floating across the Dead Sea and nobody knows who you are. I took care of you when you were alone and not even your father knows you are not his own son. But I will not have you repaying me by mistreating my real child." When Judas heard this he said not a word, but went down to the Dead Sea to drown himself. But Lot had secretly overheard this and he followed after him, shouting "bastard!" Then Judas was overcome with anger and wickedness, and he picked up a large stone from the beach and threw it at his stepbrother and smashed his head. He then stole a rowboat and rowed out to sea, and it grew so dark and stormy that he feared for his life, even though he had so recently wanted to drown himself. He rowed with all his might until the waters rose up and smashed down upon him. When he came to, he was lying on a shore with the shattered boat behind him. It was light now, and he saw a number of white-clad men kneeling on the ground, stretching their arms up to heaven; it was so quiet that he heard them cry out loudly in one voice:

"Hark, I am stricken dumb, for nothing can a man say without speaking ill to his brother. Lo, my arms are withered, for nothing can a man do without doing ill to his brother. Lo, my eyes are dimmed from looking on men's wickedness; hark, my ears are deafened from hearing of bloody murders.

"My body is like a boat shattered on the rocks of the shore. My soul is like a wasteland scorched by the winds of the desert.

"But blessed art Thou, O lord, for Thou art my shore and my wellspring. For my father has renounced me and my mother knows me not, but Thou art a father to all through whom Thou do Thy work, and Thou wilt rejoice over their weeping like a mother will pity her babe, and Thou wilt feed all that live from Thee as a nurse feeds her charge at the bosom.

"Now I am like a newborn child, and what is a child without mother and father but the prey of death. Blessed art Thou, O Father, who transforms the caves of the desert into a mother's embrace."

Judas got up to see the father they were crying out to in this manner, but could not see him. The white-clad men saw Judas, however, and asked: "Who are you?" Judas answered:

"I do not know." But to the men this answer sounded suspicious, and they asked again: "Have you been sent hither to spy on us?" They formed a circle around him and the circle grew smaller and smaller the closer they approached. Judas fell on his knees in fear, as he had seen the white-clad men do. But one of them asked: "Who has spewed you out on this dry land? Is it you for whom we are waiting?" And the circle grew bigger again because they all took several steps backwards, and Judas answered: "Yes, it is I who have spoken ill of my brother and killed him. My father has renounced me and my mother I know not. Now I am like a newborn child, and what is a newborn child but the prey of death?"

Then each of the white-clad men bent to the ground in order to gather up the first available stone to throw at Judas. But their arms stopped as if paralyzed, so that the stones fell down and struck their own feet, and they cursed loudly, while Judas ran for his life. For days and nights he ran through the desert, scorched by the wind and burnt by its sand, and he regretted having fled from the white-clad men's stones only to stumble over the stones of the desert, never to rise again. He who kills with stones shall be killed by stones, and Judas saw his guilt so plainly that he shed tears. But wherever they fell a spring gushed forth, and he was thankful for the water though not for his life; he would save it only to stand before the highest judgment seat and be sentenced to death so that judgment could be done.

When he got to Jerusalem the Roman governor lay at table with harlots and publicans. When the governor heard that a criminal was seeking audience, he let him enter at once and addressed him mockingly in Latin. But Judas had been brought up as a king's son and answered in the same tongue. Then the Roman was excited to hear what crime such a learned young man could have committed, and when he heard that he had murdered his brother, he took Judas into his service. Judas had expected to have his head chopped off, but thought that the forgiveness of all sins might be a Roman custom, and that the great Father to whom the white-clad men had cried out might be the Emperor of Rome himself. So that no one should speak ill of the black mark that had been the cause of his wickedness, Judas always combed his hair down over his forehead.

One day the governor stood in his palace looking down into a garden full of ripe apple trees. Under the trees the gardener's wife was lying asleep, almost naked, in the sun. And the governor said to Judas: "You must bring me those rare apples to bite." Judas wondered at this, because it was not difficult to get apples, but he also had noticed the gardener's wife and wanted to see her close too. And although they were not the same age it gave them great pleasure to look at one another, and Judas brought the apples to the governor, who grew very angry and threw them at Judas's head. And Judas felt unfairly treated and threw them back, until, overcome with anger and wickedness, he threw not only apples but everything else he could get hold of. With the apple juice running down his cheeks he had to flee the palace, and knew of no one else he could flee to but the gardener's wife who had received him so kindly. When he told her he had thrown apples at the governor and killed him she was still kinder, for it was no sin to kill a Roman. "But this is not the first time I have killed," said Judas, "my sin is greater than I can bear." "Pooh," she said, "I myself am married to a murderer, and I am an unhappy woman, for it was our own child my dear husband killed." They both wept and comforted one another as best they could, and she kissed the apple juice from his forehead. Then, noticing the black mark, she screamed so loudly that the gardener came running in and saw Judas lying with his wife. "You whoremonger and highway robber!" he shouted, and Judas could not stand hearing that, and his anger and wickedness made him jump up and strike his old father down before he realized it. "Unhappy one!" screamed Cyborea. "Now what was foretold has come to pass: that you should commit a greater sin here in the city than any other would ever be guilty of. For that man who lies here breathing his last is your own father, and lo, this woman you have embraced with the hands of a murderer is your own mother, for I recognized you by your birthmark. That is what comes of having secrets from one's wife, for had I known you were alive, I would have known at once that it was you. Why, I knew you at once. Would a mother not know her own child? And had you known you would commit so great a sin, you would probably not have behaved as you did." Judas closed his father's eyes and said: "There is no end to my wickedness, I am full of evil spirits who do just as they please. Now I shall leave this palace and report to the Emperor himself so as to put an end to it." Cyborea wept together with her son, and they comforted one another so well that they almost sinned again. Then she thought for a moment, and said: "Our sin is great, but I cannot understand why it should be considered the greatest sin of all, for one has heard of just as bad before, and of the Emperor one had heard worse—he would only laugh at your sins. Besides, it's a long way from here to Capri, and I have not found my son again after so many years in order to lose him immediately. And I have heard that a prophet from Nazareth has arrived in the city. He is said to forgive all sins and cast out evil spirits; we shall go to him so that you may find peace of mind."

When Judas heard that he was pleased, because he thought that the prophet from Nazareth might be on his way to the Dead Sea, and that it was he to whom the white men had cried out and for whom they waited.

2

Cyborea went with her son to Jesus of Nazareth, but he was surrounded by so many people that they were quite unable to see him, and at the back of the crowd there were so many priests and soldiers that Judas dared not approach any closer. So that Jesus should know that they had come, Cyborea raised her voice and shouted: "Blessed is the mother that bore you and the breasts which you have sucked." Judas told her to be quiet, but Jesus heard everything and answered: "Yes, blessed is he who understands my words." Then a path was formed through the crowd so that Cyborea and Judas could look straight up at the prophet, and Judas was surprised to see a man of his own age and not an old man. Publicans and harlots in uniform were thronging around him and keeping the priests at a distance; these stood at the back, shouting: "Lo, the Savior of the World is surrounded by swindlers and whores." But Jesus answered: "Is it you or they who need to be saved?" So Judas plucked up courage and elbowed his way through all the sinners, shouting: "I am the world's greatest sinner." All the other sinners laughed at him; only Jesus did not laugh, but said "So it is you," making as if to pass on. Then Cyborea seized hold of his mantle and shouted: "Savior, forgive him, for he is my son and possessed of an evil spirit, but he cannot help it because it was there before he was." And she was about to relate her sorrowful story, but Jesus said to Judas: "What have you done?" Judas looked at his mother and at the soldiers and whispered: "I have murdered." "How many?" asked Jesus. Now it was so quiet that everyone could hear, though especially all the greatest sinners who stood nearest, and Judas cleared his throat and said: "Four." "Do you not know the commandments?" said Jesus. "Thou shalt not lie." While the crowd all followed Jesus, with the priests and soldiers at the rear, who simply laughed at Judas, Judas remained standing, and said to Cyborea: "You have lied to me. He did not forgive me my sins, and I can still feel the evil spirit."

Judas no longer wished to have anything to do with Jesus, but his mother kept filling his ears with praise of the Savior and wanted to confess their sin to him, for she believed he knew everything anyway. But Judas forbade her to speak about Jesus any more. Nevertheless, one day he left his mother's house when there was nobody there, in order to follow Jesus until he could be rid of his sin. But when he had come so far as to throw himself at the Savior's feet, Cyborea lay there already, saying: "Savior, I have loved my son too well." The angry crowd began to spread out so that the soldiers could seize the sinful woman, but Jesus said: "It is hard to love too well," and Cyborea would not let go of his mantle, but shouted: "I do so want you and Judas to be good friends." Jesus answered: "He who is always with his mother cannot follow me," and Judas said to his mother: "Go away, woman, it is all your fault. Cursed is the womb that bore me and the breasts which I have sucked." Whereupon Cyborea went home alone, but Judas followed after Jesus, and Jesus seemed not to notice him.

Jesus then went up to Galilee in order to be rid of the priests and soldiers in Jerusalem, and Judas went with him although no one had asked him to. Every time he tried to push forward to speak with Jesus he was held back by the men of Galilee who walked nearest to Jesus, and one of them said: "Your accent is so strange; where do you come from?" Judas began to explain: "You see, I am from Judaea, but . . ." "In Judaea," said one of the men of Galilee, "people only think of money." Then Jesus turned and said: "Then give him our money so that the rest of you can be free from thinking about it." Judas received a purse and saw that it was empty, so he put in it half the coins he had earned while working for the governor, and which bore the Emperor's portrait.

But he who surrendered the purse was offended, and said: "Have I not handled the money as you told me to?" "Are you never going to do anything without being told?" said Jesus. "Surely you remember the man who before traveling abroad summoned his servants and divided his money between them. When he came home he asked for his money back, and those who had received the most gave him back even more. But he who had received the least said: 'Lord, I know you are a hard master who reaps where no one has sown; therefore I went and dug your money down into the ground, so that I could give you everything that is yours.' But the hard master answered: 'If I reap where no one has sown, you had no need to plant money in the ground. You could have gone to the moneychangers and let them reap it for you, so that you could have given me the money back with interest.' And he took the money from the servant and gave it to the one who had earned the most, for he who has much will receive much, and he who has nothing will lose all he has." When Jesus stopped speaking, the man who always walked nearest to him because he never understood what was said, asked: "What do you mean by that? You yourself have said that one cannot at the same time serve God and Mammon." Jesus answered: "One thing is needful, but the necessities are many," and Judas took the rest of his money and put that in the purse as well.

In Nazareth everyone knew who Jesus's mother was, but they did not know who his father was, and so they shouted "bastard" at him. Because only a few wished to listen to him, he spoke mostly to the few, and Judas said: "If it was prophesied that I should commit the world's greatest sin, is it then my fault?" Jesus answered: "Much evil comes out of prophesies. Thus it was prophesied that the Savior of the world would be born in Bethlehem about thirty-five years ago, and so that the world would not be saved, the ruler had all the little boys in the town killed. Now if the Savior of the world had really been born, would he not have been a very great sinner right from birth, since so many innocent children were killed for his sake?" Judas laughed and said: "One cannot very well be guilty of murders one did not commit." "Were you guilty of the murders you committed?" asked Jesus. Then Judas thought Jesus was going to declare him free from sin, and he said: "I myself did not intend to commit murder, but there is an evil spirit inside me that wants to." And when Jesus said nothing, Judas said: "You who can cast out evil spirits, can you not cast mine out too, so that I can become clean?" Jesus said: "When an evil spirit is gone out of a man it becomes homeless and wanders around, and it says to itself, 'I will return to my house,' and when it comes, it finds the house swept and garnished. Then it takes to it seven other spirits more wicked than itself, so that it can feel a little better, and the last state of that man is worse than the first."

Judas would have said more, but he was interrupted by some foolish laughter, and the disciples tried to hold back a shrieking boy. But the boy's father was the Roman prefect there in the town, and he said to Jesus: "Master, my son here is possessed of an evil spirit and it makes him gnash his teeth and grimace and pine away; I did not wish to disturb you and bade your disciples cast it out, but they do not seem to be able to do so." Jesus could not understand Latin, and Judas had to interpret, and when Jesus laid his hands on the boy and said: "Come out, you evil spirit," Judas said that in Latin too, so that the evil spirit could understand. The spirit charged out with such a loud scream that people came rushing up, and when they saw the boy fall down and lie as if dead they rejoiced that a Roman was dead. But Jesus took the boy by the hand and said: "Stand up and walk, be free from sin," and the boy stood up and walked and everyone was horrified to see that he was not dead. While the crowd went around scowling, Judas scowled too, and went to Jesus and said: "You are not concerned with my sins, yet you will declare a Roman free from sin." "Why, that was a sick child," said Jesus, "what sin can it possibly have committed?" But Judas kept on: "I have heard you say that there should be greater rejoicing about one sinner who repents his sins than about ninety-nine persons who have no sins to repent, but it is only the small sins you can or will forgive. How small must a sin be in order to become rid of it?" "That's a difficult question," Jesus replied. "You know that he who kills his brother is guilty according to the law. But I say to you that he who calls his brother a "tattletale" is a great sinner, and that he who calls him a "stinker" shall be cast into the eternal flames." Judas did not know what to say; instead he showed Jesus how much money he had in his purse, for money multiplied in his hands. Jesus took all the money to give to the poor. Judas thought: he says that the poor are blessed, and yet he gives them money so that they become less poor. But aloud he said: "What a lot I could earn for the poor if only you waited until I had earned more before giving it to them." Jesus smiled and answered: "Surely you know the story of the farmer whose field had brought forth such plenty that his barn could not contain the crops. So he called all his reapers home to build the barn bigger, and when the barn was ready the crops were spoilt. For he who has much wants more and more, while he who has nothing wants for nothing." Judas was silent, but thought to himself: if my evil spirit could scream like the Roman boy's, he would surely cast it out. And he tried to scream, but was stricken dumb.

When it was rumored that Jesus could cast out evil spirits, those who were possessed came to him from every quarter, screaming: "You are the son of God," and Jesus cast out the evil spirits so that they would stop screaming. But priests and wise men had been sent out from Jerusalem, and they heard the screams and thought: "Lo, the mad seek him out and the evil spirits acclaim him as their prince." Jesus knew what they were thinking and said: "Is it not madness to be divided against oneself? Then it is mad of the Evil One to cast out evil. But is it then wise of the good to be mad at the good?" But Mary, Jesus's mother, had sent all her sons to fetch him home, and they whispered to the wise men: "He is out of his mind," and they repeated aloud what his brothers had whispered. Jesus said: "Who are my brothers?" They laughed and said: "Your brothers are your mother's sons, but whether they are your father's sons we do not know." Jesus pointed to his disciples and said: "My father is father to my brothers and I call those my brothers." The wise men answered: "If you have the same father, you are all bastards and not begat according to the law." But Jesus asked: "Then can the law both beget and kill? But if you, children of the law, only call your brothers of the flesh your brothers, then you are putting the flesh before the spirit, so why do you then speak ill of bastards?"

Then the priests and the wise men returned to Jerusalem in order to relate what they had heard and seen, and Jesus's brothers of the flesh said: "Leave this place; if you are not our brother, why should we protect you?" And when Jesus had healed all those who had acclaimed him as their prince, no one protected him and he returned to Judaea.

On the way, Judas said: "I call you my brother because I have killed my real stepbrother. And I call your father my father because I have killed my real father too." Jesus said: "He who has not hated his father and his mother and his brother as I have done cannot understand me. And he who has not loved his father and his mother and his brother as I have done cannot understand me." Judas was silent for some while before he answered: "I have loved my mother." Jesus was silent and did not answer.

The nearer they got to Jerusalem the greater became the crowds surrounding them, and the priests and soldiers turned out too. During those days Jesus did not say very much to his followers, and to Judas he said nothing at all. When they could see the towers of Jerusalem they saw too that Jesus had tears in his eyes, and his feet were so tired that he had to have a donkey to ride upon. When the great crowds saw him come riding into the city they waved branches and garments, shouting: "Long live the son of David," for they had heard that David's son would come riding in on a donkey. Then the priests and soldiers realized that it was high time to arrest him, for what might happen if all the people started believing in him and stopped hating the Romans, and what might happen if the people became so disorderly that the Romans had to restore order? Jesus's followers realized that it was dangerous to follow Jesus at that time and frowned at anyone who went off on his own, and they frowned especially at Judas, who was carrying the purse. For fear that he might use their money, they all followed him, and they noticed that he spent money on a harlot and noted everything he did so that they could tell Jesus. But Jesus said: "If you are afraid of sin, then why do you seek it out? If you have sin in your eye alone you can pluck the eye out, but if you have sin in your whole body, can you then pluck out the whole body?" With the money Judas spent on her, the woman, whose name was Mary and who had heard Judas speak about Jesus, bought a costly ointment and came to anoint Jesus's tired feet. Judas was indignant and said: "That ointment could have been sold for a high price and given to the poor." "Then let it comfort you," said Jesus, "that there will always be poor people enough, whereas I shall not always be with you."

Judas had misgivings and waited until he could be alone with Jesus. Then he said: "I know that you do not care for me. So declare me free from sin and you will be rid of me. But if you do not cast out my evil spirit, I don't know what I shall do with myself, because I can only kill it by killing myself." Jesus answered: "Was it not your evil spirit that made you kill, and can one atone for one's sin merely by dying? Do we not all owe God a death, however great or small our sin?" "But my evil spirit will go on killing," said Judas. But Jesus answered: "Who makes wicked people kill? The good who call them wicked or the wicked who call them good? More people will be killed for the sake of good than for the sake of wickedness, so is it not better to be wicked than good?" Then Judas became angry and said: "Is it better then to kill you than to kill myself?"

It was the day before the Passover and Judas went to the temple to buy the sacrificial lamb, and the courtyard was full of moneychangers changing money and merchants selling bleating Easter lambs. But while he was standing there, Jesus came and overturned the moneychangers' tables so that the money chinked, and tumbled the merchants' stalls so that the lambs fled, and he shouted: "Can you become free from guilt by shedding innocent blood?" The high priests in the temple heard this, and they whispered to one another that he would have to be killed, for it was better for one sinner to die for the people according to the law than for all the people to become sinful and lawless. But Judas was now standing so close to them that he heard what they whispered.

On the eve of the Passover there were so many people in the streets that Jesus and his disciples were able to hide among them and enter an old stable unseen. As they lay at table Jesus's hands shook so much that he dropped the bread and spilled the wine, and he said: "One of you will go to the priests and tell them that tonight I shall be in the Garden of Gethsemane." Then they raised themselves on their elbows, and although most of them knew that they would not go to the priests, they all asked with their mouths full: "Surely it is not me?" Judas alone could get neither a bite down nor a word out, and Jesus said to him: "What you will do, do quickly." Then Judas ran as fast as he could to the priests, who received him kindly and paid him well. Late at night he went with them to Gethsemane. Jesus was walking among the trees, but his disciples had fallen asleep from grief. In order that the priests and soldiers would be able to seize the right person in the dark, Judas greeted Jesus with his usual kiss, and when his ear passed close by Jesus's mouth, he heard it whisper: "Brother, be free from sin." Then Judas howled like a dog and woke up the disciples, and one of them, who had exchanged his mantle for a sword, charged at the armed men; but he had only got as far as hacking off one ear when Jesus said: "Stop, I say! Truth cannot be slain with the sword." All night long Judas walked to and fro among the trees in the garden; not until it was light and they led Jesus from Herod to Pilate did he run to the priests, shouting: "I have shed innocent blood, now I am the world's greatest sinner," and they laughed and said: "You're mad." He threw his reward in their faces and ran through the streets, which again were full of the same people, and he kept on shouting that he was the world's greatest sinner. But the people all shouted louder than him: "Crucify him!" for at that very moment Pilate was showing Jesus to the people. When Judas saw Jesus with the crown of thorns on his head it was as if his eyes were scratched and bleeding and everything swam before them; and he saw himself standing beside Jesus, and heard them shout: "Crucify him! And let that one go free." Judas ran home to his mother's house, but there was no one at home and he hanged himself from the ceiling. And it is said that he did not hang himself properly, for the body fell down and was crushed on the stone floor so that his evil spirit charged out from his body, since it was not good enough to charge out through the mouth the Savior of the world had kissed.

This came to pass during the latter years of the Emperor Tiberius under the consulate of the twin brothers.

Emperor and Apostle

Paul the Apostle suffered much evil after he had been converted. In Philippi he was beaten with rods and put in prison and had his feet fastened in stocks. In Lystra he was stoned, and in Iconium and Thessalonica he was persecuted by the wicked; in Ephesus he was thrown to the wild animals, and in Damascus he was hoisted over the wall in a basket. In Jerusalem he was bound and beaten and led before the council and put in prison for two years, and in Caesarea he was brought by his countrymen before the Roman governor and said: "I appeal to the Emperor." The governor conferred with his council and answered: "You have appealed to the Emperor, and to the Emperor you shall go." So Paul journeyed to the Emperor on a vessel bearing the sign of the Twins. But when he arrived in Rome the Emperor had no time to listen to him, for he was busy acting the stage hero and star athlete, and Paul had to wait two more years in hired lodgings, where he received all those who came to him, preaching the kingdom of God and teaching those things concerning the Lord Jesus Christ, with all confidence, unhindered.

According to Haimon, Paul labored from cock-crow until the fifth hour, making tents by hand. Afterward he preached, and the sermon often dragged on until well past midnight. For the remainder of the time he ate or prayed or slept.

Whenever Paul preached there were so many listeners that

there was not room enough for them all to sit on the floor, and some of them had to sit on the windowsill. Now it happened that in the window sat a certain young man by the name of Patroclus, who had fallen into a deep sleep. As Paul was so long preaching, overcome with sleep, Patroclus fell down from the third-story sill and was taken up dead. And Paul went down and fell upon him, and embracing him, said: "Stop this commotion, for there is life still in him," and he brought the young man back to life so that he could hear the remainder of the sermon, and he went on talking until break of day, and they were all not a little comforted.

But Patroclus was employed as cupbearer in the Emperor's household, and the Emperor is said to have been very fond of him. So when he heard that Patroclus was alive he became overjoyed as well as frightened, for after his mother died sometimes his late mother used to appear before him with bleeding belly. So the Emperor asked: "Patroclus, are you dead?" "My Lord Emperor," Patroclus replied, "I am alive." At this the Emperor immediately wanted to punish those who had spread wicked rumors about his death, but Patroclus said that he had truly been dead and had merely risen from the dead. At the thought of the dead coming alive again, the Emperor Nero once again came to think of his mother and his stepbrother with the beautiful voice and his first wife and all the others he had been obliged to have killed so that he would be able to reign in peace, and he shouted: "What kind of a muddle is this? Who is bringing the dead back to life again?" Patroclus said: "It is Lord Jesus, the King of the world." "The King of the world," shouted Nero, "that's me, isn't it? Am I not lord over life and death?" "You are lord over death," said Patroclus, "but you are not lord over life." This was lese majesty, but Nero could not be angry with Patroclus, and said: "That's something you dreamed. It's not good for people to sleep alone."

But when, on top of his fall, Nero wanted to sleep with Patroclus, the quick-witted young man said that they ought not to dishonor their own bodies, for that was to change the truth of God into a lie and to worship and serve created things more than the Creator, who is blessed for ever.

As the Emperor stood gaping at him, Patroclus continued:

"For this reason God gave them up to shameful passions, for even their women exchanged natural relations for unnatural, and likewise the men, giving up natural relations with women, burned with lust for one another, so that men did with men that which is unseemly, and received themselves that recompense for their error which was meet."

"Patroclus," roared the Emperor, "is that you speaking?"

"It is not I who am speaking," spoke Patroclus, "but he who speaks through me; for just as they did not see fit to know God, God gave them up to a reprobate mind, to do those things that are unseemly, filled with all unrighteousness; fornication, wickedness, covetousness, maliciousness; full of envy, murder, debate, deceit, and malignity; whisperers, backbiters, haters of God, despiteful, proud, boasters, inventors of evil things, disobedient to parents. . . ."

Then the Emperor personally boxed his ears. But five of the slaves said:

"Emperor, Sire, why do you hit the young man? He has answered wisely and truthfully, for he has risen from the dead and no longer lives after the flesh."

So the Emperor had to throw all six of them into the dungeon. But he gave orders for Paul to be summoned, and the Prefect of the Guards, Tigellinus, fetched him at once and said that he had been accused of deception by his countrymen because he had insisted that a man by the name of Jesus, who was dead, was still alive.

"Is he alive or dead, yes or no?" asked the Emperor. But Paul answered:

"After the flesh he is dead, for . . ."

"Very well," said Nero. "He's dead. But what was he like, this man, since you go on talking about him until late into the night? Was he good-looking? Did he sing well?"

"I never knew Christ after the flesh, and if we had known Christ after the flesh, now we know him no longer . . ."

"No, I realize that's all over now. But if he's dead in that kind of way, then you are all dead too?"

"If one died for all, then we are all dead, for if it is life that is working in you, then it is death that is working in us."

"That would have pleased my uncle. 'Let me have men about me that are dead,' he always used to say. I would prefer to see statues about me—they don't bleed. Look, he's already standing like a statue! Then you too are dead, as you stand there; even you are not living 'after the flesh,' as you call it."

"It is no longer I who live but Christ who lives in me; and the life I now live in the flesh, I live by faith in him who loved me and gave himself up for me."

"Aha! He loved you and gave himself to you while he was still in the flesh, and in spite of your being a Jew . . ."

Nero, who as Imperial Actor had accustomed himself to receiving applause every time he raised his voice, glanced sidelong at his guards, who immediately burst out laughing. But the more the Emperor's glance wavered, the more fixedly the Apostle stared at the Emperor:

"He loved all, for there is neither Jew nor Greek, slave nor freeman, male nor female, for we are all one in Christ Jesus."

"That makes no difference to me—my love knows no bounds. But now that he is dead, do you now live with the memory? Has love come to an end?"

"If I have no love I am nothing. But love does not boast and does nothing unseemly and is not puffed up; and he who speaks with the tongues of man or even sings with the voice of an angel, but has no love, is like a clash of cymbals or a tinkling zither."

The Emperor, who knew that the enemies of the State despised his song and music, said:

"What have you done with Patroclus, you who have done nothing unseemly?"

"I know no one of that name."

"You don't remember all their names? But for me nothing is hidden; I have heard that at your orgy last night my former cupbearer fell and lost his life and reason, and that you embraced him, and gave him back his life, but not his reason. What am I to make of that?"

"To live is Christ."

"Christ? Is that your name for love?"

"Yes it is, for he who belongs to Christ has crucified the flesh with its passions and lusts. With Christ I am crucified . . ."

"He's mad," said the Emperor, and the guards laughed.

"But you suffer madness gladly, seeing you yourself are so wise! But since the world did not know God by wisdom, it pleased God by the madness of preaching to save those who believe. We preach Christ as crucified and risen, to the Jews a stumbling block and to the Greeks madness, but God's madness is wiser than your wisdom. I speak the wisdom of God, the mysterious, which God before the world's creation ordained to our glory, and which none of the princes of this world know, for had they known it they would not have crucified the Lord of glory . . ."

"Tigellinus," said the Emperor, "do you understand any of this?"

"Yes," said Tigellinus, who understood nothing. "He wants to be crucified."

But the Apostle said to him:

"Is it lawful to crucify a Roman citizen?"

"You're afraid to die," said the Emperor, "even though you're dead already."

"Do you not know that we who were baptized into Jesus Christ were baptized into his death? But since we are dead with Christ we believe that we shall also live with him, knowing that Christ, once raised from the dead, dies no more. For to me, to live is Christ and to die is gain. I would rather depart and be with Christ, which is far better, and yet to remain in the flesh is more necessary for you."

"Necessary for us? But we don't want to hold you back! Yes, of course we'll miss you, we may even gather together at night in memory of you. But we shall make the sacrifice and bear the loss, so that you need no longer miss your beloved Christ."

"Christ with all boldness shall be glorified in my body, whether it be by life or by death. For we must all appear before the judgment seat of Christ, so that everyone may again receive the things done by his body, according to what he has done, whether it be good or evil. But God repays tribulation to those who trouble us; in flaming fire he takes vengeance upon them, and they will be punished with everlasting destruction away from the presence of the Lord and from the glory of his power! But God will have all men saved, and knowing, therefore, the terror of the Lord, we persuade men, and I pray you in Christ's stead: be reconciled to God; do not the works of the flesh!"

"And what are the works of the flesh?"

"The works of the flesh are manifest, and are these: adultery, fornication, uncleanness, lasciviousness, idolatory, witchcraft, hatred, variance, rivalries, wrath, strife, seditions, heresies, envyings, drunkenness, revellings and suchlike, of which I have told you before, that they who do such things will not inherit the kingdom of God."

"The kingdom of God—where is that?"

"When our earthly tabernacle is demolished, we have a building of God, a house not made with hands, eternal in the heavens . . ."

"Oh I see, in the heavens! So it's not only gods who ascend into heaven like my divine great-great-grandfather did, according to the eyewitness's trusty report, but also ordinary mortals?"

"If the dead do not rise, what then is life other than to eat and drink, for tomorrow we die . . ."

"On the contrary! If we don't eat and drink, we die—if not tomorrow, then pretty soon. But tell me, you man of Rome who longs for death in order to become alive—if I were to satisfy your longing and chop off your head, would you put your head on again and leave this place as if nothing had happened, or would you be content to ascend into heaven as spirit? I don't mix myself up in ascensions, but if the dead can rise up again in the flesh and everything, as Patroclus is supposed to have done last night, there's no sense in killing people. Answer me properly, otherwise I shall have to put it to the test."

"If it is preached that Christ rose up from the dead, then how can one say that there is no resurrection of the dead? If there is no resurrection of the dead, then Christ has not risen, and our preaching is empty. But Christ *has* risen from the dead . . ."

"And ascended into heaven, goodbye and thanks? So the world is none of his concern—God's kingdom is in the clouds, perhaps?"

"God's kingdom comes when he has delivered up the kingdom to God the Father, when he has put down all rule and all authority and power. For he must reign . . ."

"He must reign? So you preach insurrection against the lawful powers?"

"There is no power other than God's—the powers that be are ordained by God. So that whoever resists the power, resists the ordinance of God, and those who resist will receive their damnation. For rulers are no terror to good works, but only to evil."

"I suppose you're saying that to please me!"

"If I still wanted to please men, I should not be the servant of Christ. And what have you which was not given to you? And if it was given to you, why do you then boast?"

"Hm," said the Emperor. "So you're not preaching insurrection—it's not you who is making bad blood between the slaves and their masters, forcing me to put six slaves in chains . . ."

"Let all those servants who are under the yoke count their masters worthy of all honor, so that the name of God is not blasphemed . . ."

"Then you respect the State gods?"

"There is only one God!"

"That's something new, but one might well suffice. And you call him Christ?"

"Christ is the son of God the Father . . ."

"So there are two of them after all?"

"The Father and the Son are one in Spirit."

"So long as they aren't one in the flesh, it's all right, eh? It's only the flesh you've got something against. The flesh is sinful, and when you're not doing the works of the flesh, as you call it, then you're busy becoming spirits, ascending into heaven when you die, and landing in God's kingdom. Have I got it right now? You are without sin?"

"Among sinners I am the chief, for . . ."

"Aha! You're nothing short of the *chief* sinner? So you have sinful lusts after all, and live after the flesh, as you call it, even though you haven't much flesh on your body."

Thus spoke the Emperor, who had himself grown rather stout. But the Apostle answered:

"I myself serve with the mind the law of God, but with the flesh serve the law of sin. For what I will, I do not; and what I hate, I do. When I do what I will not, then it is no longer I who does it, but the sin which dwells in me . . ."

"He's good, eh, Tigellinus? That's what I've always said—we all have it in us, but not everyone's willing to admit it! And so he says that it isn't he who sins, but the sin that sins. Cunning! But if it's no longer you who are living, Paul, but your God who is living in you, and if it isn't you who are sinning, but the sin sinning for you, then there isn't much left of you yourself, Paul, so you, at least, haven't got much to boast about!"

"I would rather boast of my weaknesses, so that the power of Christ may rest upon me . . ."

"But he hasn't got much power, has he, when you can't stop sinning anyway! Sin must be a mightier god than your god, since he has to put up with your sinning."

"What concord has light with darkness, has Christ with Belial? And lest I should be exalted beyond measure through the abundance of the revelations, I was given a thorn in the flesh, a messenger of Satan. Concerning this I prayed three times to the Lord, so that it might depart from me. And he said to me: 'My grace is sufficient for thee'. . ."

"Aha! But it isn't sufficient for you. Why else should you pray to him three times? You are still having trouble with the flesh, eh?"

"I keep down my body, and bring it into subjection. But is not everyone who takes part in the contests temperate in all things . . ."

"Hm."

"And they who run a race all run, while only one receives the prize. And they run to obtain a corruptible crown, but we an incorruptible one. Forgetting those things which are behind, and reaching out for those things which are in front, I press toward the goal, to the prize, which is God's call to the life above in Christ Jesus."

"So you're interested in racing. Find him a circus ticket, Tigellinus. He's an honest man—he himself admits to being lecherous, and this Christ can't be worse than so many other gods. You come from the east, don't you?"

"I am a citizen of a not unknown city in Cilicia."

"Yes, in that part of the world. That's where they have peculiar ideas about gods dying and becoming alive again, and fights between light and darkness. Even here, in the center of the world, their barbarous temples are shooting up all over the place, and they hold love-festivals until far into the night. They could be a danger to the State, Tigellinus—we must watch out. For our citizens have grown tired of fearing stern gods and prefer to love gods who suffer like human beings. But why should they love foreign gods when they can love their own emperor. That's why I appear in tragedies and let myself be murdered so that they can suffer with me, and why I take part in races so that they can win with me. But it might be just as well to ally myself with some worthy god or other, until they have become weaned and are able to appreciate art properly. I have thought of speaking to the King of the Persians when he comes to visit us, for he has such a suffering god of victory over there. But perhaps we could appoint this Christ—who promises the prizes of victory—God of Racing. They are used to fearing invisible gods, and before they can love visible people, maybe they should love an invisible god. And our friend here loves his god, and is willing to die for him because he has never seen him . . ."

But then the Apostle of the Lord shouted:

"Have I not seen Jesus Christ our Lord? Last of all he was seen by me too, as the one born out of due time; for I am the least of the apostles, I who have persecuted the church of God. I myself thought that I ought to do many things against the name of Jesus, which things I also did, in Jerusalem, and many of the saints I shut up in prison, and when they were put to death I cast my vote against them. Yes, I persecuted them even to strange cities! When, for that purpose, I went to Damascus, with authority and commission from the chief priests, at midday on the way, O Emperor, I saw a light from heaven which surpassed the brightness of the sun shining round about me and those who journeyed with me. But when we had all fallen to the ground, I heard a voice speaking to me, and saying in the Hebrew tongue, 'Saul, Saul, why persecutest thou me?' And I said, 'Who art thou, Lord?' And the Lord said, 'I am Jesus whom thou persecutest. But rise and stand upon thy feet, for I have appeared unto thee for this purpose, to make thee a minister and a witness, delivering thee from the people and from the Gentiles, unto whom I now send thee, to open their eyes, and to turn them from darkness to light, and from the power of Satan unto God, that they may receive forgiveness of sins.' Whereupon, Emperor Nero, I was not disobedient to the heavenly vision, but I proclaimed . . ."

"Thanks, that'll do. You're not only lecherous, you've also had people killed. And you had a vision of one of those you had killed, that we know. I shan't kill him, Tigellinus—think if I should have a vision of him and imagine him to be God! All joking aside—that's how gods come into being. The dead become gods when they are resurrected in people's imagination. Uncle Claudius became a god too after eating mushrooms—a true dish for gods! So as far as possible one ought to avoid killing. Without death, no gods—and gods, of course, have to have sacrifices in order to live . . ."

"The Gentiles sacrifice to demons, and not to God . . ."

"Be quiet, the Emperor is speaking! If we could close all the temples, just as we have closed the Janus Temple because there is peace and security in the whole of my kingdom—outwardly, that is to say—then people would go to the races and to peaceful dramas like the Greeks. And we could abolish the gladiator fights and use condemned persons for building an even bigger arena so that everyone could gather around me. For why do they want to see others die? In order to vanquish their own fear of death. If they didn't slave for the gods . . ."

"Because they know not God, they slave for those who by nature are not gods. Even as we, when we were children, were in bondage under the elements of the world. For the heir, as long as he is a child, differeth nothing from a servant though he be lord of all, but is under guardians and governors. But when the fullness of time comes . . ."

"Correct! So I freed myself. For I was really a slave for many years, even though I was master of the whole world. I was under guardians and tutors: my late mother, whom I had to do away with, and Annaeus—Seneca, I mean, you must have heard of him, he's quite famous. He said that the Emperor's exalted position is only an exalted form of slavery—that's what he actually said. For what other people can do on the quiet, the Emperor cannot do, because all eyes are upon him. That's why an Emperor cannot do anything wicked. For an Emperor must not do what he himself wishes but what the gods wish. And just as the gods cannot leave their heaven, the Emperor cannot walk about freely in Rome without being surrounded by armed men. That was what I learned as a child and have had to grow out of, for the Emperor is not under but above the law, and the Emperor can do what he wishes. And I went out into the city at night and no one recognized me, and sometimes I was even beaten up, so that I had to take the guards with me in ordinary clothes. But if they beat up their master when they don't recognize him, what is the sense of their hailing him when they do recognize him? I am aware of the people's cruelty, but I am also aware that it springs from fear, for Seneca said that too, and so I'm graciously disposed towards gentle gods whom nobody needs to fear. And you are not frightened, are you?"

"When we were in the flesh, the sinful passions, which were evoked by the law, worked in our limbs to bear fruit for death. But when the fullness of time came, God sent forth his Son, born of a woman . . ."

". . . rather degrading for a God. He should be able to give birth to himself . . ."

". . . born under the law to redeem those who were under the law . . ."

"What now? Are you dissatisfied with the law?"

"By no means! But I did not know sin except through the law; for I would not have known lust if the law had not said,

'Thou shalt not covet.' For where there is no law, there is no transgression . . .''

"And without any transgressions we wouldn't need any laws. Whatever is forbidden is wicked—and thus tempting, so it is better to forbid as little as possible of that sort. My late father-in-law and stepfather, the god Claudius, was so timid that he increased the penalty for murdering fathers and mothers: the little murderers were to be put in a sack together with a cock, a monkey, a dog and a snake. And the poor children seemed to become so obsessed with longing for intimate contact with so many innocent creatures at once that they killed their mothers and fathers for that very reason, for during the following five years more patricides and matricides were registered that in all previous centuries! It was Seneca who drew my attention to that. Our society was in a bad way, he said, so long as we were faced with more sacks than crosses. The law became an accessory to the murders, he said, in order to make me abolish the strict laws. For if a decline in moral standards brought about stricter laws, then milder laws would be bound to improve morals. So that is why I do not say, 'Thou shalt not covet!' "

"I'm not talking about your laws but about God's own law. For the wrath of God is revealed from heaven as being against all ungodliness and uprighteousness in men who suppress the truth with unrighteousness, for all that may be known of God is manifest in you, so that you have no excuse. For when you, without having the law, do by nature what the law demands, you have the work of the law written in your hearts, in that your conscience bears witness . . ."

"Oh, so by God's own law you mean conscience! And it's from that bad conscience Christ has exempted you, so that you can sin with good conscience until far into the night?"

"To freedom Christ has called us, if only we do not use freedom as an occasion for the flesh, but serve one another with love. For the whole law is fufilled in one word, in that: 'Thou shalt love thy neighbor as thyself!' "

"Splendid! He who has a happy love life commits no crimes! Thus I intend to introduce public love games instead of death games . . ."

"But if you bite and devour one another, take heed that you are not consumed by one another . . ."

"Of course, to start with, the games would have to be under military supervision, but . . ."

"But I say: walk in the Spirit and you will not fulfill the lust of the flesh. For the flesh lusts against the Spirit, and the Spirit against the flesh, and these are opposed to one another, so that you cannot do the things you would wish . . ."

"Why ever not—when we are free from the law?"

"The law is not made for the righteous, but for the lawless and disobedient, for the ungodly and for sinners, for unholy and profane, for murderers of father and of mothers, for manslayers, for whoremongers, sinners . . ."

"Stop! Is anyone righteous? You, perhaps? Didn't you say that you were the chief sinner, which may be putting it too strongly, but still . . ."

"It is written: 'There are no righteous,' no not one, they have all turned to the side, all alike are unfit, there is none who does good. For all have sinned . . ."

"That's what I've always said! No one is worse than anyone else. And when you see how many people there are in this city, where you can fill three theaters at once, you can see what a merciful ruler I am; for if I were to let justice be done, they'd all be executed . . ."

". . . and death passed upon all men, for they all have sinned; for until the law came, sin was in the world, but sin is not imputed when there is no law. The law came so that the offense might abound. But where sin abounded, grace became even greater."

"Ha ha! So one ought to live in sin in order for grace to become greater."

"By no means! How shall we, who are dead to sin, live any longer in it? For they slander us, those who say that we learn evil so that good may come of it. Their damnation is well-deserved. They should be delivered up to Satan so that they may learn not to blaspheme. For God commended his love toward us while we were yet sinners, in that Christ died for us so that the body of sin might be destroyed, and that it should happen as both Moses and the prophets have said, that Christ should suffer, and, as the first to rise from the dead, should show light both to us and to you!"

But when Paul defended himself in this way, raising his voice, the Emperor said:

"You're mad, Paul, it's all this eastern wisdom that's turned your head."

But Paul said:

"I am not mad, most noble Nero, but am speaking words of truth and soberness. For just as sin has reigned with death, so might grace reign with eternal life by Christ Jesus, for if he, who knew no sin, sacrificed himself for our sins, then death is no longer the wages of sin . . ."

"He knew no sin! Aha! And that was why you became angry with him and killed him! I too am most graciously disposed towards those who admit to being sinners. And you, of course, were the chief sinner . . ."

"But therefore mercy was shown to me, so that in me first, Jesus Christ might show his long suffering as a pattern, for it pleased God, who singled me out from my mother's womb and called me by his grace . . ."

"Right from your mother's womb? You believe in predestination?" shouted the Emperor, about whom it had been predicted that he would lose his empire and become King of Jerusalem.

"He who is made heir according to the law is no longer made heir according to the promise. For those whom he foreknew, he also predestinated as conforming to the image of his Son; and in such a way are they chosen when they are not yet born and have neither done good nor evil, so that God's selective purpose might stand, not by virtue of works but by virtue of He who calls."

"So what you call God is really fate! That's why it doesn't matter whether you keep the law or not—God doesn't notice whether you are righteous or not."

"Is God unrighteous? How then shall he judge the world?"

"So we cannot judge without judging righteously? Thanks . . ."

"For he said to Moses: I will have mercy on those on whom

I will have mercy, and I will have compassion on those on whom I will have compassion . . ."

"That's what I say too. I will have compassion on you if I will have compassion on you. There's not much difference between a god and an emperor."

"You are a corruptible person . . ."

"That is why I shall not let myself be deified until after my death—for naturally a living person cannot be a god, except in the provinces where he never shows himself. But your god was also corruptible while he was alive, wasn't he? For had he already been a god then, he would not have let himself be killed just in order that you could give vent to your murderous desires, feel like new and better people and find peace of mind—just as I have to sacrifice one or two for the sake of world peace . . ."

"He gave himself up as an offering and a sacrifice with sweet-smelling savor to God, so that he might deliver us from this present evil world, according to the will of our God and Father . . ."

"Oh, you *sacrificed* him to God in order to mitigate fate, because he was without sin—just like Agamemnon sacrificed his innocent daughter! Are you listening, Tigellinus? Human sacrifice in our time! How barbarous! It really ought to be punished. What kind of an authority permitted *that* to take place?

"It happened under Pontius Pilate, the Roman governor in Jerusalem . . ."

"Pilate!" shouted the Emperor. "It was a provincial procurator who deified him? Aha! So it was *we* who saved you!"

"And so the Lord takes vengeance on you who did not know God! For he sends you strong delusion, so that you should believe the lie and that you might all be damned, you who did not believe the truth, but found pleasure in unrighteousness. For know that in the last days perilous times will come! When you say 'Peace and safety,' suddenly destruction will come upon you, as labor upon a woman with child, and you will not escape. For first shall the man of sin be revealed, the son of perdition, who opposes and exalts himself above all that is called God or is worshipped, so that he takes his seat in the temple of God, shewing himself that he is God . . ."

"By God, I believe he's talking about my uncle! He who seated himself in the Temple of the Twins and allowed himself to be worshipped although he was only one! Who is this son of perdition?"

"It is he whose coming is according to the works of Satan, the lawless, whom the Lord will consume with the breath of his mouth . . ."

"Ugh! And I was about to believe him to be a gentle god!"

"But I beseech you by the meekness and gentleness of Christ—let the peace of God rule in your hearts! Be as I am! If it be possible, live peaceably with all men . . ."

"It is possible, provided all men live peaceably with me. For rulers are no terror to good works, but only to evil . . ."

"Recompense no man evil for evil, bless those who persecute you, bless and curse not, let the word of Christ dwell within you, with all wisdom, teaching and admonishing one another with psalms and hymns, singing with grace in your hearts to the Lord!"

"Have you heard me sing? But your God does appreciate singing and music? And he is—in a way—a god of love?"

"Be of one mind, live in peace, and the God of love and peace shall be with you!"

"A strange case!" said the Emperor to himself. To Tigellinus he said: "Fetch Patroclus!" And to the Apostle he said:

"Now I'll tell you something. I learned as a child that love cannot exist in company with fear. And that a state that is founded upon fear cannot endure. The people fear the old gods, so the State cannot continue to exist in company with the old gods. If the State is to endure it must be founded on love—on love of the State, not on fear of the State. But men can only love what is of flesh and blood—don't interrupt me!—and so long as they do not love the flesh, as you call it, they will see blood. For cruelty springs from fear, and fear cannot exist in company with love. The people have been accustomed to fearing their rulers, but I want them to love me. That's why I sing to them. But it is not sufficient to love at a distance, and since I cannot manage to love them all, I want them all to love one another. I have heard of the love festivals you hold in your temples. But people ought not to love one another secretly, in closed circles; everything ought to take place openly and in a body. For whatever is forbidden is wicked, and whatever doesn't gather the people together disperses them. Up till now I have let them worship whichever gods they please, but in the end there will be too many gods. I intend to abolish the fear of gods, and I intend to abolish the cruel gods who demand bloody sacrifices and harden the people's hearts and make them demand sacrifices, so that I have to be cruel and kill people and increase the fear of gods, the thirst for blood. But maybe I shall introduce new gods of love, for we need a change . . ."

Then Patroclus was led in, in chains, and laid between the Emperor and the Apostle.

"Undress him," said Nero. "Isn't he lovely, Paul? You may do what you like with him."

Paul said:

"Grace, mercy and peace, from God the Father and Christ Jesus our Lord, be with you!"

"And with you," said Patroclus.

"Is that all you have to say to one another? I couldn't quite make out what you were saying about love—you kept on contradicting yourself, possibly out of fear of me. But you've no need to fear me, for I am sheer love towards lovers, for lovers do no harm to others. I was angry when I heard that you had seduced Patroclus, but jealousy is evil, and so in order to overcome my jealousy I shall watch what you do. Well, what about it? You have made that young man describe love in terms of abuse. I rather suspected it was in order to deceive me, and of course now and again you said some beautiful things about love. But this much I shall say to you: if you call love indecency and fornication, then you won't live very long *after the flesh,* as you call it; if you have no love you are *nothing.*"

The Apostle was standing as stiff as a statue. Patroclus said:

"Apostle, you may."

"You fool!" shouted the Apostle. "Make no mistake! Neither fornicators, nor idolators, nor adulterers, nor sodomites shall inherit the kingdom of God!"

"Strike him down," said Nero.

"Have mercy, Emperor," screamed Patroclus, "strike *me* down, strike me down, let me die for the Apostle."

"Wait," said Nero. "You deserve to die, but I shall be merciful. The Apostle, whom you love, can save your life by making love to you. If he cannot make love, then you're a dead man. Do you want to be guilty of his death, you Apostle of love?"

"Do not fear," said Paul to Patroclus, "for the sufferings of our present time bear no comparison with the glory which will be revealed to us."

"Strike him down," said the Emperor.

"Which of them?" asked Tigellinus.

But Patroclus screamed so loudly that no one heard the Emperor's reply, and so he was struck down so that they could hear it.

"Oh, never mind," said Nero. "We'll keep the Apostle for a while; he can become spirit soon enough. He was handsome—that Patroclus."

The Holy Couple: Adrian and Natalia

Adrian was a heathen, though he was married to Natalia who was a Christian because Christ had suffered for her. She gave the Christians secret food, while Adrian had to go to bed hungry. They had scarcely been married a year when Emperor Maximian came to the city to persecute the Christians, and Adrian went to him in order to disclose the secret place where they ate. Thirty-three pious Christians were brought before the Emperor, who said: "You fools, daring to revolt against the good idols who are cruel to all who revolt against them!" "Cruelty means nothing, while love is all," shouted the Christians as if with one voice, and so in order to silence them the Emperor ordered their tongues torn out.

But when Adrian heard the Christians speak and saw them lose their tongues without screaming, he was seized with great remorse. "What kind of love is this for which you let yourself be torn to pieces?" he asked one of those who had no tongue and so could only answer "Mmmmmmmmm." Then Adrian shouted aloud: "I too am a Christian," and they put him in prison.

When Natalia heard that her husband had been put in prison with the Christians, she at first fell on her knees and thanked God. Afterwards she hurried to the prison and said: "Blessed be that day when you discovered the treasure your flesh has not granted you! Promise me to be steadfast in your faith in the Lord, and should your rich friends want to set you free, you must say: "Get thee hence, Satan!" "Wife," answered Adrian, "your faith has saved me and I shall gladly offer my life for our love." Then she bade him farewell with joy in her heart.

But when the day came for him to be tortured to death, he was allowed to leave the prison because he longed for his wife. When she saw him approaching, she was horrified, and she closed the door and turned the key. "You foolish man," she wept behind the door, "why did you take upon you a task that you cannot go through with? Never has my heart rejoiced as in these past days, and never have I shed so many tears as in this hour when you have fled from prison and from God. It was my greatest wish to become the wife of a martyr, and now for the rest of my days I must be married to a heathen, because divorce is wicked."

When Adrian heard his wife's voice his heart beat with joy. "Natalia, my dear sister, open the door and let me in. Don't think that I have fled from the prison and from God. I have merely been granted leave of absence so that I could come and take leave of you just as you came to take leave of me." But she did not believe him, so she said: "You're lying." "Let me in," he repeated, "this is the last time I shall see you. Many good men have pledged their lives for mine, and I wouldn't want them to be killed." Then Natalia believed him and uttered: "God be praised! Let us hurry back to the prison so that innocent blood will not flow."

Adrian was such an important man that his wife was allowed to accompany him. The Emperor also thought that she might be able to persuade him to preserve his life, but when he was kind enough to give him a ring so that he could offer it to the cruel idols, Adrian flung it away with all his might, and the Emperor's torturers beat him until the blood flowed and Natalia flushed with joy. Adrian, who wanted to please his wife, shouted out: "Cruelty means nothing, while love is all," and the torturers lashed at Adrian until his guts began to take flight from his body. Thus it was difficult to carry him down to the dungeon again, but Natalia accompanied him, holding up his guts, and she laid his unconscious head on her lap, and groaned: "Oh Adrian, you are God's martyr and my husband!"

When the Emperor heard that Adrian's wife did not wish to preserve his life, he grew very angry and gave orders for all women to be banished from the prison. But Natalia always carried a pair of scissors with her, and she cut her hair short and put on her husband's clothes so that she could see his dreadful wounds better and look like a man herself. "Dear husband," she said, "when you are admitted into God's presence, ask Him to take me to Him, for I cannot live without you." "I cannot live without you either," said the dying man.

Since he would not return to the old gods it was decided to chop off his feet. Natalia gathered up the bleeding feet and said: "Let them chop off your hands too." So he stretched out his hands to be chopped off and, this being done, he ascended to heaven. The Emperor commanded that Adrian and the other dead Christians should be burnt in honor of the supreme gods, but no sooner had the bonfire been lit than a rainshower came from heaven and extinguished it. Then those Christians who were still alive came and stole the dead bodies and gave them a Christian burial in Constantinople.

Natalia was so overjoyed to have her husband's hands and feet that she longed to see the whole body. And when the Emperor, who had lately seen so much of her courage, wanted to marry her, she fled to Constantinople and visited the Holy Graves. And despite the smallness of her hands, she dug so deep into the ground that her husband's body finally appeared, and she restored to it its hands and feet and embraced the body. And hark! It spoke to her: "Most beloved Natalia, come with me to the Lord, for it is in God's heaven that I want you now. Rest in the Lord!" And Natalia rested on her husband's body, and in her life's most blissful moment she sighed so deeply that she sighed her life away and entered into eternal bliss.

Now help us, O God, that we too may rejoice over St. Adrian and his incomparable spouse, and enter into eternal love. Amen.

The Screamer

When he was a boy he was a milk boy, and he used to whistle so piercingly in the morning that it pierced many good customers' dreams and made them complain. He was not fired on the spot, however, for in those good days it was difficult to get milk boys out of bed so early; but the Central Dairies ordered him to refrain from whistling at that hour and from waking people up while they were sleeping. So he postponed his whistling until most people had gotten up anyway, and at that hour of the morning the school children were on their way to school and joined in the whistling. A whistling chorus could be heard on all the roads leading to school, and in many schools the whistling continued because the children just couldn't stop. So the milk boy was forbidden to whistle at all.

But on the street corner the school children stood waiting expectantly for him, and called out for him to start up the whistling. And when he refused, because whistling had been forbidden, they crowded around him and employed the most commonplace methods of schoolboy torture in order to make him whistle. At that painful moment it became apparent that he could produce sounds even more impressive than his whistle. It wasn't so much a song as a kind of scream, and the screams sounded so pure yet so easy that some of the other children thought they could copy them, and they screamed too from sheer enthusiasm. The others told them to be quiet because they preferred to hear the milk boy scream solo, but no sooner had they let go of him in admiration than he stopped screaming and they had to tackle him all over again.

This time he was more experienced; his screams became rich and colorful and, although the others would have preferred merely to listen to him, they couldn't help screaming too. They had to see if they too could produce the same sounds, and their chorus of screams summoned so many people to the spot that the police were summoned too and turned up at once with police dogs. But the dogs set up such a howl that they completely drowned the police sergeants' orders, and since the great crowd had brought all traffic to a standstill, they had to draw their truncheons and set upon the children in order to make them move on silently—though this only made them scream more loudly. Nevertheless, several policemen managed to seize the troublemaker and to carry him off in a screeching police car. The children raised an outcry, but as soon as he was out of earshot silence descended on them; not even with a combined effort could they produce the sounds the milk boy was capable of.

Now the milk boy was dismissed and sent to a reform school where it was forbidden to scream. But in an institution of that type a new boy is often treated roughly by the others, and this treatment produced the screams again and again. The former milk boy had to be isolated and forbidden to scream or talk to anyone, though this called forth screams of protest from all the badly brought up boys who were being raised in the reform school. The teachers tried to keep them quiet by promising that they would be allowed to hear the savage screams for a few minutes every day. But as time went by the number of minutes became fewer and fewer, because whenever they heard the screams the other boys were almost bursting to scream too, and quickly began to join in. Soon they were back where they started, and even the Board of Governors went so far as to admit in secret that they wanted to scream too. While the children were screaming out to hear the screamer, who was locked up in a sound-proof cell, the

Board of Governors held Board meetings and in the end they became so excited that they all screamed at once and couldn't hear a word the others said.

However, a well-known impresario happened to hear of the screams, and arrived in order to hear them and see their originator. The latter was not as good-looking as he had hoped—he was a bit tubby, even though he hadn't been fattened up in the institution. But the screams sounded so promising that he was nevertheless willing to pay quite a large sum for the screamer, and the Board of Governors—who wanted to get rid of him at any price—accepted the price.

The impresario brought him up most carefully, and experimented on him for hours on end in order to discover where and how he had to be touched in order to produce especially touching screams. Naturally, while the primitive force of the scream had to be preserved, it had to be brought under control before the screamer could be allowed to appear in public. But fearing that the scream should lose its childlike charm and savagery when the boy's voice began to change, the impresario decided, after all, to let him perform before he could be sure how the scream would affect the public. He started by letting him perform in small provincial towns—under the name of Cry. But the rumor about the savage scream immediately spread from the small towns to the large ones, whose citizens rolled up at the concerts in big coaches, and so it was easier to drive Cry to the large towns in a cab. Soon his screams could be heard everywhere, both on records and portable radios, and the screams were still so uncivilized that they made all the uncivilized people join in, though with several civilized people as well. This had not been the impresario's intention; nevertheless, he earned as much as he could wish, because even though all the other youngsters tried to copy Cry and hold screaming concerts, their screams were only a pale echo of the great scream that only Cry could produce.

Of course, such a talent for screaming was essentially due to a biological abnormality, and that was probably why Cry's voice never broke. He went on screaming just as boyishly—or rather girlishly, as ever, for there was something feminine about Cry. And that was possibly why his picture was pinned up on everyone's walls, both the boys' and the girls', and eventually even on the grown-ups' walls, for he was still just as childlike and chubby. And on Cry's own walls, which he acquired more and more of (because the impresario didn't keep all the money himself and because Cry had to be more and more protected the more popular he became) there hung only pictures of Cry—Cry striking all kinds of poses, making all kinds of grimaces and wearing all kinds of hair styles and clothes; for to all the various poses and facial expressions and hairstyles and costumes there corresponded variations on the scream, which nobody in the whole world could imitate. So he became famous all over the world and everyone tried to imitate him, and in front of every television set people waited longingly for Cry's latest screams; every new pose he struck altered the scream a bit, and he appeared at all possible angles and from all possible sides so as to provide novelty.

But when this had been going on for some years, nobody in the world could hear themselves speak. Everyone was screaming and striking strange poses and wearing strange new clothes and affecting peculiar hairstyles in order to keep up with *le dernier cri;* and Cry had to be surrounded by more and more walls and by bigger and bigger bodyguards so as not to be crushed by fans wanting to squeeze new screams out of him. Eventually even the bodyguards struck such threatening poses that the impresario had to dismiss them and hire only deaf people instead. But Cry couldn't possibly scream for deaf ears and succeeded, therefore, in making the deaf hear; and for those who had never heard anything before, his scream was such a marvel that they felt obliged to squeeze more and more screams out of him—and that is how they came to squeeze him to death. His last scream was recorded and preserved for posterity; there were always microphones around Cry's mouth so that no sound should be wasted.

After his death there was a deathly hush in the world, and the deaf could no longer hear. But not until peace had descended on the world did people discover how peaceful the world had become. All the peoples who otherwise spoke totally different languages which nobody could understand found each other in an outburst of mutual loneliness, and the *Weltschmerz* of the whole world was expressed in screams; and if it happened that people started speaking incomprehensibly to one another again, they needed only to play Cry's last scream in order to find each other in that profound humanity which humanity essentially is. Cry continued to hang on every wall, and special Cry Centers were established, containing large pictures of Cry in the strangest poses. In the Centers people gathered and listened in rapt attention to his voice, which had tuned the world anew.

The Boss

Let's see if we have the whole story now. It began when you attended a meeting of the Personnel Association, a thing you had never done before because you were not exactly part of the personnel. But since the lecture was to be on shop-floor democracy you had felt obliged to go, all the more so because you didn't feel at ease in your own home. A father can at some point or another in a son's life be reduced in his eyes to a fixture that may in certain situations be useful but is otherwise in the way, and it seems that you were sufficiently youthful to see yourself with your son's eyes. During working hours you were omnipotent and were met with smiles and respect, and you knew they were all acting a part toward you, just as you were acting the part toward them, of being omnipotent, of being the boss. But when the personnel left the building in the afternoon, as a rule you remained sitting because you couldn't get through your work. The work of a boss is never done, because all expansion must in some way or other go through him personally. Or perhaps you remained sitting, after having told your private secretary to go home, because you used to experiment at being yourself when there was nobody who could see you and therefore get a wrong impression of you. You generally went home so late that you imagined your wife looked reproachfully at you—and when you attended the meeting of the Personnel Association that evening, you thought she thought you had gone somewhere quite different.

How did you feel, then, the evening you attended the personnel meeting? It was obvious that it made a great impression on the personnel. Anyone who met the managing director during working hours would nod respectfully and pass on (incidentally, you yourself had noticed that the closer your subordinates were to you in rank the more respectfully they greeted you, whereas the lads in the warehouse were content to wink), but outside working hours the personnel couldn't very well nod and pass on, leaving you, the boss, standing there all alone while all the others formed contented little groups. The least subordinate members of the staff naturally had to put themselves out and go to pay their respects to you, and some of them may even have felt it a great honor to stand beside you. But since no one is accustomed to addressing the boss, it was you who had to find something to say to the others, and what were you to say here, in a situation where you had no more to say than anyone else? You came to remember that a king never arrives until all the others have taken their places, and you regretted having come too early—even regretted having come at all. And yet in one respect you may for once have been looking forward to standing among your personnel without standing there as boss. But you *had* been standing there as boss. And, one by one, all those who had stood beside you for a while withdrew, smilingly and somewhat deferentially. You didn't quite know where to look, but felt that all eyes were upon you, especially when you weren't looking. You didn't feel welcome, even though the chairman of the Personnel Association—the warehouse inspector—had spoken of the great honor, and you were surprised to find that it was apparently undemocratic of a boss to turn up at a meeting concerned with shop-floor democracy.

And it was then—to come straight to the point—that you, who didn't know quite where to look, chanced to look at the young man who obviously knew he had to look at you. All the others instantly looked away when they met your gaze, but he stared so fixedly at you that you had no other alternative than to look away yourself. But you nevertheless become so curious that you immediately glanced at him again, and apparently he had not taken his eyes off you in the meantime. So for the second time it was you who had to look away. And then the lecturer arrived—some young author you had never heard of, who had written books on modern class barriers. And in order to be truly democratic you didn't sit in the front row, as the warehouse inspector had indicated, nor did you sit in the middle of the hall among the personnel, because you were not exactly part of the personnel, but instead you sat in the back row, which you had all to yourself because the hall wasn't filled. And no sooner did you sit down than you regretted sitting where you did: it might seem too consciously modest, or might be interpreted as a way of keeping watch on the personnel from behind, which you couldn't have done if you had sat down in front after all. And the chairman bade everyone welcome, and especially you—who had always shown such a great interest in the personnel and especially in the Personnel Association—and of course the lecturer, who had shown such a great interest in democracy.

I have forgotten to say that you may have attended the meeting simply because of your interest in the evening's topic. Up there on the platform the young intellectual was saying something to the effect that class barriers and all other barriers between people were products of a development he could sketch in very broad outline, and it was easy in retrospect to see how unreasonable and unjust the barriers were. But so long as they prevail they are regarded as quite natural—not as man-made, but as products of nature. When people no longer accept their position in life as predetermined and unavoidable, their occupation included, a state of crisis prevails, and roughly speaking this has been the case since, let's say, 1789. All that talk of a specifically modern cultural crisis is simply talk, since in our day there are in fact signs that the gulfs in society are narrowing, not only the economic gulfs—that is obvious to everyone, for nowadays the richest man is the one who pays the least tax—but also the intellectual gulfs. I suppose that is roughly what you remember, and it didn't interest you particularly. But then he said something which did interest you, and which you have since forgotten;

and if he said anything at all about shop-floor democracy you didn't hear it, because you suddenly discovered that the young man, whom you had forgotten about in the meantime, was staring at you. This was impolite to the lecturer, to whom he had almost turned his back, and the thought struck you that you should have sat in the front row after all. Naturally you were surprised to find that you had never seen the man before, since you thought you were democratic enough to be able to recognize the entire personnel. On the other hand, it was likely that he hadn't seen you before, for if he had he scarcely would have found you so fascinating, even though you were the boss. What does a boss do in such an awkward situation? The most dignified thing would be to not take any notice of him, but not only had you never made a point of standing on your dignity towards a subordinate, but you found it impossible. You tried to keep your eyes on the lecturer and follow his train of thought, but the fixed stare constantly attracted your gaze. The strange thing was that it gave nothing away; you couldn't tell if he was really fascinated by the boss—by you, that is to say. He was at any rate dissatisfied with merely meeting the boss's gaze, for it had repeatedly met his, and when you eventually went so far as to contort your left cheek into some kind of friendly, good-humored grin, his expression remained unchanged. It wouldn't surprise me if your face hadn't been slightly flushed at that moment, because you had in any case suffered a slight loss of dignity, and if that was so, I wonder whether he had been sufficiently close to notice it? You decided that from now on you would not look in that direction at all, but although you did in fact stop doing so for some minutes, you sat there trying to see the situation in your mind's eye so that you could analyze it undisturbed, and it was at that moment that you discovered the splitting headache you had had for quite some time. You had been slightly shocked when he failed to return your grin; until then you had, after all, been rather proud that the sight of you could be so fascinating. But now you realized that it wasn't that, but couldn't understand what it was. To him you must be an eyesore—for why else should his gaze remain fixed on you? You had always fancied yourself to be a popular boss, and surely the very fact that it was possible to speak about democracy in your factory must also be a sign of the harmonious relations between you and the personnel. Was he perhaps a revolutionary—a communist? Was his gaze still an expression of that hatred the oppressed could feel for their oppressors in olden days? In your firm! In that case, it was all rather ludicrous and you could easily look him in the face. Were you not an employee just like him—even if your function was a different and certainly more demanding one? So then you looked him straight in the face—but he was no longer there, and you didn't even manage to find the place where he had been sitting, for you hadn't noticed what he looked like and so couldn't recognize him from behind. You had only seen his eyes, and yet you wouldn't even be able to say whether they were blue—or brown, for that matter.

You were ashamed of yourself and concentrated on hearing the lecture to the end, and when it came to an end the chairman thanked the lecturer for the interesting talk and invited everyone to an informal gathering where there would be an opportunity to ask questions; and you thought it would look strange if you were to leave now, and that it would also look strange if you did not, so you remained standing where you were, letting most of the others leave the hall before you, and you had succeeded in forgetting the young man in question—until you saw him standing at the end of your back row. You tried to look questioningly at him, but your question remained unanswered. You thought his glance was more imploring than accusing, and it was not until now that you saw his entire person—a man about average height, rather thin, and with a conspicuous head of hair, which was so voluminous and stylishly arranged that it even looked a bit feminine. And so you walked hurriedly past him and out into the cloakroom, where the chairman was so eager to help you on with your coat that you realized he was anxious to get rid of you. And so you disappeared into the four-person elevator and waited for the other three. But no one entered, even though the corridor was full of those members of the Personnel Association who didn't want to take part in the informal gathering and ask questions, and could be going down in the same elevator as you. And this irritated you, and you began closing the sliding door; but at that very moment your persecutor entered wearing a raincoat, and you were alone with him and could have asked him for his name and department or something of the sort. But it only takes a few seconds to descend in the elevator, and before you had made up your mind to say something you had already reached the bottom, and he held open the door for you, so he was not a revolutionary or a communist, and you thanked him and, somewhat relieved, you wished him good night. But those few words sounded so strange in your ears that you kept on hearing them, especially since he did not answer.

You walked quickly over to the carpark—quicker than usual—and after you were already sitting in the car and were swinging open the door in order to slam it, you almost hit him with it. So he had been following you (which, incidentally, you had known all the time)—that was why you had walked quicker than usual. And although you knew it was ridiculous, you were trembling all over and couldn't get the car started, and he stood there looking at you, imploring rather than accusing, you think. Then why didn't you ask him to jump in, so that you could at least have found out what he wanted? Maybe he simply wanted a raise or an advance, or maybe he was in trouble and viewed you as omnipotent, since otherwise he wouldn't behave so strangely—everyone must have noticed it. Those thoughts didn't occur to you until you had started the car and were no longer trembling so much as before. And it was not until your head had cleared that you turned around to let him in. You could at least drive him home, even though that wasn't the job of a managing director; but he was no longer standing where he had been standing. And you felt annoyed with him because he wasn't still standing there, and you saw him before you quite clearly—not his eyes, which he had turned away (and you hadn't noticed what color they were), but his raincoat and his hair. And you thought: "He is in fact a bit feminine!"—and only then did it occur to you that this was probably the explanation, as simple as that, and you were annoyed at having allowed such a trifle to upset you. You were inclined to put it all down to your headache, although in the meantime you had most probably forgotten it.

Then why didn't you drive straight home? Why couldn't you banish the thought of this slightly feminine youth? Why did you constantly have to tell yourself, even on your roundabout way home, that he was not feminine except for his hair; for feminine men—if the word is to have any meaning—must be feminine in form, and this was not the case. And why did you get up again as soon as you had sat down at your desk the next morning? Why couldn't you remain in your own office where your private secretary, as usual, did everything to make sure that no one disturbed you? Why did you constantly find some pretext for visiting all the departments where you otherwise never set foot? The personnel must certainly have thought that you had learned something from that lecture on shop-floor democracy that you had not taken in. But of course you knew, without really wishing to admit it, that you were searching for him in order to put him in his place—the place where he really belonged.

For you were beginning to let your imagination run, even though it had been years since you had let your imagination run about anyone. During sleepless nights, and eventually even during drowsy days, you held long conversations with him, without quite knowing what they were about. Or rather—they were about everything. Everything turned into a conversation with him, an extremely friendly conversation, for he never contradicted you. For instance, you talked about your son, with whom you no longer talked; about your wife, about your business problems, and about shop-floor democracy. You were in constant agreement that the most important thing of all was understanding. Although your working day became longer and longer, you managed to get less and less done. You felt you needed an assistant, or rather, someone to relieve you, but you didn't take the matter up with the Board, only with the slightly feminine young man, who wasn't really feminine. And once again you attended meetings of the Personnel Association, even though you didn't feel welcome; and you sat in the back row again, even though you had regretted it the first time. But the young man wasn't there.

So you gave orders for the entire personnel to be photographed for the purpose of the firm's archives. This was no popular measure—there was even some talk of a police album—and a couple of shop stewards turned up, and you explained that it was more like a family album, to be used when writing the history of the firm. In the old type of firm you would find pictures of past managing directors hanging on the walls, but this wasn't the case here—here everyone had to be photographed, and so on. And everyone was photographed, and you spent several days studying those hundreds of photos, and you thought you could recognize all of them and didn't find what you were looking for.

It was then you began to read books on psychiatry—on hallucinations, to be precise. But you couldn't find any examples of a hallucination being able to act as strangely as the young man in the Personnel Association had acted that first evening.

You didn't attend the Personnel Association meetings any more, even though you said so to your wife, who didn't believe you. Whenever there was a meeting you sat in the restaurant opposite, trying to see who came out after the meeting, but it was impossible to see anything in the dark, and you went outside, terrified at the thought that your personnel might be able to see you—and he wasn't among them. But although to start with you had not really known what he looked like, now—so long afterwards—you saw him so clearly in your mind that you felt disgusted with yourself. He stared at you with large brown eyes and long lashes—and you went to the place where managing directors oughtn't to show themselves, and where young men stand with beseeching eyes, and you realized that it wasn't that you wanted—and in your previous life, as you say, there was nothing really to indicate such a thing. Nevertheless, you remained standing there where you oughtn't to be standing, possibly for hours on end, because you didn't know where else to go—until suddenly he seemed to pop up out of the ground in front of you, looking quite different from what you had remembered. Not particularly good-looking, although you didn't remember him as particularly good-looking. Not particularly feminine, although you didn't remember him as particularly feminine. Without his raincoat, without visible eyelashes, but of course still with eyes that kept on staring at you as if they were asking for something. And you managed to stammer, "What is it you want?" And he contorted his left cheek into a humorous though mocking grin. And suddenly you stood there, having knocked him down . . .

Certainly it's an unpleasant story, my dear Sir. But it's not quite so strange as you yourself imagine.

Bird in Maid's Guise

I sat at my mother's table glancing through picture books, and all the pictures were of animals.[1] I thought that animals could speak like real people, and since I was an only child, I wanted a dog of my own I could talk to. But my mother was afraid of dogs, so I got an aquarium with fish. The fish could not talk, even though they opened and closed their mouths as if they were trying, and because they couldn't talk, and maybe because they were always surrounded by wetness, my eyes became wet with tears whenever I stared at them. Later on I got a yellow bird with a curved beak, and the bird sang all day long, and I learned to sing like the bird did.

But the bird didn't learn to sing like I did. I sang the old songs about animals that turned into people when a human being kissed them, and I kissed my bird, and it bit my nose with its curved beak and didn't turn into a human being.

I was sent to school among other children and no longer knew why I wanted to turn animals into people, since there were enough people already. I understood their language better, and now I learned to spell it. I sat at my mother's table glancing through many books, and there were no longer any pictures in them.

---

1. Translator's note: This story is based on an old Danish ballad: "Jomfru i Fugleham" ("Maid in Bird's Guise").

My schoolmates seemed like birds to me—they twittered like birds—and yet I couldn't sing as merrily with them as I used to do with my yellow bird. I didn't believe they could become people if I kissed them, for they were people already and I didn't want to kiss them.

I thought that maybe human children were not proper grown-up people, and that I myself was not yet a proper person either. When I grew I got growing-pains in my knees, and I felt there was no room for myself in my skin; in the mirror I saw myself grow bigger and bigger, but I didn't care for myself in my own form. It was not myself I should be facing in the mirror, but another—whose thoughts I would know as well as my own. By now I knew more and more words, though I still didn't say very much; perhaps I got that from my mother—even though she was really my stepmother—for she was always silent.

At school I learned that in the beginning people were animals. I remembered the old songs, and asked whether animals had turned into people by being kissed in those days. Then they all laughed. The boys with their broken voices laughed the loudest, as if they were all about to be changed into wolves. The teacher just smiled to himself and spoke some words I couldn't understand, and so have never been able to forget: "In those days people used to feel sorry for animals because they were not human beings. Nowadays people are sorry for themselves because they are not animals. For this is the difference: whereas an animal can feel pain, a human being can feel pain on behalf of others—or himself."

From that day on the boys were always chasing me, panting like dogs. "Wouldn't you like a kiss to become a person?" they howled, circling around me, and I scratched their hands until they bled. "Isn't she a wild-cat!" they shouted, and wherever I was they were always jumping around me shouting "Kiss, kiss, kitty-cat!"

One of the boys was called Rolf because he was stronger than the others, and so I was afraid of him most of all, and he always seemed to be after me. But when the others were chasing me with their "Kiss, kiss, kitty-cat," he drove them all away; his voice was louder than theirs and he could drown them all out. To me he never spoke, though he used to follow me like a dog on my way home from school; and when I left school he left too, and used to stand outside my gate looking in, while I sat inside looking out, for when I was that age my stepmother would not let me go out. But when darkness fell and she no longer saw so well, I went out just the same, and we stood on either side of the gate not saying a word; and I felt almost like when I had stood in front of the mirror, dreaming of the one whose thoughts I would know as well as my own. And yet it was different now—I no longer needed to think of myself, for he did that, and it was of him I thought now. But we couldn't go on being silent, even if that would have been the best. He seemed always to be wanting to say something, but it was as if he had forgotten the language after he had left school—they were strange sounds that passed his lips, and I skittered back into the house. But I couldn't sleep, although it was night—I kept on hearing him and saw him pacing to and fro in the light of the moon, and I didn't know whether he wanted to protect me from every danger or make sure that I didn't escape.

Thus it continued, night after night—for he knew that my stepmother wanted me to leave the house and find a place. "You're a cuckoo-child," she said, "and it's high time you flew out of the nest." I didn't care for those words, and when I had to leave I shouted for Rolf, but he had fallen asleep and just growled.

I didn't find a place anywhere, for there was a shortage of places, but stood in a flower shop selling roses and lilies. I received my wages in flowers, but I had no one to give them to, and the air in my attic room was sickening from sheer red roses. In the daytime I went around in a daze, during the night I didn't sleep, and the roses turned yellow in the light of the moon.

Every day a young fellow used to visit the shop and buy large bouquets of flowers although he was dressed in a page-boy's uniform. His movements were strangely nervous, and when I turned my back on him to bind up the flowers he leaned right over the counter—I saw that in the mirror. In my vanity I thought he wanted to see more of me—until I realized it was the cashbox he was after to get money to pay for the flowers. I pretended not to notice, for I thought he might have someone to give his bouquets to. Then the florist sent for me and threatened to dismiss me because some coins were missing. When my page boy came again I told him I was not allowed to sell him anything, but if he were to come to my attic in the evening I had flowers in plenty, for the air was growing more and more sickening in my room. When he came he didn't want the flowers—he was nervous and hardly able to stand on his legs. With his strange chattering voice he told me he had come to the shop for my sake, and that his own place was already full of roses and lilies.

He came every evening and talked about this and that, and I didn't like his chattering voice and his shifty eyes. One evening he brought two silver rings with him and wanted to give me one. He wanted to bear me as if on wings, and in the place where he lived grew roses and lilies. And I was tired of my faded roses and was yellowed from the light of the moon, and accepted his ring, but our hands shook so much that the ring rolled onto the floor. The following day the silversmith's daughter came and told us to watch out, for two rings were missing in the silversmith's shop. In the evening he brought me trinkets of silver and gold, and I accused him of being a thief. Then he wept so much that his voice grew soft: whenever he saw shining objects he could not resist the temptation to steal; that was his nature, he said, for he was an unhappy creature and I alone could help him to hide the stolen goods and discover the good that lay hidden within him. I embraced his page-boy uniform, and he kissed me for the first time in my still young life. But I did not feel the transformation I had dreamed of—I didn't turn into a proper human being, and neither did he, for when there came a knock on the door and it gave way to police uniforms, he crawled out of my attic window; the bird had flown. He had done me no good, for the trinkets shone in the moonlight, and they put me behind bars as if I were a bird.

When I came out again I went to the silversmith's to protest my innocence, and he stood there behind the counter with the silversmith's daughter, shaking his head. On all the chimneys I passed on my way, large magpies were sitting chattering, and wagging their proud tails.

I returned to my stepmother's house. I was full of wicked thoughts and wanted to see Rolf again so that he could tear my page boy to pieces. But I saw only my stepmother; she, like me, had aged, and was now so old that she needed help. "Stepdaughter," she said, "I wanted you out of this house so that you could become different from me and have real human children. And yet I grudged you a different life from mine, for I took you into my house so that I could love my own unhappiness in you, and I knew you would return."

As hoarse as a crow my step-mother had become, and never before had human speech sounded so raucous to my ears. I realized that when people have to speak in order to understand one another, it is already too late. It was muteness I loved now, and I remembered the fish of my childhood, which only pretended to speak; I remembered Rolf too, who could not utter a word and made do with strange sounds. I never said a word to my stepmother, just as she had never spoken to me before; I knew that if I were to speak I would use wicked words, and I felt sorry for her on account of her wickedness. In the daytime I could not leave her—only at night did I go out into the dark garden. But wherever I walked the leaves rustled; I walked along the quiet streets where the street lamps shone stronger than the light of the moon—there too I heard whispering behind me. I caught a glimpse of him in the lamplight, but I had no wish to see him, for I despised the creeping nature of man. But I left the door ajar nevertheless, for I was soon too old to be young. Hissing, he bent over me and kissed my dank lips with his. Suffocating me, he twisted round my breast and buried his fangs in my belly. Then, wild as an animal, I screamed as I had always wanted to scream, while his froth ran over me and loathing stank in my mouth. When I came to myself he had crept away, and that same night my stepmother died, perhaps frightened to death by my screams.

I sat alone at my stepmother's table, which was full of aquaria with fish and terraria with snakes and showcases with squeaking mice. I never left the locked garden after darkness had set in and the streetlamps shone, but on summer evenings I sat behind the hedge, listening to the animals running past. There was no need for me to kiss a human being in order to know its animal guise, and when Rolf passed by— driven by memories of old, perhaps—I saw him, four-legged and hairy, for more than I had kissed his mouth. I flew up into the lime tree and hooted— though not as loudly as I had screamed in my youth, for I had learned to control myself. But he ran off, howling, nevertheless, and I heard him moving farther and farther away. All through that summer night up in the lime tree I sat and disgorged the remains of my mice.

The Foster Daughter

During the civil war many children were sent out of the country so that they could return home and repopulate it should all their parents be killed in the war. But by the time the war was over the children had spent so many years in exile in their new countries that they no longer thought about the old one. Since only a few exit permits were issued after the war, only a few parents were able to travel out of the country to bring their children home; most parents could only write letters to their children, who were unable to read them, for they had forgotten their own language.

The foster daughter knew that the many letters with foreign stamps on them were for her. She put them in the drawer of her bedside table in a stack that grew higher and higher, and every day the letters became longer and longer, and she ran her eyes quicker and quicker over the many unreadable lines. Her foster parents were kindly people and didn't know whether she could still remember anything of her mother tongue. Every day they asked her: "Elna, was there anything special in the letter today?" But Elna never answered, so they thought she might be hiding something from them. However, she cut the stamps off the envelopes and swapped most of them for other stamps, so that her stamp collection grew.

Elna didn't hide things from her foster parents any more than children usually hide things from their real parents, but she continued to conceal the fact that she didn't understand her own language. It was not one of the languages she learned in school, and it never occurs to a school child that it is possible to learn things outside school. In geography lessons she learned about her native country, about its old minerals and hot springs, and about its fruits and animals; and in history lessons she learned about its lost might and, finally, about the civil war. But when questioned by the teacher, she knew neither more nor less about her country than her schoolmates did, and none of them knew that she was born there. True enough, she had darker hair and blacker eyes than most children, and the teachers called her Dark Elna. But that was only so as not to confuse her with another girl called Elna, who had fair hair.

When Dark Elna was around confirmation age she came home from school one day and found a note asking her to fetch a registered letter from the post office. Her parents had received the postman kindly, but the letter could only be delivered to Elna in person, and they were sorry they couldn't receive a letter on their own foster daughter's behalf. Elna went to the post office and was handed a letter that was so thick and heavy that it was completely plastered over with stamps, and it was full of printed forms inside, which possibly had to be filled in. Her foster parents studied the forms anxiously and asked what they were for, and Elna replied quite truthfully: "I can't read them." But she didn't say it as if she spoke the truth, so her foster father said: "We have fed you and clothed you without expecting any gratitude and without hiding anything from you. We could have made you forget about your other country, but we felt it our duty to remind you about it while you were still small. We could have hidden all the letters from you, as well as the note from the post office, but we have hidden nothing. And yet you still have secrets from us." At the thought of these secrets Elna's foster mother began to cry, and at the thought of not knowing her own secrets, Elna cried too, and so she went out of the house with her letter in order to swap stamps with Fair Elna.

When Fair Elna asked where she had got all the foreign letters from, Dark Elna replied that she had got them from her homeland, for that was where her real parents lived. Surely Fair Elna could remember what she had learned about it in school? No, Fair Elna could remember nothing about it, for after all, it wasn't her own country. So Dark Elna had to remind her about the hot springs and about the civil war which had put an end to the old Empire, so that the Emperor's entire family had had to go into exile and hide themselves under cover names so as not to be caught and murdered, and "Dark Elna" was just such a cover name. "Golly!" said Fair Elna. And while Fair Elna's eyes popped wider and wider open, for the first time in her life Dark Elna related her life history, of which she knew so little that she made most of it up. She was in fact the Emperor's daughter, but no one else knew that, and no one must ever know it, otherwise it would cost her her life. "Golly!" repeated Fair Elna, who got all the stamps in return for keeping it secret, for Dark Elna had more serious things to think about than stamps, and had them all already anyway. Fair Elna became so interested that she got out her geography and history books in order to see if there was anything about all the things Elna had told her; but there was next to nothing, and so she had to ask Elna, who knew all the answers. The revolution had started because the Emperor, her father, had no sons but only one daughter, and most of the men in the country wouldn't even consider being ruled by a woman. So they murdered the Emperor, and Elna only managed to get out of the country in the nick of time before all little girls of her age were killed so that there wouldn't be any Crown Princess. Yes, but then Fair Elna couldn't understand how the letter with all the stamps could be from her parents when she was the Emperor's daughter and the Emperor was dead. Dark Elna flushed and said that her mother, the Empress, had married again in order to get a surname, because empresses normally only have Christian names. Fair Elna counted up on her fingers and said: "So you've got three fathers and two mothers." But then it was time for supper, and Dark Elna arrived home late, and her parents had already begun to fear that she might have run away from home. But they said nothing and ate in silence.

The next day the whole school knew that Elna had three fathers, one of whom had been an Emperor. During the history lesson one of her schoolmates put up her hand and asked the teacher whether he couldn't teach them about Dark Elna. During break Dark Elna spoke to Fair Elna for the last time and said: "If I'm murdered, it'll be your fault." So Fair Elna told the others that if Dark Elna was murdered it would be her fault, and she couldn't bear it. So Dark Elna was surrounded by countless school children, who were loudly protecting her from murderers. From then on, saving Elna's life became a cherished duty for her schoolmates; they encircled her faithfully on her way to and from school and discussed the possible murderous intentions of all the passers-by.

Every time Elna was brought home safely in this way, she expected to find a personal note from the post office, but she never found one. Then she remembered her foster father saying that they could have hidden the note, and in secret she searched all over the house, but, finding no note, she imagined they must have thrown it away. She went to the post office and asked if they should have a registered letter for her, but the post office said that letters could only be handed over to people with notes. Since no new letter ever came, Elna went on reading the old ones which she couldn't understand, and spent no time on her homework. Her foster mother sighed, while her foster father said: "It's just a phase."

One day, when Elna had run home from school early in order to escape her bodyguard, she found her mother sitting reading her letters. Elna snatched them away, so that some of them got torn, and she told her foster mother off for reading her letters and tearing them up. But her foster mother complained that it was Elna herself who had torn up the letters, and that she herself couldn't read them anyway. "Then why are you reading them?" asked Elna, and since her foster mother couldn't answer this question it struck her that her parents might know what the letters contained and simply be hiding them from her. Both foster daughter and foster mother spent such a long time imploring the other to disclose what she was hiding that in the end one of them promised the other to tell the whole truth if the other would do the same, and then both of them stood there with nothing to say to one another.

Elna came to think that there must be many other girls in the country—and boys too, of course—who had left her homeland at the time of the war. Since she knew of no other compatriots, she had nothing to go on but her own appearance, and so every evening she walked the streets looking for people of her own age who looked like her. But none of them looked quite like her, and in any case she wasn't able to speak her own language to those who looked just a bit like her, and if any of the others were to speak her own language to her she wouldn't be able to answer, and that would look silly.

One day Elna left school. She no longer wished to be surrounded by the others and wanted to be able to read her own letters. She could have taken the letters to a wise man or woman to have them translated, but she thought they might contain secrets that shouldn't be disclosed to just anyone. But in order to pay for the necessary language tuition she had to earn money, and so she became a waitress instead of a schoolgirl. Her foster parents pleaded with her to give up the waitress job; they thought they had a special obligation towards her because she was their foster daughter, and if Elna needed money her foster father would give her what she needed. But Elna didn't wish to be ungrateful; her foster parents had done enough for her even though she was only their foster daughter, and she must soon leave home. So her foster parents said no more lest she should leave home.

In the hotel where she was a waitress she heard many foreign languages, and she asked the others what the languages were. One fine day she learned that she was listening to her own foreign language. It didn't sound as pleasant as she had expected; it was full of terrible sounds and was being spoken by two elderly gentlemen with moustaches and small black eyes that kept on winking at her; but Elna kept both her eyes and her ears open. From that time on Elna recognized her own language as soon as she heard it, and she also recognized her compatriots; they always used to wink at her as if they recognized her too, and if she dared approach in order to hear the language better, they would pinch her cheek and make it quite red. They were always elderly gentlemen—the younger ones probably couldn't get exit permits yet, and probably not the women either—and she didn't know what to make of them. Those who were given permission to travel abroad were likely to be especially faithful opponents of the Emperor, and Elna didn't yet know whether she sympathized with the Emperor, though she already suspected that she was not the Emperor's daughter.

When Elna received her first wages she went to a language teacher who advertised that she taught her language. She too had small black eyes and a large hooked nose that made all the sounds sound peculiar. She spoke so brokenly that Elna wondered how she could possibly teach anyone languages. "Why do you want to learn that language?" the language teacher asked. Elna couldn't very well confide in her, and said: "Just for fun." Then the language teacher laughed so terribly that at first she couldn't speak. But then she said: "People don't learn that language for fun. Take my advice and learn one of the other ones." But Elna was adamant and wouldn't listen to her good advice. This made the teacher angry, and she conjugated verbs with Elna until Elna could no longer utter a verb. Exhausted, she went home and read through all the letters in order to find the verbs she had learned. But she couldn't find them, and for many weeks she was afraid that the language teacher might be deceiving her and teaching her a different language. But eventually, as the months went by, she began to make out single words—words like 'daughter' and 'mother' and 'father'—and when she had learned the words for 'return home' she found them in all the letters and realized that they were concerned with asking her, as their daughter, to return home. There was nothing about the Emperor, nor was there anything about money, although that was most important if she were to travel so far. She spent more and more time serving guests at the hotel, while the rest of the day she spent learning her language, and so the language teacher received all of her wages and she couldn't afford to leave home.

She didn't feel she was getting any further, and from sheer

impatience she wrote down all the words that kept on cropping up in the letters and asked the language teacher what they meant. But the teacher clasped her hands and screamed: "What kind of words are these? Where have you got hold of these words at your age? I hope you're not reading texts that are above your level. Stick to the beginners' book—it doesn't contain horrors like that. Practice the language so that you gain control over it. A language must be commanded. You mustn't let yourself be tyrannized by it! Decline the words together! Don't give them any peace for a single moment. Don't let them stay as they are—convert them, put them into the plural, into the past, but leave the future until later. Now, let's translate 'the child's father was its mother's husband.' " But Elna couldn't translate anything at all; she kept on thinking of all the horrors she had stored up in her letters all through her childhood, and which the language teacher wouldn't teach her—and she suddenly broke off her lessons. "About time too, my child," the teacher said. "That wasn't anything for you. Stick to your mother tongue, it won't lead you into trouble."

So if she wished to become more fluent, Elna had no recourse but to try to speak to her own countrymen, even though it made her cheeks red. The head waiter noticed it and said: "You are good at languages, I see." Then Elna asked whether she could have a raise. But the head waiter answered: "We pay you for your ability to wait, not for your knowledge of languages. On principle, we prefer you not to be able to speak to the guests, for conversations tend to revolve around irrelevant subjects. There is much personal pleasure to be gained from speaking foreign languages, but that is a private concern, unless one happens to be an interpreter or a language teacher."

Elna took this as a warning, but now she really had to learn her own language, and she realized that the more she got to know her compatriots the better she would learn it, even if they were all elderly gentlemen old enough to be her father. The longer she conversed with them, the more irrelevant subjects the conversations revolved around, and Elna was dismissed. Her compatriots had often offered her money, but she had been obliged to refuse so long as she was on duty; now she was unemployed and able to accept. She was never at home with her foster parents anymore, so she left home. "To think you would cause us this grief," said her foster mother. "Can't you see you'll be the death of your father?" Elna looked in astonishment at her foster father, who had become old and white-haired, and walked with a stick. "No," she said, but her father said: "It's that foreign blood."

Soon Elna was able to understand nearly everything her fellow countrymen said, and they all said the same irrelevant things. But at home she had learned some of the words in the letters by heart, and to her compatriots' surprise she managed to weave them into the conversations and, in so doing, to get to know both her language and her letters better. Already in the first letter Elna had been asked to write her name on a postcard at once and send it to her parents, for they wouldn't have a moment's peace before they knew whether she was alive or dead. Elna could naturally have written her name on a postcard at once, but she didn't, because the letter was many years old. And in the next letter her parents thought she must already have been old enough to write a proper letter, but Elna was not yet fluent enough to be able to write a letter without mistakes. The older Elna had grown, the longer and more difficult became the letters. It was her mother who wrote them, and she mostly wrote about her father; he had been wounded in the war and he still lay ill and thinking about Elna, for she had been the apple of his eye ever since her birth. Elna had to ask one of her compatriots what 'the apple of his eye' meant, but couldn't quite understand his answer. But her father continued to be ill in letter after letter, and her mother wrote to say that Elna could make him well by returning home, and that if she didn't return home she would be her father's death. For since Elna didn't write he could only think she must be dead, and he would never be able to survive her death. Elna looked at the last letters, which she couldn't yet understand, but could find nothing about her father's death.

A certain young man used also to frequent the place where Elna went to meet her compatriots and learn her language;

he had fair hair and never winked, but he was always staring at her with wide eyes. She thought he might have been set to watch over her by the Immigration and Naturalization Service, or was employed by her foster parents as a private detective. Whenever she went out with one of her compatriots he used to follow her, and one evening he drew nearer and nearer, and since there was no one else in the street but herself and her compatriot—a man so old that he could scarcely walk without support and had to lean on her—he came right up and seized hold of Elna, while her compatriot fell to the ground. Terrified, Elna's heart beat so wildly that she could scarcely stand; so the young man had to carry her, and Elna didn't dare kick him for fear that he was from the vice squad. But he carried her home and put her on his own bed, and Elna cried because she didn't learn any more of her own language that night. The young man wanted her to call him by his Christian name, which was Tom, and asked why she was crying. Elna couldn't very well confide in him and said she was crying because she had no money. So Tom drew a large bill from his pocket; Elna could have one like that every night, he said, if only she would sleep with him, for he hadn't slept a wink since he had seen her leading that kind of life, and now he could no longer live without sleep. Elna quietly decided to buy a dictionary in her own language and to go on teaching herself, for if she were to sleep with Tom for a sufficient number of nights she would have enough money to journey to her fatherland.

After his long period of sleeplessness, Tom did nothing but sleep. But during the course of her private studies Elna learned that her father lay sleepless day and night from thinking of her, for he was obsessed with the idea that he had to keep his daughter in his thoughts day and night, and that if he stopped thinking of her for a single moment she would die in a foreign land. And it was even fortunate that he had such an obsession, for it forced him to stay alive for Elna's sake. But she herself, Elna's mother, could no longer believe that Elna was alive and couldn't understand why she kept on writing letters just the same. For if their daughter was alive and wouldn't write a single letter—not even her name on a postcard—she was a bad daughter and not worth writing letters to. But when she was little she had been a good daughter, and her mother couldn't believe she had become worse with the years. They could only believe that the letters must have got lost on the way or been snapped up by customs officers or by her foster parents. But she had nevertheless been given a note with her name and address on when she left home, so she should be able to write on her own if she wasn't dead. But she couldn't believe that their daughter was dead without their having noticed it or their clocks having stopped. She had better write at once if she didn't want her parents to go out of their mind.

By now Elna had become fluent enough to write an intelligible letter to say that she was alive. But if she were to write now, her parents would be bound to think she was a bad daughter because she hadn't written for such a long time, and since she was going to make the journey in any case it was no longer necessary to write letters. She had already realized from the last letter, which she had fetched from the post office in her childhood, that it was full of entry permits, and at night she lay working out how many nights she still needed to lie beside Tom in order to have enough money for the ticket. Whereas Tom always slept, Elna lay sleepless from thinking of her sleepless father, and sleepless people always become angry with those who are sleeping. But Elna didn't want to be angry with Tom and tried to wake him with kisses and pats, but however hard she patted him Tom always went on sleeping. Not until the alarm clock rang did he get up and pay Elna her night's wages.

During the day Elna became more and more sleepy from lying sleepless at night, and her eyes smarted so much that she had to buy glasses in order to read the letters, and they cost so much that she had to put off her departure. "Dearest daughter, this is my farewell letter to you," her mother suddenly wrote, even though Elna still had three letters left, "for since you never write I can only believe you are dead. Indeed I hope you are dead, because then we have done right in grieving over you, whereas if you are alive our great sorrow has had no meaning. If you are dead I beg forgiveness for my wicked thoughts, but if you are alive, receive herewith my motherly curse. Your mother." For the first time Elna understood every word in the letter, but she had no reason to be pleased with her progress, for she was now afraid of meeting her own parents again. When she got as far as that she would not make herself known to them all at once; she could say she was Elna's foster sister and that her foster sister was dead, and only if they appeared upset about their daughter's death would she please them by saying she was still alive.

But Elna had identified herself so daughter-like with her parents' feelings that she had already begun to grieve over her own death and was no longer pleased to be alive. From sheer grief she couldn't see what was written in the last letter—she reread only the printed entry permits she had read before, anxious lest they should have expired in the meantime, but there was nothing to indicate that. And she realized that since the last letter still permitted her to travel into her native land her mother could not have gone on cursing her for still being alive. So she took the last letter but two, though waited until Tom had come home and fallen asleep before reading it.

No sooner had she begun to read than she found reason to be pleased that she could read so well. "Dearest daughter," wrote her mother again, "now I am writing to you for the last time and without your father's knowledge. For your father wishes you to return for your parents' sake and not for the sake of your inheritance. But I will lose my dignity as a mother and ask you to come for reason of your inheritance, if you know of no other reason. For you were so little when you were a child that you must not remember that your father is a very rich man and known by almost everyone. We even own the big hotel beside the hot springs that can heal all illnesses, and after the war there were so many poor sick people that our wealth is greater than anyone can imagine. If only our beloved country were not so poor that we cannot spare the money, we would have sent money to you long ago, but money may not be sent out of the country and your father thought you could probably make that sacrifice. But I must tell you that your father is still lying at death's door, and if he dies without knowing that you are alive, he must cut you out of his will, for he still has the obsession that his thoughts are keeping you alive and that you will die when he can no longer think of you, even though you will be his last thought. But a mother is never as stern and just as a father, and so I am writing to you in secret to ask you to write your name on a postcard before your father dies, for that may save his life and keep your name in his will . . ."

Elna couldn't read any more; her eyes filled with tears at the thought that her mother no longer cursed her. Impatient at the thought of still having to sleep three nights with Tom, who merely slept while her father lay dying, she began to shake him. But he just shook his head and started to snore. And suddenly Elna began to think longingly of her own countrymen, who may well have been old enough to be her father, but who had nevertheless been able to stay awake all night long with her. If she was to save her father she could wait no longer, for the last letter in which he lay dying was already several years old. She had to get hold of the remainder of the money that very night. Tom was snoring so loudly that he wouldn't be able to hear what she was doing, and she felt in all his pockets and found nothing. And although she stood there empty-handed, Tom suddenly said: "What do you want the money for?"

At first Elna thought he was talking in his sleep; but he was staring at her with eyes as wide open as she had ever seen them. "Answer me," said Tom, since she didn't answer. "I'll pay it all back," she said. "That's no answer," he objected. "I'm rich," said Elna. "Then you don't need any money," said Tom.

But then Elna begged for her last wages and two nights in advance so she would be rich enough to bring back her fortune. And for the second time in her life Elna related the story of her life hitherto, and this time the story was quite true, and she told it so eagerly that she didn't realize she was telling it in her own language. Tom's eyes opened wide with terror at the thought that she was speaking the same language to him as to the lecherous foreigners, and maybe was also feeling terrible feelings of inferiority because he was no good at languages. So he cried: "It is only whores who neglect their mother tongue," and he felt justified in treating her as he thought a whore should be treated. Afterwards he sobbed violently and said he would never do it again. It was his nerves that were on edge from working overtime every day in order to earn money enough for Elna. He would give her everything he owned, but he had no more to give.

But Elna laughed and said: "I am rich." And she drew out all the money Tom had given her. She wrote her name on a postcard and sent it to her original parents and never received an answer. On her wedding day she burnt all her letters and her foster parents came to the wedding. It still occasionally happened that she spoke her own language to Tom, and he became violent. But after a while she forgot it. She often planned to brush it up, but then she got twins and other things to do. Even as small children, they began to collect foreign stamps; their father bought them from stamp dealers, and their mother quite forgot she belonged elsewhere.

In Strange Country

As he stepped out of the airport bus and stood in the city he had heard so much about, he said to himself: "So this is the city I have heard so much about," and he looked around in order to see it too. But in particular he was looking for a hotel, and so for the time being he didn't take much notice of anything else, even though he was standing in the middle of a large square, which was full of foreigners (who were naturally not foreigners there) surrounded by big dirty brown buildings. In such a frequented spot he expected there would be countless hotels just around the corner, but when he got that far, this was not the case, unless "hotel" was called something quite different in that country. He put down his suitcase and was surprised to see in his pocket dictionary that "hotel" was called "hotel." He walked for some time along a long avenue before he discovered that it bore the Dictator's name on every corner. Then he turned round one of them. Until now it had been the corners he had chiefly noticed, for they were not proper crossroads as he still remembered them from home. No, wherever the streets converged they swelled up into octagons, and if you went straight on you had to make a detour in order to cross over them, for the pedestrian crossings were in the narrow places beside the octagon. So it was better to turn all the corners, and this he did, until he stood in the Dictator's avenue again and turned the corner once more.

He ought to have jumped into a cab immediately and said "hotel"—that one word would probably have been understood. But since he had been walking for such a long time anyway, it seemed absurd to suddenly start driving, for then all his trudging would have been wasted energy. The large buses which passed him every now and then were so full of people going home at this time of day that there would hardly have been room for both him and his suitcase, and he couldn't be sure that they went past the hotel district anyway. If he hadn't encountered any solitary hotels until now it must be because they were all clustered together in one particular spot that he hadn't yet discovered because he had been walking in circles on account of the inconvenient octagonal shape of the crossroads. He sat down on his suitcase in order to get his bearings. The sun was about to set in the west. Should he himself walk in the same direction or in a different one? He took the opportunity of looking at the passersby who were not well dressed enough to be living in a hotel, and it wouldn't be much use asking them, all the more so because he wouldn't be able to understand their reply. Besides, they were all in such a hurry that something was probably brewing, and he became nervous and walked on without knowing where.

Although the country was poor there were fountains in all the large squares, and sidewalk cafés with so many guests that he didn't think he'd be able to find a seat. Moreover, in the gutters swarthy men were squatting, or sitting on footstools, lying in wait for the guests like a pack of jackals. They were apparently only shoeshine boys, but dangerous nevertheless. Now and again they would suddenly jump up and grab a café guest by the leg so that he fell backwards in the chair, and then set about polishing his shoes with violent gestures. His own shoes had become so dusty from the many hours of walking that he dared not even go near the cafés, even though his legs were so tired that he could scarcely walk, let alone stand on them. Late at night he realized he had been walking for several hours without either hearing or seeing, for now he suddenly saw so many hotels shining in front of him, while all the other houses were hidden in darkness, that it was quite unlikely that he hadn't seen them before. Happy at having found them all by himself, he walked determinedly from one to the other, though he became less and less happy as all the night porters shook their heads without listening to what he had to say. At first he was sensible enough to enquire at the medium-sized hotels with names like The Post, The Station, Denmark, or Victoria; now he made a desperate attack on the Excelsior, Royal, Ritz and Majestic, but in the luxury hotels whole crowds of uniformed porters and elevator boys stood shaking their heads. "Surely it can't pay for you to run a hotel in that fashion," he said in his righteous desperation, but received no comprehensible answer. He thought they might have had strict instructions not to admit foreigners who might tell the natives about the hospitality, much less the freedom, in their homelands.

In the early hours of the morning he was staggering through streets so narrow that he and his suitcase were constantly bumping into the houses, and looking for accommodation in bars and pubs with names like The Parade, The Dragon, The Hare, and The Hearth. Since he had been met everywhere by shaking heads, some old and cross, others young and smiling, he got the cunning idea of keeping his mission secret until he had drunk so much that he was already an old and respected customer. But in the places where he had drunk enough to be taken into consideration they apparently didn't rent rooms, and when he eventually reached a hotel that advertised empty rooms even at that hour, he learned with great effort that there were no rooms for rent to drunkards. By then the sun was about to rise somewhere in the east; he thought he could recognize it from the day before and started to shout at it, since he didn't think he would be able to make himself understood by merely speaking at such a great distance. And those were his last words that morning, for just then he was seized by two policemen carrying pistols, and he couldn't utter a word from sheer terror, even though they asked him one question after the other. Then his guardian angel turned up and answered for him—a half-naked boy, who talked the police into silence, took hold of his suitcase in one hand and him in the other and walked off with both of them without their knowing where.

He woke up having dreamt that he had been lying in a bed that was too short for him, so he got up and noticed that the bed was too short. Although his clothes were rumpled he was relieved to find he had them all on. Beneath his window the buses were still driving around an octagonal square in sunlight that was already as tired and dusty as the day before. Amid all the noise of the traffic he heard someone snoring and, seeing that his door was not shut, he noted that its two sections couldn't be made to close; this prompted him to make sure that neither he nor his suitcase had been robbed. Other doors of the same double nature opened out into a dark hallway, which he entered; these doors couldn't be closed either, and narrow shafts of light fell through into the passage. He followed the snoring sound and found a half-naked young man lying open-mouthed on a bed that was too short for him; and when he opened the other doors he saw nothing but half-naked young men with dark hair lying asleep. "A lazy people," he thought, with a slightly better conscience, but still feeling sick. Only one door was locked; probably a young girl was lying asleep behind it—in that case noiselessly, even though he listened at the door. The corridor opened out into a steep staircase which he descended—down into a restaurant with a sidewalk café outside, though without guests and shoeshine boys; behind the bar, from which glistening tubes and taps were protruding, stood a solitary grinning boy to whom he gave a coin to stop him grinning. Grinning, the boy pocketed it and thanked him. At least he assumed so. The boy was not as half-naked as he seemed to remember him, but was wearing a white shirt which was half dirty in comparison with his grinning teeth.

"Sit down," said the boy, but he didn't understand and remained standing, until the boy pushed him down into a chair from which he could stare straight up at the Dictator's portrait. He turned the back of his chair on it, which to his astonishment made the boy call out "Mamma, Mamma." Through a door that was obviously used as a kitchen door entered a woman of such vast proportions that she entered sideways, and she took a good look at him with her large black eyes, even turning him around in order to see him from the back he had hitherto turned on the Dictator's portrait. She was taller than he was, although he considered himself far above the average height in that country; she was covered with earrings and necklaces and bracelets on the appropriate places, her dress was red, but despite her apparent age her cheeks were even redder. "Passport," she said, and she took it and stamped it and kept it, saying:

"Do you want breakfast at this hour?"

"I am a foreigner," he answered.

"Perhaps you don't understand me?" she said, and, not having understood her, he nodded; and she shook her head so violently that he almost shook too. Then she said something to the boy, and the boy fetched a glass and a bottle that was smaller than the glass and so could be emptied into it, and grinned and said "cheers" in his own language. He dared not drink the yellow liquid while the landlady was watching him, which she was:

"Would you like worm soup for supper?" she asked.

"Soup," he nodded, happy to have understood so much—so happy that he was still nodding when she said:

"And starfish?"

And since she too said "cheers" and walked sideways out, he drank and, feeling immediately better, he grinned at the boy, though without showing his teeth. Thinking of something else, he knew not what, he glanced up at the Dictator's portrait. A cat was winding itself around his leg and, pointlessly, he said: "You understand me."

"Pardon?" said the boy.

"Cat," said the man, pointing at it.

"Cat," corrected the boy.

"Cat," said the man, feeling he had learned something. Perhaps in the end he would learn to understand them. He had been given to understand that they didn't like to say anything for fear someone would overhear it. He turned the chair around again and surveyed the life in the street, which was getting darker and darker again until the lamps were lit on the corner and on the cars. A few customers came in and looked at him, and he looked at them too, so as to get to know the country's inhabitants before they went again. He drank another little bottle and, feeling still better, began to write a letter, not because he had anyone to write to, but in order to look busy. "So now I have arrived," he started, though got no further, for it was apparently dinner time; the smell of food streamed in through the kitchen door, and the young men—who no longer slept and were no longer half-naked but were awake and wearing white shirts—streamed in through the door by which he himself had just entered. They distributed themselves among the tables, and he nodded at one of them—the only one who had fair hair—because he himself had fair hair and wanted to come into contact with the population. But the fair-haired boy turned his back on him and began to fight with the boy behind the bar. A couple of the dark-haired boys nodded at him, but here in this country nodding at people one didn't know was apparently not done, and he continued his letter: "I am sitting here among nothing but young men; there are no women here at all apart from an elderly landlady who nevertheless looks younger. I imagine that nearly all the fathers must have been killed in the civil war and that nearly all the fatherless sons live in this relatively cheap type of boarding house (the proper hotels were full up). One should think that the young girls would generally be just as fatherless as the boys, but in such a backward country young girls are probably not allowed to live alone, not even two together. At any rate you don't *see* as many girls as boys; perhaps large numbers of them are being brought up in convents or suchlike, and in any case they don't receive the same education. Presumably I am sitting among students, but they don't learn foreign languages, so I don't get much out of talking to them—I suppose one is afraid of their being able to understand what we say to them. I myself have begun to learn the language now: 'thank you' means 'thank you,' 'cat' means 'cat' and 'soup' means 'soup.' Incidentally, I have ordered soup for supper today, but that's the only thing I've ordered. The first steps, as one says . . ."

"Thank you," he said, as a lame little man placed a large though only half-full bottle of wine in front of him.

". . . are the hardest. It is typical that the waiter who works alone here—apart from a boy who minds the bar during the day when there apparently aren't any customers—is so old that he hasn't had the opportunity of being killed in the war, but even he is marked by it, for he limps heavily and his hands shake so much that he spills on the floor all the soup he is serving the students."

He was interrupted by a sudden silence. All the young men, who may not have been students at all but just other young men, screwed up their eyes and mouths into curious grimaces; he looked in the same direction as their winking eyes and saw a young woman coming over towards them with a plate of soup which she didn't spill on the floor although it was so full that she stuck her tongue out between her lips in order to keep her balance. Otherwise he tried not to look at her, because he felt that all the young men were looking at him; intrepidly he met their gaze, which pierced first him and then her, and not until he smelled the soup on the table and she had already turned her back did he say "thank you"—so brokenly that all the young men broke their silence and laughed, while she sought shelter behind the kitchen door. The soup tasted even worse than it smelled, but in order not to incur their scorn he swallowed it with a screwed up nose and scalded tongue and palate and stomach, while the conversation in the room grew more and more noisy and angry-sounding. They were almost certainly envious of the fact that he alone was being served by her, and they merely by the lame waiter who was still limping around and saying "oooooh," presumably so that he too should be able to understand it. He felt as hot as the soup—even the chair burned beneath him—and when he resumed his letter writing so as to appear busy, his handwriting became a scrawl. "The soup was strong and nourishing," he wrote nevertheless. "As an exception it was brought by a waitress whose appearance made a great though for me embarrassing impression upon those present. The relationship between the sexes is obviously not of the best. Because the girls are usually hidden away, a visible girl gives rise to lecherous nasal sounds on the part of the young men. Apparently one of the beauties *also* to be found in this country. Now what does such a beauty look like?" He tried in vain to remember what the beauty looked like, but since he had not seen her properly he could only visualize the landlady, who was probably her mother anyway, and he blinked in order to get rid of the sight, though in the end he couldn't open his eyes again. All around they were speaking in hushed, even whispering voices; it sounded as if his own ears were at fault, but although he rubbed them hard he could hear no better. So they were in fact afraid of someone hearing what they said. On the other hand he managed to open his eyes, but he couldn't see anything because of the thick cigarette smoke— not even the waitress when she came again. He had struggled halfway out of his chair when he was struck so heavily on the shoulder that he sank down into it again.

"Be warned," sounded a loud and penetrating voice in his ear. But he couldn't understand.

"I am a foreigner," he stammered.

"Be warned nevertheless. Mosetta . . ."

"Who? Mosetta?"

But no sooner had Mosetta's name been mentioned and repeated than the bartender boy leaned over the table between them, saying, with demonstratively shut eyes:

"Sleep? Upstairs?"

And he nodded in relief and said "cat," which he confused with "thank you," and was helped to his feet by the boy and dragged up the staircase, which grew longer and longer. Not until he got to the top of the stairs, however, did he manage to make out that the boy had been trying to introduce himself on the way up as Tesso, and when he wanted to introduce himself by name he found he had forgotten it.

Scarcely had they entered the door, which still couldn't be shut, when it was pushed open and Mosetta stepped inside with the starfish. The smell of fish and oil was so overpowering that he nearly choked, and the soup inside him churned about so violently that it splashed right up into his mouth. Without being able to take note of Mosetta he sank down on to the bed, and Tesso noticed that it was too short and took it away with him, so that, dizzy and lonely, he had to stand up again, supporting himself on Mosetta, until Tesso came back with such a large bed that he needed her help—it was both twice as long and twice as broad as its predecessor. He had an improbable suspicion that he could have kept Mosetta, but he let her go away with the starfish instead. People don't usually feel very well on their first day abroad. The foreign taste of the soup filled him right to the brim, and yet this new fullness was something to do with Mosetta, who had brought the soup. Its taste stuck to his palate so that his mouth extended, but it still couldn't contain the splashes that kept coming up into his mouth. Despite his tired legs he got onto them in a flash, tried all the doors in the corridor before finding the lavatory and sank on to his knees as before an altar; after the soup the wine came up as well, and finally the yellow liquid which tasted so much nicer that he began to feel a little better. Each of the lamps in the hallway was formed like a picture of a mother and child—it was the eyes that shone. And in the lamplight he saw all the dark-haired heads sticking out between the door panels; he didn't think he ought to nod at them in that undignified position, and it was as if the soup from his inside had filled everything with its smell. He didn't feel safe with a door that couldn't be closed, all the more because one of the boarders had had his own bed exchanged for his, and could be expected to make good the bad bargain under cover of darkness. Carefully, so that his defensive measures should not make the others become aggressive, he pushed the rickety table in front of the door and placed his suitcase on top. But his reassuring barricade worried him, since he might have to go out in a hurry again. And he probably would have to, so he removed the table and suitcase again.

In the morning nothing had happened to him after all. He had dreamed more than was good for him and had to chase away unpleasant memories without knowing what they were memories of. He knew that a bad stomach and erotic stirrings were inappropriate in his situation and that both of them had something to do with Mosetta. He really ought to move, but apart from the fact that the hotels were probably still full he was better concealed, at least from the authorities, in that rather out-of-the-way place. And maybe the young men, who—apart from in his dreams—had let him sleep in peace although they had him outnumbered, seemed so unhostile that they might even become his allies. Understandably enough, they were a bit jealous because only he was served soup by Mosetta while they had to make do with the lame waiter; it was a discrimination he ought to complain about when he got a chance. But now it was time to prepare himself for his task and to buy a pistol, and for that he needed help. He looked up the word in his pocket dictionary, but in a country like that one can't just go and buy a pistol, even if one should happen to know the word. One would have to strike down an armed policeman, which was something of a risk, considering one was unarmed oneself until one had gotten the pistol. Or else one had to find a black market for weapons, but he couldn't even find the expression in the dictionary. Naturally it was more a job for the country's own children, but those who speak like the others also adopt their use of the language; they speak respectfully of the Dictator as the country's father, at least when others are listening, and they are afraid to speak of freedom because there is no freedom of speech. Only for one who did not speak the language was there freedom of speech, and so he had to act before he learned to speak. While reasoning in this fashion in his own free language he thought vaguely about Tesso, who had already saved him once before from the armed men and found him shelter for the night and a larger bed, and who did speak the language, though possibly still as freely as children normally speak, and he went downstairs and found Tesso behind the bar as usual.

"Pistol," he said, drinking his morning coffee and glancing towards the kitchen door.

"Pistol," grinned Tesso, producing one from his trouser pocket. He choked over his coffee, coughed, and thought that that was what prohibition led to, that was what rearmament led to—that children, at any rate small boys, carry pistols in their pockets. And even if it was for revolutionary purposes, it nevertheless served to uphold the martial regime.

He put so many bills on the table that Tesso pocketed them at once.

"But does it work?" he asked. "Bang? Bang?"

"Bang!" confirmed Tesso. But then he was terrified to see

Tesso point up at the Dictator and then, with the same hand, at him. Was it a warning or a challenge? In reply Tesso reached out and touched first his moustache and then the Dictator's. He felt extremely uneasy—it was apparently the same kind of moustache. He sat up straight and looked dictatorial. Tesso could take it as he liked. He grinned. The man with the moustache gave Tesso yet another of the big bills that he might not have any use for.

It was now a question of taking his bearings. He was once again on good terms with his own body—just a bit exhausted from yesterday's soup, almost pleasantly exhausted, and conscious of his own body in an unusual way. He consulted his dictionary to see what a city map was called and set out to buy one. But just as he was leaving he heard a woman's voice, presumably the landlady's, loudly telling someone off in the kitchen, and in the same instant the kitchen door opened and Mosetta came rushing out, half-naked and so persecuted by the landlady that she anxiously sought refuge with him and stood pressed up against him, while the landlady smiled at him for the first time and presumably said "good morning" and several other things he didn't understand either. He couldn't very well take the landlady to task for her behavior now that she was suddenly behaving quite differently, and for the same reason he couldn't say anything to Mosetta either. He held the pistol well hidden in his pocket. Tesso grinned and the landlady told him off instead and chased him out into the kitchen, so that he was left alone with Mosetta. Her presumably black eyes were still obscured by tears, and he was tempted to dry them but had no handkerchief. "You're beautiful," he said, now seeing Mosetta properly for the first time, more in order to comfort her than to establish a fact, for he had discovered that Mosetta's skin looked older than herself, wrinkled as it was by so many tears. Mosetta betrayed nothing other than her sorrow and eventually not even that; she was as stiff as a doll, and standing as she was then standing resembled a mannequin, apart from the fact that the torn dress she was wearing would never have been worn in a display window. Since Mosetta might nevertheless be a temptation, as women sometimes may be, he left her standing and went into the city to buy a map of it.

But when he had got the map, at present it seemed less important to find out whether it was also correct. The thing that had struck him most during the short distance he had covered was that so many men had moustaches like the Dictator's. He already felt so much at home that he walked straight across the octagonal squares where the traffic was the thickest, so as to return in the shortest possible time. To Mosetta? Possibly—because the more men with moustaches and the fewer girls he saw in the street, the more he realized that in a tyrannical state it was especially the women who were tyrannized, just as the terror-stricken Mosetta had been tyrannized by the landlady, who might even be her mother. The pistol-armed Tesso would never have needed to seek refuge with him in that manner. So his task would be to liberate the women, and in such a situation it was Mosetta who was the woman nearest at hand. Of course, her mother too was a woman, but she seemed less in need of liberation. Naturally Tesso winked as he went past, but up on his extended bed without batting an eyelash lay Mosetta. He imagined that such immorality could only spring from unreasonably strict morality, but sat down on the bed nevertheless, with Mosetta's soup tingling in his body again. Since understanding without words is better than all other kinds of understanding, he didn't say a word to her, and she didn't answer either. Instead he looked into her eyes, which—quite rightly—were black, and winked like Tesso, but she sat staring vacantly at him, so he said "Mosetta" after all. Irritated because not even that form of address met with any response, he began to shake her and came thus to shake tears out of her eyes. Then he was seized with pity again, and kissed all the tears away; but all he could taste was the soup, and he realized that Mosetta must be snatched away from that slightly foul atmosphere. He went over and shut the door, which immediately opened wide again. Mosetta was more of a reason for him to move than to stay.

"Mosetta," he said, since in any case she couldn't understand him, "you are maladjusted, but it is to your credit that when in Rome you do not shout as the Romans do and prefer to stay silent altogether. Your country's language is corrupt, and the most important words are especially loaded—words like father, mother and loved ones—because the Dictator is called the country's father and the country is called the mother and they both demand to be loved. In my country it is not nearly as bad. You might ask, then, why I came here, then—was it really to set you free, or because I am just as badly off myself?"

Scarcely had he posed that interesting question than Mosetta pointed at her ear with one hand, at her mouth with the other, and shook her head.

"No, I know you don't understand me," he laughed, "but if I could teach you my language from the beginning, don't you think it would become different—for you, of course, but maybe even for me?"

But Mosetta was still shaking her head so that the tears began to flow again; and he was about to kiss them away as before, when suddenly he had the answer as to why he hadn't heard Mosetta say anything until now—she was deaf! And probably also dumb, for some reason or other. And this might be why she had so plainly been offered to him—nobody wanted to have a deaf wife who couldn't take orders by ear.

"Are you deaf?" he roared in her ear, and she nodded through her tears. The young men must have come home from work, and it was possibly already the time when they lay down to sleep. But they must have heard his shout just the same, for now they all crowded together in the doorway, approaching nearer and nearer; he was standing with his back against the wall and Mosetta with her back towards him. But when he had already seized his pistol, one by one they stretched out their hands in reconciliation or congratulation, for they all smiled and nodded and most probably said "Congratulations!" though he didn't understand what for. Tesso came in with the two policemen, who disarmed him and looked menacing, and the landlady appeared wearing even more necklaces than usual and accompanied by a fat clergyman, and he dimly realized that if he didn't marry Mosetta he would be arrested for carrying a pistol. He said bravely "no" when the clergyman asked him, and they all laughed because the answer should of course be "yes," and the landlady answered "yes" when Mosetta was asked. The bride's eyes were full of tears and the bridegroom's full of astonishment. Tesso brought large glasses and the small yellow bottles, and he felt a little better, and the clergyman made a speech and didn't say anything he could understand.

The celebrations went on all night in the restaurant, where the lame waiter served the soup which he spilled on the floor. Mosetta sat beside him, glancing anxiously at him, and as the night drew on he returned her glance more and more frequently—more ashamed over having failed his task and lost his pistol than in actual despair over having been married to Mosetta. The black-haired young men never stopped talking for a moment; even the fair-haired one confided something to him which he didn't understand, and it was quite a relief to look at Mosetta's dumb though red mouth. The landlady, who was now presumably his mother-in-law, embraced him until he lost his breath, and Tesso grinned. Not until the early morning when the sunlight fell admonishingly across the tables did the cars arrive—one for him and Mosetta and another for a chosen crowd of young men who were to act as escorts, and as the sun rose higher and higher, they drove farther and farther on deserted roads along the coast, which now was full of seaside hotels where there was apparently room for everyone, and now full of small wooden shacks in which there was hardly any room at all and which had donkeys and goats and sheep standing outside. At such a wooden hut they stopped. As Mosetta touched the doorhandle he looked around for the car, but the first car had already driven away; only the second one was still there, the black-haired young men standing outside it with raised pistols. When the door opened, out of it tumbled several black dogs and naked toddlers, who were not dumb but who nevertheless shouted "Mamma" at Mosetta; but when they saw him they grew silent, and the biggest, who looked like Tesso, drew out a knife. Then a pistol shot was heard, but it was only a car door that slammed to and disappeared. And a little girl who looked like Mosetta took him by the hand and said: "Story, story," and he didn't know what to say.

A Tale of the Future

PROLOGUE

The President of the country had introduced birth investigations. Every human individual was carefully investigated immediately after birth, and the results of the investigations were fed to an electronic brain that was commonly called the Soothsayer because it was able at birth to predict with a high degree of probability the entire span of a human life. Sometimes it was sufficient to analyze the parents' characteristics before birth; but these preliminary investigations often resulted in the parents not being allowed to have the child at all, so that they couldn't truly be called parents.

The technicians who operated the Soothsayer were the first to admit that it was still a rather primitive apparatus, for at present its statements could not be regarded as totally devoid of errors. But so as to avoid overly large discrepancies between an individual's life and its card in the State files, control investigations were undertaken at short intervals so that the individual could be appropriately adapted to the files. Only a very few trusted men, the prophets, had any knowledge of the files; their wisdom was not allowed to get into the hands of people who might think of misusing it, and who would in any case become acquainted with it soon enough when they got older.

But some people had no wish at all to partake of the Soothsayer's wisdom. The President's most bitter opponent was a man called Philip Rose; they had once been rivals for the presidency. When the birth investigations were just beginning, Philip Rose, who had long since grown to manhood and whose future was therefore undetermined, began to attack both the investigations and their originator in fiery speeches. And when the President—naturally, for the sake of the common good—went so far as to have people arrested because the Soothsayer had prophesied that they would commit crimes in the future, Philip Rose gave speeches from morning till night and drew people's attention to the laws that were still in force, and that did not permit anyone to be imprisoned without trial and verdict.

"I prophesy," shouted Philip Rose, "that I myself will be arrested in the near future. Certainly, I do not intend to commit any crime, unless the government intends to regard my actions as criminal. But, mark you: before long every human action will be branded as criminal, for a human action is a free action. But when people are permitted only to follow orders, then freedom vanishes, and the enslaved people must commit crimes in order to become free. The government insists that I am not telling the truth. All right—but if I am lying, the government has no reason to fear me, for its good actions will put my wicked words to shame. But if I should be arrested, you will know what to think of the government."

"Yes, let's now see if he is arrested," thought the people who were interested in politics and who were all adults, for children are not interested in that kind of thing, and the adults were less worried about the new system, which was only in its infancy. When they heard the President speaking about how beneficial it was, both to the general public and to the individual, for the authorities to possess as much information as possible about individual talents so that it was possible to quickly and correctly place everyone in the right job and thus save time and money, they thought the President was right. But when Philip Rose said that to choose one's own human life was a human right, they thought he was right too, but the very fact that everyone could say what they felt, and freely discuss others' opinions if they didn't have any themselves, just went to show that they were living in a free country.

"It makes one feel uncomfortable," said a philosophically-minded person, "to know that the fate of our children is already determined in advance—it's almost as if they don't need to live at all."

"Oh, but they don't get to know their fate themselves. If everything is predetermined, then it has always been predetermined—we just haven't known our destiny."

"Yes, but if everything has been determined beforehand, who then has been determining it until now?" asked an old priest.

"You mean God, I suppose? But if He has really been determining things, then He is still determining them—even determining that we people should now know what He has determined, so that we can make better use of His foresight. If science points the way to God, what shall we call those who denounce science?"

"Now Philip Rose is what I call a brave man. He has the courage to say what he says, and there are not many people who do that."

"What if his saying that was predetermined? He's only saying it because he himself has not found his niche—unsuccessful presidential candidates never do."

"Not if they were destined to become presidents—like perhaps Philip Rose."

Thus the discussion went; some were for and some were against Philip Rose, even though the presidential election was over. The President has his ears everywhere and knew everything that was being said. He dared not arrest Philip Rose, for in that case everything he had predicted would come true; nor did he dare to leave Philip Rose in freedom, for his words were not without influence on the public—that his secret public investigations confirmed. For the time being the press reported that Philip Rose was in the service of a foreign power, for in the rest of the world, where it hadn't been possible to construct quite such an infallible Soothsayer, most people still opposed the new forecasting system.

For years the President had sacrificed his private life for the sake of his public one. He was already President before he married—and then it was to his private secretary in a private ceremony. But when she gave birth to his firstborn—a son, who was immediately birth-investigated—the picture of the naked child appeared on the front pages of all the newspapers so that everyone could see that the President had had his own child investigated as thoroughly as everyone else's. But the other parents were not told the results, for these were not accessible to the public. The President was informed, however, and the prophets entered his presidential office with gloomy expressions, and said:

"We regret that we are destined to bring the President these tidings."

"Speak," said the President. "Is my child soon to die?"

"No," said the prophets, looking very worried. The President had to thump the table in impatience before Teresius, the head prophet, hurriedly began to speak, explaining the laws of genetics, which often relentlessly demanded that the child of a man who combined all good qualities in his own person, as, for example, the President, may well inherit some of that person's positive qualities but also some of the less good qualities that the child's exalted father had not in his perfection been able to develop, but which could nevertheless be found, so to speak, as recessive genes.

"I'm not a schoolboy," interrupted the President.

"No," said Teresius.

"Did the answer come out of the machine will all these evasions?" asked the President, and Teresius answered:

"The Soothsayer answered clearly and comparatively unambiguously—but of course the Soothsayer doesn't have the same human feelings as the rest of us—that the child, when it stops being a child—here there is a slightly ambiguous date, and one may question whether the use of a Soothsayer is at all possible in the case of someone who is out of the ordinary . . ."

"Are you suggesting that the apparatus isn't functioning satisfactorily? That we are building our society on an uncertain foundation?"

"Forgive me, Mr. President. You will soon understand me.

It is predicted that as a child your son will be more intelligent than is normal for his age and will receive a good education."

"Naturally," said the President.

"Yes. But it will not be sufficient just the same. For it has also been predicted that he will cause his mother great sorrow."

"That is not unusual," said the President.

"No. But this is not an entirely usual kind of sorrow. And just before that time comes he will be separated entirely from his mother."

"That is sad," said the President, coolly.

"Yes. But it is even sadder, that when the time comes—a time when you are apparently still alive, he will . . . murder his father."

Even the President paled. Teresius hastened to add:

"But everything indicates that such an act will not be repeated. His future shines bright."

"Why will he murder me?" asked the President.

"The card doesn't say why. As you know, the apparatus chiefly registers facts—rarely motives."

"Is it correctly adjusted? Are you sure that . . ."

"Mr. President, we have questioned the Soothsayer time and time again, and the answer remains the same."

"Do the investigations often reveal that a child will come to murder its father?"

"It does happen. If the father cannot be regarded as subversive we see to it that the child is removed from its home. In the earliest cases the ignorant fathers protested and demanded the children back again; so then we switched to swapping children, so that the murderers-to-be could be placed with subversive fathers . . ."

". . . who are not the children's fathers—and whom they therefore will not murder . . ."

"The children will presumably murder their presumed fathers. How could they murder the right ones—they don't even know them. Would you like to have a good and harmless child instead of your own? We have found one that looks like yours—your wife needn't know anything."

"What was it you said about genetics? Is it *my* hidden qualities that will make my own son murder me and cause his mother sorrow?"

"Of course not, Mr. President. The dangerous qualities may be inherited from earlier generations. They may—so to speak—be a relic from the past."

"Thank you, gentlemen. You may go," said the President, and the prophets went.

"You read in the newspapers that our President's newborn son has been birth-investigated, and you exclaim: 'See, his own son's life has been determined right from the start, why should he then make an exception with our sons?' Do you then believe that the Soothsayer predicts the same future for the President's son as it does for your children? Don't you believe that it predicts that he will become President one day? The laws proclaim that no father may know the fate of his own son—only the President and the prophets may know the future. But now the President himself is a father. The laws permit the President to know a child's future, but forbid the child's father to know it. Yet the President is himself his own child's father, and is therefore guilty of a breach of the law. We demand, therefore, that the future of the President's son be made public, for if we tolerate *one* father knowing his child's fate, then *all* fathers ought to know that child's fate. The President has stated that he does not wish to assume dictatorial authority; he does not wish to rule for the sake of power, for he hates power, but he wishes, he says, to rule for the sake of the people, for he loves people. I say to you: demand that the future of the President's son be made public. If no great future has been predicted for him, then we can understand the President's unselfish motives. But if the future government of the country has already been placed in his hands, then you ought to question all prophecies and regard them as instruments of power in the hands of the government!"

While Philip Rose was making speeches his wife was alone at home, for she had no children. Her husband didn't want to be a party to the conception of a child that would have no opportunity to shape its own destiny. Since Philippa Rose was very fond of children and of her husband too, she had reason for much sorrow and anxiety, for her children would never be born, and her husband was in great danger. Whenever there was a ring at Philippa's door she was afraid of seeing a body of people in uniform outside instead of her husband. One evening the bell rang, and she found the President himself standing outside her door.

"My husband is not at home," she said.

"I'll wait," he said, and waited right until Philip Rose opened the door, looked at him, and said:

"Am I seeing you in the flesh, or am I only seeing your shadow, which finds its way into all homes and darkens men's faces and disturbs the peace of private life?"

"Nice to see you, Mr. Rose," said the President. "I think you are overestimating my shadow. At the moment it is falling only on you."

"It is falling on our entire future, and wherever it falls nothing can grow and nothing can thrive."

"Children always grow up. We more experienced adults must endeavor to organize the world according to their needs."

"According to the needs of the President's children, you mean?"

"That question leads to the heart of the matter. You have made a speech today . . ."

"I make speeches every day."

"You talk too much. Now listen to what I have to say . . ."

"Here you have nothing to say. Outside that door it is you who rule, alas. But here it is me."

"You have greater freedom of speech there where I rule than I have here where you rule. In the speech I refer to you made certain statements that ought really to be regarded as personal insults and punished accordingly. You have intimated that the birth investigations are fraudulent and that I intend to use their inaccessible evidence as a means of ensuring that my son succeeds me as president."

"Make the prophecy public! Satisfy us that your son will never become president and you will have won a victory over me."

"If one prophecy were to be made public, then all prophecies would have to be made public."

"As you like."

"Yes, but I don't like. Neither would you, if you thought of the people's needs. How many people would care to go on living if they knew the whole of their life in advance? Would you, for example, be quite as energetic as you are now if you were sure you would never become president?"

"You keep on confusing my motives with your own. I am fighting for the truth, not for myself."

"I am delighted to hear that you do at least know the difference between yourself and the truth. You will have the opportunity this very day of proving whether you are speaking the truth when you say that you put the truth before yourself."

"You too have the opportunity of proving it. Make your son's future public!"

"Philip Rose, it would be delightful if we could both prove that we are both honest men simultaneously—both with much lower opinions of ourselves than of truth itself. Would you like to adopt my son and bring him up as yours?"

After lengthy consideration, Philip Rose said:

"There is a catch to this."

"Yes," said the President. "I need the confidence of the people. You are making people suspicious of me by casting public doubt on my unselfish motives. If I were to arrest you, the people's suspicion would be increased. Everyone knows that you wouldn't bring up my son to be president—that is why I am asking you to take charge of his upbringing. Presumably, you will refuse. But then tomorrow all the newspapers will know that you have refused so as not to have to abandon the political role you are playing with such dexterity. And the people will think you are putting your own career before the welfare of society. Well, what is your answer?"

"What did the birth investigations show?"

"I didn't know it interested you. You officially regard the birth investigations as fraudulent."

"While you only do so on the sly!"

"If I thought that they had no significance I wouldn't be standing here. I am willing to sacrifice my son in order to cleanse the birth investigations of grave suspicions. What is your answer?"

"Are you not hiding your real intentions behind an unselfish gesture? If you wish to win the people's applause for that noble gesture, how noble is it? It would be both praiseworthy and farsighted of you if it were concern for your own child's future that made you hand it over to me. But it is concern for yourself."

"And as long as you refuse you cannot prove that it is concern for the people and not for yourself that makes you refuse. But I will go even further in order to persuade you to take charge of the child you have deprived me of, for the suspicious eyes of the entire population are focused on it. You would not be adopting the son of me, the President, but would be bringing him up as if he were your own child—no one will be told that it is my child. In a few days' time the public will receive the tidings that my son is dead—after all, infant mortality is still the most frequent type—and I shall not be praised for any noble gesture. What's more, you will not have to suffer the defeat it would have been for you to confess that you had mistaken my motives."

"There is a catch somewhere," said Philip Rose. "You have certain conditions?"

"Yes, indeed. That you never let anyone, even the child, know that he was originally my son. That is in your own interest, and beyond that I have no other conditions. Though, naturally, I hope that in the future you will consider my motives a bit more carefully before slandering me in public. I demand nothing in return—on the contrary, I even offer to pay for your son's upbringing. I will not—not even by you—be called an unkind father. Do you still refuse my proposal?"

"No. But now it's my turn to impose a condition. I demand that the card representing *your* son in the State files be destroyed upon his death, and that *my* son will be subjected to neither birth nor control investigations at any point of his life. You complain that I have deprived you of your son—but *you* have prevented me from having my own children, to their mother's great sorrow, for I will not breed children if their life is to be determined beforehand. *My* son shall be a free man—otherwise he can go on being *your* son."

"I myself have a weakness for human freedom," said the President. "You have said that in our State-controlled society every free action acquires the nature of a crime. When we in government limit the freedom of our fellow citizens, it is in order to deprive them of possibilities that are not open to them anyway, and thus are not even possibilities. Think of the energy we waste in losing our way in this dreadful society. Isn't it a shame that people have to become something other than what they are? The more dreadful the society, the more highly organized it must be for the benefit of the unintelligent masses. Your son is scarcely one of them, and I am sure he will receive such a good upbringing that he can find his own way and choose between the possibilities. But remember—if he has more possibilities than others, he will have a greater possibility of . . . well, of freedom of action. Will you shake my soiled hand?"

With this handshake they parted. The President's son was buried, and the sympathy of the entire population converged on the child's father. At the same time Philippa Rose received, to her joy and astonishment, a little fair-haired son without having given birth to him herself. She asked her husband whose son it was, but received no answer, and it reassured her that the child didn't resemble her husband, even though small children often change appearance and hair color when they grow up. Philip Rose was already impatient with the child because it was little, and since he didn't make speeches in public, so as not to conflict with public mourning, he spoke to Philippa:

"Can't you use a bigger bottle, so that that puny child can grow up and carry on my great task?"

"But Philip," said Philippa to her husband, "how do you know what Filius is going to do when he grows up?"

"I shall see to his upbringing," said Philip Rose.

A LESSON IN WORLD HISTORY

When Filius reached school age he didn't go to school. Children were enrolled in those schools that specialized in training them for their particular kind of future. Filius had no future and so was not enrolled in any school. That suited his stepmother, Philippa, very well, for she would have hated for Filius to learn naughty words from naughty schoolboys. It also suited his stepfather, Philip Rose, for he would have hated for Filius to learn what the other children learned. He was the President's son and had to be brought up strictly. But he was also Philip's own stepson and was to have a proper education.

"Do please remember that Filius's head is not yet fully grown," said Philippa, glancing anxiously at Filius's head, which was still fair-haired.

"Knowledge is power," quoted Philip Rose, adding himself "and by force is knowledge impeded."

Philip Rose had always considered world events to be the most important events, and so he immediately made world history the main subject. But history was not "free": the only textbooks available were those that arranged the march of world events according to official hindsight, and so he had to teach Filius history out of his own head.

In the history books Hannibal was portrayed as a scoundrel who delayed the *pax romana,* an epoch once again regarded as a forerunner of the coming world peace: when the new forecasting system gained universal acceptance everyone would receive what was due, and so would no longer come into conflict with anyone else as to who owned what. But according to Philip Rose, Hannibal was so brave a hero that Filius cried when Hannibal took poison. Philip Rose didn't like the childish tears—he wanted Filius to be angry with the Romans, and when he just went on crying Philip Rose tweaked his ears and said that he would never be a Hannibal. So Filius stopped crying.

Then Philip Rose realized that it was no good for Filius to be a Hannibal, even though he fought against greater odds, for even Hannibal's powerlessness in the face of the Romans couldn't be compared with his own powerlessness in the face of the President. Hannibal had at least had his own people and several elephants with him, but Philip Rose had support from neither man nor beast, and so he would have to bring Filius up as a rebel!

He got as far as the noble Brutus. It said in the history books that he regarded himself as Caesar's son, which of course he wasn't, and therefore he wanted to become Caeser's successor and murdered him, who was after all nearly his father. Since Philip Rose couldn't really remember anything about Brutus, he mixed him up with himself, but when he was about to mix Caesar up with the President he grew doubtful, for Caesar had after all been a brave soldier, while the President had only been an office executive who had married his private secretary. However, Caesar himself may merely have written the Gallic wars while letting the others fight them; he could remember having heard that Caesar couldn't swim and that he was deaf in one ear. And he said to Filius:

"Once upon a time there was a President called Caesar. He wanted to rule over all men, and if they were unruly he killed them. And since there were many people who wouldn't obey him because they wanted to be free and do what they liked, he killed a great many people."

"If there were so many of them," said Filius, who like all children was interested in hearing about people who got killed, "couldn't they all have joined forces and killed him?"

Philip Rose was overjoyed to discover such determination to resist in his pupil. But he was not happy about the question just the same. It was that dreadful unanswerable question, and if Filius already knew all the things he intended to teach him, maybe he could understand the incomprehensible fact that people preferred to be controlled rather than to control themselves. If people could be taught to realize their own power, then being a schoolteacher was of incomparable value. But by the time people are old enough to understand, those in charge have already taught them to misunderstand everything. He would have to teach Filius to understand before he could understand anything!

"It was he who was in power," explained Philip Rose, "and those who are in power always have weapons, and people who have weapons can kill those who haven't any weapons—even if they are in the majority. If Caesar had had to fight his enemies personally he wouldn't have been able to win, for he wasn't very strong."

He suddenly saw himself fighting the President. Filius asked:

"Father, are you very strong?"

"Yes, you can be sure of that," said Philip Rose.

"Haven't you any weapons then?"

"Yes, Filius, I have an old pistol."

"Then is it you who are in power? Do you kill people?"

Philip Rose looked angrily at Filius, who was his father's son:

"Be quiet, now, and pay attention! Of course I don't kill people, because I'm not in power. And then there was also a big boy called Brutus, and he had no father. And because Brutus had no father, Caesar said: 'I shall be a father to Brutus.'"

"Does one always have to have a father?" asked Filius.

"Yes, one does," said Philip Rose. "But Caesar didn't like Brutus. For Brutus was tall and thin, much taller and thinner than Caesar, and Caesar preferred people who were smaller and fatter than himself. So one day they were out swimming off the shore. And Caesar didn't swim very well and was about to drown. But Brutus rescued him and said: 'If I rescue you, will you then promise to stop killing those people who want to decide for themselves. And Caesar had to promise, for he was afraid that otherwise Brutus wouldn't rescue him. But as soon as they came ashore Caesar went on killing people."

"So Brutus should have drowned him!" said Filius.

"Then Brutus assembled all his tall and thin friends and they decided to kill Caesar, so that he wouldn't kill any more people and so that they could all be free."

"And be rid of Caesar," nodded Filius. "But wouldn't it have been enough to catch him and lock him up, if they didn't like people being killed?"

"No, because they were afraid he might be set free."

"But who would do that, if they wanted to be rid of him?"

"It wasn't all of them who wanted to be rid of him. For most people always side with whoever is in power, for in that way they themselves obtain power over the others."

"But if Brutus had locked Caesar up, he himself would have been in power and most people would have sided with him."

Philip Rose was about to tweak Filius's ear and tell him to pay more attention. But Filius was paying attention, and Philip Rose sighed:

"It is much more difficult than you might think to catch whoever is in power. It is easier to kill him, for that is quickly done, and once he is dead people stop siding with him."

"That's clear," said Filius, "for then he's dead."

"And so Brutus and his friends decided to kill Caesar without telling anyone about it. For if anyone got to know about it, they might warn Caesar and prevent him from being killed, and then Caesar would be sure to reward them because he was still alive."

"That's clear," said Filius.

"Good," said Philip Rose. "But someone did warn him just the same—a soothsayer."

"A soothsayer?"

"Yes, that is someone who knows what is going to happen in advance."

"But how can he know that?"

"Why, he doesn't know that either. But at that time people used to believe in all that kind of thing that one cannot know—they still do, in fact. And the soothsayer told Caesar that he would be killed on March 15th—or was it the 13th? It doesn't matter, for Caesar wasn't paying attention anyway."

"That was stupid of him, wasn't it?" said Filius.

Philip Rose wiped the sweat from his brow. If only he hadn't brought up that silly soothsayer! If Filius kept on remembering it, then how could he explain that it was stupid to believe in soothsayers—and that the President was consequently stupid?

"Caesar didn't hear," shouted Philip Rose, "for he was deaf in one ear. And on March 13th—or maybe not until the 15th—Caesar went out as usual and people stood everywhere shouting 'hurrah,' for that's what people are like—they shout 'hurrah' for those who control them so that they don't have to control themselves, while they boo those who tell them they shouldn't let others control them. And so Brutus and his friends said nothing, but lay in wait behind a column Caesar was going to pass by."

"A column?"

"Yes, Filius, there's a lot you don't understand. And when Caesar passed by, they rushed out and stabbed him with their daggers. Those were the weapons they used in those days."

"But didn't you say that it was those in power who had the weapons and that you had an old pistol. Why didn't Caesar have any?"

"He did, but he was only one against many."

"So it must have been easy for them. But couldn't Brutus have killed him by himself? For Caesar wasn't very strong."

"It was usually Caesar who was many against the others, you remember. And when he was about to die he recognized Brutus and said: "You too, Brutus, my son . . ."

"But he wasn't his son, for he wouldn't have killed his own father, would he? Surely, one only kills one's own father because he isn't one's father and wants to control one just the same? Did Brutus become like Caesar, then?"

"Like Caesar?"

"Yes, like he who is in power, whom all the others side with?"

"No," said Philip Rose. "Just pay attention! Brutus was killed by the others."

"That was silly. He should have killed them first, like Caesar, shouldn't he?"

"Oh, Philip," said Philippa, who had apparently come in without anyone noticing, "is that something to tell a child of his age? Isn't there misery enough in the world already?"

"That is precisely what he has to learn!" In his fury, Philip Rose had shouted that out before he remembered that what he really had wanted to teach Filius was that good always triumphs in the end.

"Bedtime!" he ordered, unable to hide from himself the fact that the story had missed its point. Clearly world history was useless!

A BIBLICAL STORY

The unfortunate thing was that Filius could only understand stories. In order for him to understand history it had to be retold as stories with some relevance, so wouldn't it be more educational to dispense with history altogether and make do with stories?

Was fiction the truth, then? Philip Rose had always been a man of action and had never thought much of daydreaming and poetry. The truth was what really happened, but apart from the fact that it was difficult to remember what had actually taken place between Caesar and Brutus, was it the kind of truth that would be beneficial for a child?

From sheer irresolution Philip Rose spent long school days teaching arithmetic and writing—deadly subjects which bored him even more than Filius.

But how was he to teach his pupil that man is free—history did not prove that, nor did science. He tried to make up some stories to prove it, but couldn't think of any. But then he happened to think of Adam and Eve who ate of the tree of knowledge because it was forbidden them. Were they not the first free and disobedient people? Were they not the first to set mankind an example? But how could he, who demanded Filius's obedience, bring up the same Filius to disobedience? He could, of course, bring him up to revolt against those who were in power outside the house—but Filius didn't know them yet. Everything pointed to the fact that Filius would have to learn the ways of the wicked world before he could stand up against it. But before he let him go out into the world he would have to teach him to defend himself against it, for otherwise he would be defenseless.

Then couldn't he alter the story of Adam and Eve so that it taught Filius how to tell the difference between good and evil? In the old story, which Philip Rose could remember very well even though the Bible wasn't free, the free action was depicted as criminal, which of course it was—Philip Rose had himself made speeches about it. So couldn't he represent the crime as a free action?

Philip Rose had forbidden Philippa to speak about the

Father they both remembered from olden days. God had naturally been abolished from the official education, but was that reason enough for introducing him in Filius's?

Nowadays the President had come to replace God, and in the old stories God corresponded very well to the President. The President too laid down people's future, said what they might do and might not do, and called man-made society a paradise. Those who didn't comply with the future that had been determined for them were cast out, like Philip Rose himself had been cast out. Thus he himself was like Adam, and Philippa was like Eve. And Filius—well, Filius was like Cain. It was true that Cain had a brother and Filius hadn't, but he fitted into the story nevertheless. Abel was the one who did what God said. Cain was the one who did what he himself wanted to—or what Adam wanted. And Philip Rose was now well into the story.

He began to understand something he had never understood before—that poets are people who revolt in their imagination because they cannot do so in reality. And that was possibly why the President had forbidden poets and ordered his yes men, who were not rebels and therefore not poets, to write stories that taught people to regard good as evil and evil as good!

Philip Rose began to relate:

"Once upon a time there was a boy called Cain. He had a father whose name was Adam, a mother whose name was Eve and a brother whose name was Abel. And Adam said to Cain and Abel: 'In this house it is me who decides, and I say to you that you may do what you like.' But outside the house there was another man who decided, for he was the President and called Jahveh, and he said to all men—to Adam and Eve and Cain and Abel, and to all the others: 'I am your ruler, and you must do what I tell you.'

"But Jahveh was very rich, and when people did as he told them he rewarded them.

"Adam and Eve had a garden, and in it there stood an apple tree with big juicy apples on it. Those Cain and Abel liked to eat, and Adam said: 'It is healthy to eat apples.' They also had a sheep which was covered in wool, and when they clipped the wool off they could wear it themselves. When Cain and Abel became old enough, Adam said that Cain should pick the apples, but that Abel should clip the sheep, and this they did.

"But Jahveh said: 'He who eats of the fruit on the trees, he shall be slain, for the fruit must be plucked and brought to me. And he who clothes himself in sheep's wool shall likewise be slain, for the sheep must be clipped, but the wool must be brought to me.'

"Then Cain asked: 'Is Jahveh so big, then, that he needs all the wool in order to clothe himself, and all the fruit in order to be satisfied?'

"Of course this is not so, Filius," commented Philip Rose, "But Jahveh wanted everyone to believe that he owned everything. And when they were hungry, they were to go and ask Jahveh for the fruit, and when they were cold they were to go and ask him for clothes.

"But Adam said: 'We will not take what we own to Jahveh in order to fetch what we own from him. We shall go on eating our own apples and wearing our own clothes.' And many others said the same.

"Then Jahveh said that all animals were to be given to him, he would then set shepherds to mind them all, and people would no longer have to mind their animals. And all the land was to be his, he would then set husbandmen to till it, and people would no longer have to till their earth. But so that Jahveh should have sufficient shepherds and husbandmen, the people all had to enter his service. For if one person minded many sheep instead of many people minding one sheep, many people would be out of a job, and they could go and work for Jahveh and become his soldiers. For Jahveh needed many soldiers in order to slay those who wouldn't do what he said.

"But Adam said: 'I say to you that you should not offer our sheep and our ground to Jahveh, but that you should till the earth and care for the sheep.' And Abel became a shepherd, while Cain tilled the earth.

"But most people were afraid of Jahveh, and he acquired more and more sheep and more and more soldiers, and these went around the country forcing those who were still shepherds to offer their sheep and become soldiers. Cain made himself a cudgel from his apple tree so that he could defend himself, and he also wanted to give his brother Abel a knotted branch. But Abel was afraid and said: 'What can we do if a hundred soldiers should come, for then we two are in the minority.'

"Then they heard the drums coming nearer and nearer, for the soldiers were beating their war drums, and many people dared not offer any resistance, and the fewer the people who resisted them, the more people they had to fight against. But when Abel heard the war drums he said: 'Now I shall go and offer my lamb to Jahveh, for it is he who rules over the earth.' But Adam said: 'Our sheep is ours and Jahveh shall not have it.' But Abel contradicted his father and said: 'You have no soldiers, and if the soldiers come they will kill me!' "

"Then didn't Adam think it a pity if Abel were killed?" Filius asked.

Philip Rose looked at Filius in annoyance, but the boy was so absorbed in the story he was all but making up that he relented:

"Yes, he did, Filius. He thought it a shame for any man to be killed, and that was why he wouldn't obey the President. Had they all been as brave as he, the President wouldn't have had so many soldiers and couldn't have killed so many people. Ought Abel to have been a coward, then, just because all the others were?"

"No, of course," said Filius, "but it was a pity for Abel."

"Cain, though—he did what his father said," said Philip Rose, "while Abel went to Eve, his mother. And Eve didn't understand what Adam said, and she said to Adam: 'Isn't a man worth more than a sheep?'"

"Yes," Filius answered, and Philip Rose regretted that Eve had come into his story.

"Eve liked Abel better than Cain, but Cain liked his father best. And when it grew dark and they were all asleep, Eve woke Abel up and said: 'Get up, flee to Laban, my brother, who keeps sheep for Jahveh, and take your sheep to him, for then you will not be killed and you can help him look after the sheep. But when your father's wrath has cooled and he forgets that you have fled, then I will send for you and fetch you home. Why should I lose both of you on one day when I need only lose one?'

"And Abel got up and fetched his sheep. But Cain was only pretending to be asleep, and they met in the field, and Cain said to Abel: 'That sheep is not yours alone; you cannot do what you like with it.' Abel answered: 'I am not doing what I like but what Jahveh likes.' Then Cain rose up against his brother and slew him."

"Oh Philip," said Philippa Rose, who had apparently entered the school room, "is that something to tell a child?"

"Be silent, Philippa," said Philip Rose. But when Philippa was silent Filius said:

"Then when the soldiers came, did they decide not to kill Cain because they realized he could kill people like they did?"

Philip Rose was silent, while Philippa Rose said:

"Cain was not killed! But Jahveh said to him: 'The voice of your brother's blood is calling to me from the ground. You shall be a fugitive and a vagabond on earth.' And Cain said to the Lord: 'My sin is greater than I can bear.'"

"Yes," said Filius, "it was a pity for Abel."

Philip Rose said:

"Philippa, you don't understand what I am saying, and I command you to be silent while I'm speaking."

"I was only saying what I had learned in school," said Philippa.

Philip Rose thought: "It is all society's fault! It forces me to become a schoolmaster. *And* a poet, which is not at all my destiny."

YET ANOTHER LESSON

The social conditions were still the same, so Philip Rose made the same speeches to the people, and the people grew tired of hearing them. He spoke more and more to deaf ears and his speeches became mere interior monologues:

"I am bringing up Filius to be a rebel at the same time as I myself am learning that rebellion is impossible. I am teaching him that he who rebels against murderers becomes a murderer himself by rebelling. Should he then be taught to rebel against his real father in order to be able to follow in his bloody footsteps? Or should I teach him that good rebels rebel for good reasons, and therefore in vain? I want Filius to become a good person, but aren't good people always those who don't rebel, and who are good only because they don't? Then is it not better to suffer wrongs than to do wrong?"

Philip Rose stayed at home and educated Filius. But soon he had taught him everything he himself knew as regards writing and arithmetic, and he realized that Filius had to go out among other children so as not to become an eccentric. Philippa wanted Filius to sing in a choir, but her husband didn't like the songs the choirs sang—he took Filius by the hand and said: "You shall join a sports club!"

Out on the sports field many boys were running fast, jumping high and throwing far. The very sight of them made Filius swing his arms and jump up and down. Philip Rose's fatherly feelings were aroused—he thumped him manfully on the shoulder and said:

"You'd like to join in, I see!"

"Yes," said Filius, with such childlike enthusiasm that Philip Rose came to think of how he had wanted him to understand about Brutus and the serious side of life.

"This is Filius," Philip Rose said to a man, so half-naked that he could only be the trainer.

"I don't think I have the honor . . . " he said, hurrying to get on to the track although it was right beside him. Philip Rose seized him by the arm:

"That is not strange," he said, "for you haven't seen him before. I'm bringing him for the first time. He'd like to join the others running around."

The trainer stared at Philip Rose with open mouth:

"Join the others? Running around?"

"Yes, damn it," said Philip Rose. "He's got arms and legs, hasn't he?"

The trainer looked at Filius, who couldn't keep either his arms or his legs still.

"I can see that. But have you a card?"

"A membership card? Surely he has to be a member first!"

Suddenly the trainer, who had been in so much of a hurry before, had plenty of time. He propped himself up against the fence surrounding the boys's running track, folded his arms and looked at Philip Rose and Filius in turn with equally great astonishment. When he finally broke the silence he said:

"Aha!"

"Pardon?" asked Philip Rose.

"Aha," repeated the trainer. "Do you think we are sadists?" he continued, looking as if he might be. "Do you think we try to scrape together as many youths as possible just to chase them around for our own amusement? These boys..."—he pointed at the track—"... are carefully selected after as many medical examinations as they have years behind them, and after countless school competitions. And here you are, saying that this boy here—presumably your son, though he doesn't look like it—wants to join the others running around! Have a look at the boys, and then tell me: do you think he can keep up that pace?"

Philip Rose looked at the boys, who were running so fast that he began to feel dizzy.

"They are running faster than they can," he said.

"There, you see! And your son here probably can't even run as fast as he can, can he?"

"He's only a beginner, after all," said Philip Rose, quietly.

"That I don't doubt," said the half-naked man. "But it's in school they begin—he must surely know that, even if you don't keep up with the times."

He looked inquiringly at Filius, but withdrew his eyes in contempt when Filius continued to stare in wonderment.

"At the moment we are training for the Olympic Games which are going to be held here in eleven years' time. It is not just anyone who is chosen to represent the nation. I don't know what you imagined."

"No," said Philip Rose.

A boy went by, panting, on his way to the locker room, though he paused to salute the trainer. Filius clumsily saluted the boy, who was so astonished that he let his hand drop.

"Fall out," said the trainer, while Philip Rose was suddenly ashamed of Filius.

"That boy," said the trainer informatively, "is destined to win the Marathon in eleven years' time. One must start training early in order to live up to such a destiny. Your boy there is much too old. You must surely have received other instructions?"

"Sorry to trouble you," said Philip Rose, walking hurriedly away with Filius. The trainer wiped his brow.

"It wasn't here we should have come at all," explained Philip Rose. "Look at those boys, look at the half-naked men running after them and telling them what to do. They are not allowed to run however they please. They are not running around for the fun of it."

"It's fun to watch," said Filius, who was seeing something of life for the first time.

Philip Rose wanted to leave the training establishment as quickly as possible, but Filius only followed him reluctantly, and Philip Rose felt sorry for him and remained standing where he was, glancing more and more angrily at the the boys' display of strength. However small the high jumpers were, they were already jumping higher than themselves. Philip Rose looked despondently at his son, who made yet another feeble attempt to salute when the Marathon runner went past, now fully clothed. The boy stopped in curiosity, and Philip Rose listened curiously to his conversation with Filius.

"What's your name?" he asked.

"Filius," divulged Filius, who was not experienced enough to ask what the other boy's name was.

"My name is Feidippides," said the other boy of his own accord: "That also begins with F. Are you going to run too?"

"I'm too old," said Filius. "I'm ten."

"I'm eleven," said Feidippedes.

The boys stared at one another, equally astonished.

"Feidippedes," said Philip Rose, "do you like running around?"

"I'm going to be a Marathon runner," said Feidippedes, saluting. "There's a long way to go. I'm going to win at the Olympic Games."

Philip Rose realized that it might be necessary to disclose the delights of the future for those children who had such a great future in front of them that there was no place for the present.

"And what are you going to do after the Olympic Games?"

Feidippedes frowned:

"True Marathon runners always die at the finish line," he said finally.

"A beautiful death," said Philip Rose.

"One dies for one's country," said Feidippedes, glowing with pride.

"Undeniably," said Philip Rose.

Filius had understood only very little of the conversation and so he looked at the boy in amazement, though also with anxiety, because he realized he was going to die, which to Filius still represented something unpleasant. They reached the exit and Feidippedes saluted. Philip Rose again felt ashamed to see his son mimic the martial gesture. When Feidippedes was gone Filius still stood with his hand flapping in the breeze.

"Daddy," he said, "couldn't we go and see the old people's running track?"

Philip Rose laid his hand on Filius's head:

"You are a child," he said.

From that day on Filius became difficult to manage because he wasn't allowed to run with the others, and Philip Rose too had a more difficult time. The world was closed to Filius, and while it might be his real father's fault that the world was closed and nobody could walk in freedom, it was also his own fault that Filius was shut out and couldn't choose his walk of life. He couldn't think of any more stories to tell Filius, and so he took him to the zoo in order to teach him the names of the animals, although they were not very important. But the more Filius enjoyed seeing the animals running around behind bars, the more Philip Rose got worked up about the wild animals being caged in for people's enjoyment. He hauled Filius over to the monkey cage in order to teach him that people were originally monkeys. But instead of laughing about people being originally monkeys, Filius laughed at the monkeys because they were dressed up like people, and they were riding on wheels in a way people would never think of doing.

"That's nothing to laugh at," said Philip Rose, and Filius stopped laughing, because his father pulled him away from the monkeys. But from then on Filius not only wanted to go to the running track but also to the zoo, and he became twice as difficult.

By then Philip Rose had already begun to regret having agreed to bring up the President's son as his own. The more time passed, the easier it was for people to forget freedom; they didn't want to hear it mentioned any more, or to listen to his speeches. One of the speeches in his mind was: "When I adopted him, was it to be free of my task, to foist it upon him? But if my task was impossible in my own time, how would it then be possible for him when the future, which was determined, had already begun? Does the only thing I have achieved against my enemy consist of my revenging myself on his son now that he has become my son! And if I have become a bad rebel, is it because I have become a better father than the President? He was more foresighted than I was; he foresaw that a father is a weak man."

Since only a few wished to listen to him, he spoke only to those few, thinking that if the world was to be improved it was the individuals who had to be improved. But one cannot make speeches to individuals, one must talk to them, and Philip Rose went from one to the other in order to talk. But most people had no time to listen to him, and only the fewest care for someone who knows better than they do. So Philip Rose had no other choice than to pretend he knew nothing and ask the others what they thought; he realized from their answers that they thought the same as the rest. When he came home, Philippa said that Filius had been quite unmanageable, and that he was neglecting his son, for she couldn't tell him stories.

So Philip Rose had to relate:

"Once upon a time there was an old man called Socrates. He knew what was right and what was wrong."

"Just like you," said Filius.

"But he kept quiet about it, for he knew that people

wouldn't want to listen to what was right but only to do what was wrong. So he didn't bother to make long speeches but spoke to people one by one and asked them what it really meant, to do good. And most of them naturally said that it meant doing what the authorities wanted them to do. So then he asked them if doing what the authorities wanted them to do was good if the authorities themselves were not good. And what do you think they answered?"

"I bet they didn't want to answer."

"Quite right. They didn't answer. But that was probably because they didn't dare. For if they said that the authorities themselves weren't good, do you think the authorities would think sufficiently well of them to give them good jobs?"

"Well, if the authorities were good, they would hardly want people saying that they weren't, and would probably kill them. But if the authorities were not good, they probably wouldn't care one way or the other."

"You mean to say that bad authorities are those that treat people well—and good authorities are those that treat them badly?"

Filius didn't answer. Philip Rose said:

"When Socrates asked questions like that, no one could answer. So he asked them: 'Can the good be what people do because they are forced to do it? Surely, the good must be what people do because it is good.' What do you think?"

"Who knows what is good apart from Socrates and you? Did they never ask Socrates what he himself thought? And what did he say then?"

"He said that he knew nothing."

"But then he was lying, if he really knew what's what. And lying is not good."

"Now try to think it over, Filius. If the good is what one does on one's own accord, can other people tell one what is good?"

"No, but then they could just as well keep quiet. For then one doesn't have to listen to anyone."

"But if the person one has to obey really intends to do good, shouldn't one do what he says?"

"But if one does what he says, then one doesn't do it of one's own accord, and so it isn't good. So it was stupid of Socrates to talk so much."

"Yes, it was stupid. For the authorities killed him, Filius. Do you think that was good?"

"I don't suppose Socrates thought so, and he knew what's what."

"Now suppose Socrates had a son who was not allowed to run around with the other boys because the authorities had forbidden it. Don't you think he did right in questioning whether the authorities acted rightly?"

"Not if it was better for the son not to run around—and I understand that it was better for me, if that's what you're thinking about."

"But do you think it was right of them to make the others run around if they didn't want to?"

"So Socrates was thinking more about the other boys than about his own son."

"If one is free oneself, is one then free from thinking of others? Can one feel happy if the others do not feel happy?"

"I don't know," said Filius. "I don't know any others."

"It is high time you got to know the others," said Philip Rose.

MATERNAL SORROWS

When Filius went out into the world in order to get to know the others, first of all he went to the running track, but Feidippedes wouldn't stop running, and so he went to the zoo. He soon left, though, for now that he could freely walk around among the animals it was no longer amusing; even the monkeys weren't amusing because they did the same thing all the time.

On the street the street urchins were fighting. Filius didn't realize that those who could run about and make as much noise as they wanted were not destined to be anything but rowdies, and so he watched them enviously. In the end they noticed him too, and asked if he'd like to be beaten up. Feeling honored, he agreed, and he came home so bruised that Philippa said "Little Filly, my dear!" and told her husband that one wouldn't believe he was Filius's real stepfather, the way he neglected the boy's education.

Then Philip Rose had to explain that there was no place for Filius in the world, and that he would have to venture out into the world in order to find himself a place. But when he had gone, Filius went out too, to ask the street urchins why they had beaten him up. This question proved too difficult for them, and he came home even more bruised than before. So Philippa asked her husband to forbid Filius to go out. But Philip Rose wouldn't forbid him anything, because Filius was a free human being and had to get to know the others.

So Philippa herself went out into the street to tell the street urchins not to hit Filius. But she found Filius standing in front of the others, making speeches:

"If we beat each other, then we all suffer from it. So wouldn't it be better for us all to stand together and beat up some others? When we and the others have beaten each other up, we will all understand that it is better to stand together and beat up some others; in that way there'll be more and more of us and we can beat up more and more, until in the end there are enough of us to beat the grownups who want to control us."

While the street urchins howled with enthusiasm, Philippa was thinking that Filius was his father's son. Nevertheless the speech didn't please her. It was high time that Filius found a place now, and if her husband couldn't find him one, then she would have to do so herself. But she had no contacts, until it occurred to her that she had once had contact with the President. When he heard that she was Philip Rose's wife, he immediately listened to what she had to say:

"My husband musn't know that I've come here. But I would be so pleased if Mr. President could find Filius an apprenticeship, for otherwise he might become a rowdy. He himself used to be beaten up to start with, but now he gets them to beat each other up in order to get them to gang up on the grownups."

The President smiled kindly:

"Of course he'll soon be that age."

"Yes," said Philippa, "it's high time he did something sensible. And Rose cannot find him a place."

"But I have promised your husband not to mix myself up in your son's education. He's probably very fond of your husband?"

"He is after all his father," said Philippa. But since the President said nothing, she added:

"Mr. President knows quite well that I didn't give birth to my son. Mr. President must tell me whose son he is!"

"Do you think I know everything?"

"Everyone thinks so."

The President rose, saying severely:

"Your son must never get to know that—that he isn't the son of you and your husband. For if he does, something terrible will happen—why, you know yourself how unhappy children can be about not being the children of their parents."

"But you don't know how unhappy a mother can become about not being the mother of her child."

"Indeed I do," said the President who knew everything. "But you should think less of yourself and more of your . . . foster son."

"But that is what I have been doing—ever since Rose told me there was no place for him in the world. Do find him an apprenticeship, so that Rose doesn't have to go out looking all the time."

"Is he always going out looking?"

"That is why he neglects Filius, so that Filius turns to fighting."

"But you know that Philip Rose is my old opponent. He was opposed to my finding places for all children. I handed him over a child without parents and told him to find a place for the child himself."

"If he is your opponent, then why do you take his side? You men are always siding together against the rest of us. Why should Filius have no place and become a rowdy just because you two cannot come to an agreement?"

"If I find your Filius a place in the world, your husband would find out, and then what?"

"Yes, then what? If you don't, I'll tell Filius that Philip Rose is not his father, and that he should go to the President and ask for a place."

"If your son comes here," shouted the President, "I can find him a place in prison."

"But he's a child!" Now Philippa too was shouting: "What has he done?"

"He has done nothing so long as he is a child. I mean so long as he doesn't know that your husband isn't his father."

"Then he *is* his father?" Philippa shouted, so illogically that the President had to pause and think. At length he said:

"Mrs. Rose, you are clever. You are a woman, I cannot of course allow Philip Rose to have control of a child he has no connection with. You see, there is no reason to tell Filius that he isn't his father's son."

"I knew it," said Philippa.

While Philippa was drying her eyes, and she had to do it several times, the President was thinking: "Good old private life. Rebelling against parents. He will murder his father while I'm still alive." And suddenly it occurred to him that he would also cause his mother sorrow.

"Philippa Rose, you are a good mother. But boys are boys, and it is not unusual for them to fight. Your son is not destined to be a rowdy in the long run. At the moment his father is in charge of him, but maybe one day I can procure him a better future. Trust in the future, Philippa, and tell no one that you have been here. If one day your son should—for one reason or another—be without fatherly protection, then bring him to me. There's sure to be a place for Filius!"

A SUPERFLUOUS CONVERSATION

"Excuse me if I am disturbing you," said Philip Rose, who had entered the room unheralded, "but I have a son who is interested in the concept of freedom, which is natural at his age. Strangely enough, freedom does not become a problem until one acquires problems. Yes, perhaps disobedient children feel they are not free, but they don't feel that until they are disobedient. When one is obedient one is free, isn't one, and nowadays all children are obedient. And not only children. In the olden days nature didn't come into its own. People were forced to be something for which nature hadn't intended them—slaves, for example, or civil servants—and not much thought was given to the individual. Nowadays the individual is carefully investigated from birth, and everything is expected in the natural order. Progress, indeed! Previously people were forced to be other than what they are, now they are forced to be what they are. That is why people used to write books about freedom. Now they no longer do—freedom is simply what one wants when one hasn't got it.

"My son, then, is at an age when an interest in freedom becomes necessary because one begins to feel the lack of it. Is anyone placing obstacles in his path, you might ask—in this society which removes all restrictions on people's freedom? No, it lies in the blood. Freedom is something you start thinking about when you feel you are tied to your body. A purely biological phenomenon.

"That is why the priests of old said that the desires of the flesh were sinful. They don't say it any longer, of course. The desires of the flesh are a necessity.

"But my son is in a special position—it's rather difficult for a father to speak about it. Abstinence has been prescribed. He has not been allotted a—a helpmate, as one used to say in olden days. He has to help himself. Perhaps he is to become a poet. Who knows? So he thinks about freedom a great deal. And then it occurred to me that from the olden days—for you yourself are an old clergyman—you might have some books about that sort of thing. I have never collected books myself, and he asks so many questions I cannot answer.

"For me, freedom was first and foremost freedom of speech. Maybe you can remember my speeches from the olden days? Then so much the better—I can't remember your sermons either. Now we are both silent.

"But there is something paradoxical about freedom, and that is what my son has discovered. He says that if you want to prove that you have a free will you must take your own life, for that is what one says at that age. A bit negative, isn't it? But take freedom of speech, for example—if you want to prove that you have freedom of speech, you have to say that society is unjust, for if you say it is just, you are simply saying what you are supposed to say, and not speaking freely. And I used to speak freely, until I discovered that it was superfluous because no one was preventing me from speaking. In maintaining that there was no freedom of speech, I was contradicting myself, for had I been right I wouldn't have been able to say what I did. Those are the kind of philosophical problems that interest my son. There is no freedom in a free society. Odd, isn't it?

"In the olden days one used to say that if God decided everything, man could not be free, and I suppose that is why one didn't find it practical to go on speaking about God? I am asking you as an old clergyman, because I cannot answer my son's questions. Man can only prove his freedom by not doing what God wants—that is what one called sin, isn't it? But man didn't know what God wanted—Adam and Eve in the old story knew it, to be sure, but other people didn't."

"God," said the old priest, "caused His son to be born on earth so that He could tell people what they should and shouldn't do."

"Precisely," said Philip Rose, "but now that no one is allowed to speak about God's son any more, how are people to know what He said? Nowadays it is the President who tells people what to do and what not to do."

The old priest didn't answer.

"I know quite well that God is said to have less power than a policeman walking a beat . . ."

"God has no power in the world," confirmed the old priest.

"Then it is not God who has determined people's fate in this world?"

"That is a question no one dares to answer."

"It demands courage, that is true enough," said Philip Rose. "But my son asks so many questions that are not generally asked—perhaps he is destined to ponder over freedom and to solve problems for those who have such problems. And I have pondered a great deal about whether it is God who decides what people should do—or whether it is God who decides that people should decide for themselves."

"Saint Paul wrote: "The good that I would, I do not: but the evil which I would not, that I do.""

"Yes, that is what he wrote," said Philip Rose. "But what did he mean? Did he mean that when one is doing nothing, one is doing evil?"

"I cannot believe that," said the old priest. "For then the crimes one wants to commit would become good deeds!"

"Paul offended against the State, didn't he? In God's name!

He was executed as a criminal. Was that because he did the evil he didn't want to do?"

"You are confusing the issue. It is written: 'Render unto Caesar the things which are Caesar's, and unto God the things that are God's!' And Saint Paul wrote: 'Let every soul be subject unto the higher powers, for there is not power but of God.' "

"Did he really?" said Philip Rose. " I didn't know that. I suppose you couldn't lend my son a Bible, so that he can read it for himself?"

"You know as well as I do that the Bible is not freely available."

"That is why I have come to you, I couldn't find the book in the bookshops. I thought perhaps that you as a clergyman . . ."

"I am a former clergyman."

"Yes, but so are all clergymen. And you render the President the things that are the President's because he is of God."

"God has no power in the world," repeated the former clergyman.

"No, for then he wouldn't exactly forbid God's own Scripture. In other words, if one were to try to give God power in the world, it would be an offense?"

"Against the State, if the State has forbidden it."

"But wouldn't one in that case be offending against God? And wouldn't one be offending against Him too if one failed to spread His word upon earth?"

"Society doesn't dare to be a judge of that," said the old clergyman.

"But presumably God does dare?" asked Philip Rose.

"No one knows God's judgment. And it is written: 'Judge not that ye be not judged.' "

"Thank you," said Philip Rose, "I had forgotten that. I haven't got a Bible. My son hasn't got one either, and he is very interested in God—one usually is at that age. Forgive me for troubling you."

He was already on his way out of the door when the old clergyman said:

"It isn't a question of outward freedom but of inward truth."

"And the two things have nothing to do with one another?"

"One can be free in one's prison."

"Free from worries, you mean?"

"You don't understand me."

"That is what one usually understands by freedom, though. Having no difficulty in becoming oneself. Becoming oneself as one was at birth. Is that what you mean by "inward truth?"

"You don't understand me," repeated the old clergyman.

"No," said Philip Rose.

It was usually old people whom Philip Rose went to see when he set out in search of fellow fighters. He trod dangerous paths without any success and tried to keep Filius out of it as long as possible. However, in the meantime, Filius, who had now reached the dangerous age, struck out a path for himself.

A LOVE STORY

There were two rivers in the same town, and one of them never grew tired of flowing into the other—full of water both summer and winter, it had done so as long as anyone could remember. In this very town it had just been raining, but now the rain hovered above the treetops, not having the heart to touch the ground, and all the white flowers were full of water. Standing in the square, which had long ago been named after the President, were newly sprung-up houses with illuminated news bulletins playing on their roofs; and the colors were unable to keep up with the scurrying letters, but floated out into the damp air, flowing together in a rocking rainbow. And all those out walking asked one another politely: "Are you out for a walk?"—replying in the affirmative if they had nothing to hide. And the cleverest of them added: "It is an optical phenomenon."

Two of these people met quite by chance in the same spot; it was an odd coincidence, and so they said "good evening" in accordance with the time of day. In the same moment they were each filled to the brim each with their own past, which had nevertheless taken several years to reach that point; but their pasts had nothing in common, and so it was strange that they had recognized one another immediately.

"Excuse us for greeting each other," they said, as if with one voice, "but we thought we had met each other before."

"Are you out for a walk?" asked one of the voices.

"Yes," said the other. So they walked along together. He took her arm and pointed with the other at the optical phenomenon, and it grew darker and darker as is proper in the evening, though only very gradually, because it was gradually becoming summer. They walked along by the river, reminding each other of many different things. They remembered quite clearly when they had met for the first time, for it was that same evening, and yet it seemed as if it were not the first time, for the first time people meet they seldom recognize one another.

"Am I to believe the tales of the poets," he said, "that when one sees the beloved for the first time, one believes one has already seen her long ago?"

"All people resemble one another," she said. "Everything suddenly reminds one of everything else."

"But there are some people who don't resemble any other," he objected. "You don't remind me of anyone else."

On all the benches beside the river people were sitting kissing one another, all of them in couples; the river flowed discreetly past, and they walked in the same direction, while the stars came out in company with the darkness, because opposites often accompany one another.

"There where the river is the smallest it is both the oldest and the youngest," he explained, as she listened with wide eyes. "That's where it once trickled out, but not once and for all—it trickles out every day. It had to twist in order to make its way in the world, and it still has to twist, even though it became known in the world long ago, for every child knows its name. I know its winding path—I have sailed on it and swum in it, I have walked along its banks and mirrored myself in it—I have stood thinking of drowning myself in it."

"Oh," she said, "what a shame."

"Here," he said, "it takes eternal leave of itself, meeting the other unceasingly."

"Listen," she said, and they listened. Their words were almost lost in the rush of the waters; the rivers rushed at one another's banks in an attempt to wash them away and lay the whole world at their feet. But men understand how to consolidate river banks, and all access to the rivers was forbidden at the point where they met, because work was always in progress, summer and winter. So they had to retrace their steps, walking back upstream; but they scarcely noticed it, for the ground on which they walked was a path trodden by human feet. And soon they heard dance music coming from somewhere close by where people were dancing as loudly as the river, and they sat listening on a bench that was covered with moist darkness. Maybe it had been too much for the girl to walk upstream after all, or maybe she was just tired because it was past her bedtime, for—confusing past and future—she said:

"I wonder when we shall meet for the first time."

He was not so pedantic as to correct her. And past and present have known each other for a long time; often they meet, and maybe one day one of them will entrust to the other the duration of that curious acquaintanceship. And the river became full of the rain's expanding rings as if with expanding kisses, and the scented moisture flowed down over the brims of the flowers and poured down them. The girl got wet; he put his jacket around her, though without taking it off, for then he would have got wet too, and she wouldn't allow that. Under cover of darkness only broken by stars, sounded her voice:

"We shouldn't—because we don't know each other properly."

"There is so much we don't know," he whispered. "What is your name?"

"Filia. And yours?"

"Filius," he replied.

They remembered having heard one another's names before, but they had never before known to whom these names belonged. And as they repeated them many times in order to learn them by heart, they felt the joy of repetition and remembrance stronger and stronger.

Evening after evening they walked along by the river, and sometimes they couldn't find a bench to sit on because all the benches were already occupied. So then instead of kissing they had to talk, and in the end it was not sufficient for him to say "Filia" and she to say "Filius." He spoke of freedom and said that he had never known what freedom was until now. Filia said she had never known it either. But the longer they knew each other, the stronger the past began to assert itself, until past and future became separated, and Filia said:

"You never speak of your parents. And yet your mother has given birth to you."

"I don't remember that."

"Has no one ever reminded you of it?"

Filia laughed, but Filius didn't laugh:

"No," he said. So Filia stopped laughing too and asked:

"What does your father do?"

"I don't know."

"Don't you even know what you yourself are going to be?"

"Isn't who I am more important than what I am?"

"Yes, Filius. But—are you going to be a father?"

Filius laughed, but Filia didn't laugh:

"I am going to be a mother," she said.

"What did you say?" shouted Filius, so that the heads on the benches parted company and stared at them: "Who is the father?"

"I don't know."

Filius would have been angry if he hadn't been so surprised:

"But don't you know anything?"

"I would so much like it to be you—then I can have a Filius just like your mother."

"Yes, but how have you managed to go out with others when we have been together all the time?"

"I don't want to go out with others—but I don't know whether we match one another."

"Surely you know whether we match one another, since you don't want to go out with others? And how can you say that you are going to be a mother when we haven't . . ."

"You are so clever, Filius. You know all about freedom and

things like that, and yet you are still a child. You must surely know it is decided by means of the birth investigations whether one is going to be a mother."

"Not before?" said Filius, thinking himself ironical. Filia thought so too, but took no notice.

"My parents have told me not to be afraid, for we'll be sure to suit each other. But they'd like to speak to you."

"Have you spoken to them about me, then?"

"What else should I speak about? Come home with me, Filius. Perhaps we shall be allowed to be together."

Filius went with her.

"Do come in, Mr. Rose, or should I say, Filius," said Filia's father. He was a watchmaker and had the house full of clocks that were so busy ticking and striking that Filius felt it was high time.

"Nothing is as beautiful as when young people go courting," said the watchmaker. "But it is also satisfying to make clocks synchronize. And difficult. There are always some obstinate ones that refuse to do so, however much you screw and adjust them. I could, of course, sell those first, and then all the others would tally, but the customers have a right to clocks that keep time. And what does that lead to? I sell all the reliable clocks first and get left with more and more unreliable ones."

"Husband," said his wife, Filia's mother, "clocks are not people. They don't know any better."

"And if one doesn't know any better, good luck is better than good management," laughed her husband. "Yes, when we were young it was a stroke of luck if people suited one another. It all went by eye—love at first sight, we used to say. Then any girl could become a mother, if she was sufficiently incautious."

"But Filia is recognized as being worthy to become a mother," said her mother, and Filius thought: "So she gets it from her."

"And so we should like to have a good look at you. As parents, we don't mix ourselves up in mild flirtations, but if you persist in the flirtation—and that is what you are doing—then you *have* to be the right one, otherwise it will turn out badly.

So we must ask you straight out: what is your serial number?"

"Serial number?" said Filius, suddenly coming to think of Feidippedes.

"For long engagements have gone out of fashion," continued Filia's father, thumping Filius on the shoulder. "That was in the olden days, when people had to take stock of each other by themselves, and to think of their livelihood and all that. Now we think of the future of the race as quickly as possible. Just give me your number, and I'll go to the Registry Office and make sure that the numbers fit into each other. But if they don't, then the sooner you part the better, for our little Filia is terribly fond of you. Aren't you, Filia?"

Filia blushed and Filius paled.

"Don't worry, Filius," said the watchmaker. "However difficult it is to make all the clocks synchronize, the world is not so unpractical that there are only two clocks in the whole world capable of ticking together. It's just the same with people. Once upon a time we used to think there were only two people who matched one another; it is from then the expression 'my better half' comes, which I myself can still apply to my wife—it's playful but unscientific. There are possibly thousands, or even tens of thousands, of men who could match Filia, so you mustn't be nervous. Why, you are already tall and fair in the interests of the race. You match each other beautifully, standing there, and I suppose the inside only differs from the outside in not being visible. Cheer up, future son-in-law, and tell me the number!"

When the watchmaker finally stopped speaking, to Filius the regular ticks of his clocks felt like blows on his head. He glanced at Filia, who blushingly smiled at him as though she expected to hear a really beautiful number.

"I haven't got it on me," Filius had to confess. There was a general hush, and Filius dared not look at Filia any more. Then the watchmaker spoke:

"You mean that you don't have it in your head? But surely you've got the number on your shoulder?"

The missing number—that was the answer to everything he had not hitherto been able to work out! He knew he was different from the others who had gone to school, and who were destined to become Marathon runners, rowdies, or mothers. He had learned that he was free, and that the others were not—and so it was a number he was free from . . .

"But his name is Filius," said Filia suddenly, "and my name is Filia."

"Isn't it a curious coincidence," said the watchmaker. "As if you were made for each other. The number is really only a formality."

And while the clocks ticked louder and louder and Filius still couldn't say anything, suddenly, in a friendly or perhaps fatherly fashion, the watchmaker took him by the shoulder on which he thought the number was, and led him out of the room:

"I quite understand," he said. "You are shy of exposing your shoulder when there are ladies present. The bathroom's over there. You can just come out and tell us the number—my daughter tells me that you are good at remembering other things, so don't be ashamed of not being able to remember numbers. We'll wait for you," he said, giving him an extra hard and friendly punch on the shoulder.

Filius remained standing in the corridor, thinking that he not only lacked a number today, but would always lack a number. A clock began to strike and all the others chimed in, and under cover of their noise he crept along to the front door and down the steps. Not until he was down in the street did he hear Filia shouting "Filius."

All evening he walked along by the river, and people sat kissing one another on all the benches beside the river, but he didn't meet Filia. He stood beside the river thinking of drowning himself, but heard Filia saying, "Oh, what a shame." So he spat in the river and went home to have it out with his father.

PATERNAL SORROWS

Philip Rose had always been older than the President, but that was not the only reason why he looked so much older when once again the two gentlemen faced each other.

"I have been expecting you," said the President.

"Yes," said Philip Rose. "Now I realize that you foresaw everything. Perhaps I scarcely need to say anything."

"I suppose it's about your son. I recall you have a son. Has he had a good upbringing?"

Philip Rose didn't answer.

"I suppose it is difficult for him to feel accepted. It was always difficult for young people of that age—in the past. Can you remember how in those days one was full to the brim with terrible feelings and was unable to get rid of them—even the psychologists used to say that people had the most terrible lusts! The greatest reform of all was therefore to ensure that those who are destined for one another come together at the biologically correct age. It is lonely people who get ideas in their heads, in order not to be alone. All the ideas one used to have at that age about a just organization of the world, eh? I can remember it from my own youth. Can't you remember it from yours, Philip Rose? One feels the world is unjustly organized, doesn't one? All that energy that goes to waste—and one has of course a great deal of energy at that age, purely physically speaking. Now, though, young people say nothing about the world being unjustly organized because all their energy is put to use at the right time. All except your son's."

"I have come to you . . . " said Philip Rose, ". . . to admit my defeat. You know how that feels."

"No," said the President, "that's the one thing I don't know."

Philip Rose bowed his head, possibly in order not to have to look at the President:

"I have come—for my son's sake, but also for my own, for I cannot rest until I have made peace with you. I have brought him up—and I think he has learned to think more about the world than those who have been allowed to live in it. One has to stand outside . . ." said Philip Rose loudly, suddenly raising his head. Dropping it again, he continued quietly: ". . . or be raised above the others, in order to understand people."

"I understand," said the President.

"I wanted to make him free—and forced him to become an outsider. That was what you foresaw."

"And now you come knocking at the door for his sake. Nice of you. Fatherly."

"I think he hates me," whispered Philip Rose.

The President smiled:

"And who is it he loves?"

"Her name is Filia, of course. But despite that, they cannot be united. He has no number."

"You are an unhappy man, Philip Rose."

"Because he is."

"That is what one understands by the joys of being a father. You are a happy man. The freedom to be unhappy—that's happiness, isn't it?"

"I don't want my life to be different," said Philip Rose. "But I want his life to be different, otherwise it will be my death."

"Who speaks of dying at your age, in these peaceful times . . ."

"He speaks of it. He said: 'If you were not my father I would murder you.' As you see, you have won."

"If you were *not* . . ." repeated the President, looking worried. But having thought it over, he smiled:

"Well, then it's a good thing you *are* his father. And what am I to do for a son who speaks like that to such a good father? Children who do not attend the Schools of the Future become street urchins and rowdies. One never feels safe from them, and that is why the world was so full of vice in the olden days. Not even we two could agree at that time. Will you shake my hand in parting?"

"Will you give him a serial number?"

"You know it's too late. Your son belongs to the past. You've had the son you wanted. I've had none—and that's your fault. But I shall not punish you. Predestination—the future—will punish you."

"It is not I myself I am worrying about," groaned Philip Rose. "But why must he suffer for—our sins?"

"Sins? Oh, you must be thinking of the old saying, that the sins of the fathers are vested upon the sons. Yes, that was in the old days before we knew how to handle heredity. Heredity is all very well, if only it's used in the right way. But you used a human being in order to prove your crazy ideas. It went wrong, didn't it?"

Philip Rose was about to answer, but didn't manage to.

"Shall we part as enemies?" asked the President kindly. And with these words they parted.

No sooner had Philip Rose gone than the President clutched his breast. But after a short while he summoned Teresius, the head prophet, and had him bring the index card of the son that was once his. Then he gave orders that the former rebel Philip Rose was not to be arrested; if Philip Rose was murdered, the murderer was to be brought to the President unpunished.

At that time preparations were in progress for the President's silver jubilee, for which there were special reasons for celebration, because the President had originally been elected President for five years only, yet had remained in office for such a long time. Flagpoles were erected on all the streets along which Philip Rose trudged his laborious way home. And the closer he got to his home where Filius was angrily awaiting him, the more slowly he walked; but suddenly he had an idea and turned around, his old self-confidence restored.

The following day more and more people heard that Philip Rose was making speeches again. By that time he had been silent for such a long time that most people had forgotten about him. But those who did remember him felt nostalgic when they thought of that prominent figure of their youth, or even of their childhood. Those who had grown tired of listening to him twenty years ago were eager to hear him again. People felt mildly indulgent, as when a famous opera singer makes a comeback, and they didn't expect to hear anything of much value, except possibly of sentimental value. Perhaps Philip Rose would be reminiscent of himself and bygone days.

His hair was white, although his age scarcely warranted it. He had also grown thin; but thin men are often particularly fanatical speakers. How could anyone avoid being surprised when Philip Rose raised his voice and spoke—his voice was feebler than in the olden days, and quite without fanaticism. Only those nearest to him could hear what he said, so most of them crowded around him when he said:

"Those of you who refused to recognize me in the old days, do you still recognize me? The many of you who did not vote for me at the last presidential election, and the few of you who did, are now able to unite in celebrating the jubilee of my defeat..."

There was a general murmur among the crowd, so that Philip Rose had to be silent. Was he being ironical?—or, on the contrary, was he being humorous?—yes, apparently so.

"You are right in doing so! Had I been President, you would not have been so enthusiastic about your President as you are now—quite apart from the fact that I would have ceased to be President twenty years ago."

People were now laughing openly.

"I, who said such bad things about the President's new regime that no one would listen to what I said, I have now become its best spokesman. Who better than I can testify as to how pitiful a person can become by not finding his proper place in society. And wasn't it the President who put everything in its proper place—all except me, who is standing here. Yes, here I stand in a public park, on a rotten platform that was used in the olden days—when people were not as self-satisfied as they are now—by preachers who prophesied misfortunes if people didn't become dissatisfied with themselves and seek to become different. Is this a worthy pulpit for a man who has no misfortunes to offer, but who wishes to proclaim a great joy which shall come to all people..."

There were policemen standing at the foot of the platform, though only in order to keep the people back; they were not allowed to arrest Philip Rose and apparently had no reason to do so...

"Can you remember what I said twenty years ago, when you wouldn't listen to it? I asked whether we could be guaranteed free presidential elections in the future..."

There was a deadly hush among the crowd, who therefore heard Philip Rose continue:

"... for naturally I was dissatisfied that people had not been free enough to vote for me."

Laughter.

"You remember that I regarded predestination as fraudulent—yes, I applied that term then, but I wouldn't do so today—for I thought that the future was hidden from us all, since we hadn't yet seen it, and if we were to make ourselves masters of it it would be a different future, and in time we would come up against the real future. In the meantime we have learned to know what was then the future—the one I didn't want to know in advance. And I have been thoroughly refuted. You have become what the State has made you, and know nothing of the anguish we old people felt in seeking to become what we are. See what has become of me! I shall not become President in any case, but the President still continues to be the President. The future was his."

Applause.

"Thank you, dear friends, it does one good to be applauded in one's old age. And now I shall confess my great mistake—my great sin, as one would have said in the olden days. But in our just society sin has been abolished because sinners have been abolished—and yet, if people haven't been able to keep up with the times, surely they still have the right to be called sinners. The President had at one time a son . . ."

Once again there was a deathly hush. Everyone looked at the policemen, but Philip Rose continued:

"But he was not allowed to keep him. Who was it who forbade him? Was it fate? No, it was me."

Everyone spoke at once and shushed one another, though not Philip Rose, who shouted:

"I had thrown suspicion on that little child from birth, just as I had thrown suspicion on its great father. I asked whether a President's son would have the same prospects for the future held out to him as are held out to ordinary children. I intimated that he was predetermined to become president after his father so that you would be free from electing a new president yourselves. You didn't listen to my words so attentively then as you are listening now, and in that you did right. But one person did listen to my words—he for whom nothing can be hidden because he knows everything beforehand. I mean the President. And the President is an honorable man. In a vanquished opponent he still saw a worthy opponent. It was not I who was pushed aside but the child."

"Louder!" they shouted.

"The child was honorably pushed aside," screamed Philip

Rose. "I said at the time that if we were not to believe that predestination was the same as the President's pleasure—yes, that's what I said—then the future of the President's son ought to be made public. But futures are not allowed to be made public, unless the children are to become marathon runners, and the President's son was not destined to become a marathon runner. So the President could not do what I demanded without infringing on the law of the land. And lest you should back me up (which you didn't) the President had to get rid of his own son. He put society before his private life, for the President is an honorable man. But a happy man he is not. He sacrificed his happiness for the happiness of all."

"Hurrah!" shouted the listeners.

"Unlike myself, who demanded that everyone should be just as unhappy as I myself was."

"Hurrah, hurrah!" shouted the listeners again.

"Especially the President's son, who may have been destined to become president—not by the president personally, but by the impersonal providence that rules over our State—though who was at any rate destined to become the President's son. Which he never became.

"You may remember that when the child disappeared I remained silent for some time, for what could I say? The child was said to have died, but how can a father be so cruel as to let a child die even if it dies for the good of society?

"I knew the child was alive. Yes, I promised the President to keep quiet—not about my opinions, which you were in any case too clever to listen to—but about the child. I had said that the child was a threat to free elections—to the free presidential election. The President sacrificed his child for the sake of free elections—I knew that, but I couldn't say so, nor did I want to, for then you would have learned how honorable a man the President was. And what a scoundrel I was.

"Now, dear friends, the President has grown older—the flagpoles bear witness to it. He is not an old man like me, but he is nevertheless older than when the last presidential election took place, for that is a long time ago and the time is now approaching when he will need a successor. You have made a collection towards a jubilee present for the President who laid down our future so expertly. Not the President's future, though—for that, on the contrary, lies in your hands. You must choose a successor yourselves—choose one who is just as worthy of that high post as the President. Choose his own flesh and blood. On the day of the great jubilee you must assemble in front of the presidential palace, odd and even numbers alike! Present him with a successor. Present him with his son.

"He is alive!" shouted Philip Rose, and the crowded shouted "Hurrah!" And since more new people kept on joining the crowd than those who went away to tell the others about the great sensation, Philip Rose had to keep on speaking. He said, among other things:

"I can see that you are not as mistrustful as I myself once was. But should any of you be standing and scowling among yourselves, then remember that no one can be wrongly passed off as the President's rightful son. Even if he has no card in the files he can be investigated just as thoroughly as at his birth, sufficiently to dispel any doubt. Maybe the President will not want to accept your gift, for he has always been against private life. But then you ought to bear in mind that you are the people to whose will he bowed when he didn't want to make the question of his successor a family affair. He thought it was your will I was proclaiming at the time—but that was not so. But isn't it your will I am proclaiming now?"

And the listeners shouted "Hurrah!"

He for whom nothing was hidden naturally frowned when he heard everything Philip Rose was saying.

"A demagogue!" he said to Teresius, the head prophet, "a ghastly demagogue."

"He is paving the way for the son," said Teresius.

"Whose son? Now the son has only reason to kill Philip Rose if he thinks the same as Philip Rose used to think before. And how can I use a son like that as successor? He can only qualify himself to be my son by ridding me of that gasbag. But the people worship the ground he treads on—and on the day of the jubilee they will lead the son here in triumph. It's a revolution! Why have you not foretold this? What have you got soothsayers for?"

"The soothsayers are especially good at predicting the future of individuals. Unfortunately, crowds are still somewhat unpredictable."

"Teresius," whispered the President, "is it true what the soothsayers predict?"

"Mr. President!" exclaimed Teresius, the expert.

"Caesar, my predecessor," said the President, "didn't believe in the prophecy and was murdered for his disbelief, wasn't he? If only I knew whether he has told his son that he is my son. Couldn't one tell him that he could become the President's son—and later the President—if he were to kill Philip Rose?"

"We have had some bad experience," said Teresius. "If a person's unspoken thoughts are spoken aloud, the thought will often come to stand in the way of the action. A future regent, when told by his mysterious father to kill his stepfather finds it difficult to make up his mind—the history of literature illustrates that. Though it is easy for him to make a mistake and murder the wrong person."

"But which is the right one and which is the wrong one?"

"The President is right," said Teresius.

"Yes, of course," said the President, dismissing him. He himself kept on walking up and down the floor, so distraught that he came to think of his wife. Couldn't she go and tell the boy—no, not that he was his son, but that he could become his son if he—yes, couldn't she say that it was Philip Rose who had deprived him of his future—hadn't she herself hated Philip Rose because she had an idea that it was he who had stolen her child. But she had no reason to hate him any longer—on the contrary, she had reason to hate him, the President—then couldn't he tell her everything, except for the prophecy—but naturally without that everything was incomprehensible.

Although the President didn't know what he should say to his wife, he tried to find her, but couldn't find her anywhere, even though she was usually always at home.

Then when night came he received the message that Philippa Rose was waiting to speak to him. Impatiently, he shouted:

"Has it taken place? Is your son without fatherly protection?"

"Yes, President," said Philippa. And the President was about to embrace her, when she said:

"For Rose has gone out and Filius has found his old pistol. You must come and take it away from him."

"I!"

"For I am afraid he might do his father some harm, and he is after all my husband."

"Your husband is sure to come home again," said the President. "He has probably just gone out to find a place for Filius."

"But he won't be able to find him any place. And he mustn't come home because Filius is on the warpath. You must take the pistol away from him. You must find him a place. You are the President."

"The President is father to all the fatherless. But for children with fathers I can do nothing. If he does do away with his father, it may be for the best. You are a mother, you know that Philip Rose has not been a good father. Go home and tell your son that."

Philippa stared at the President, who nodded smilingly at her. But Philippa didn't smile in return.

"Now I can understand Rose," she cried. "You are wicked. You wanted to revenge yourself on Filius because he is Philip's son. You want to set Filius up against his father because he cannot find him a place. I shall go home. I shall tell Filius that it's all your fault."

The President had to ring for the guard:

"Mental hospital!" he ordered, and remembered that Filius would be separated from his mother just before the time came.

MOTHER AND SON

Filius was alone at home and wanted to put his solitude to use by taking his own life because it couldn't be used for anything. He had brought out his father's old pistol, but before using it he had to write a farewell letter to Filia—a letter that became longer and longer. He realized that he had led an unusual life because he had not had a number, and when he had read through his own life story he couldn't help grieving over the fact that such an interesting life should already be at an end, and continued his letter:

I have an old-fashioned pistol lying beside this letter, for when I started the letter I was going to shoot myself when I had finished it. I have never tried to shoot before and no one uses that kind of pistol now, but it isn't difficult to aim, and how can I go on living without a number and without you, Filia?

Alas, if I could only make you understand everything I cannot understand myself. I would have murdered my father with the pistol for deciding everything for me without ever consulting me. Yet how could he have consulted me when I was only a newborn baby? Anyway, since he has disappeared I have begun to feel sorry for him. For isn't it strange that even if he has wronged me, he may very well be right. In fact if he were right, he would have to do me wrong, for otherwise he would be just as wrong as the President and all of you who follow him. My father wanted me to decide things for myself; you others cannot do that, and nor can I, but I could if all the others were like me (without numbers).

And now, when I consider how meaningless it is that I cannot come to you even though I miss you and know the way, so that I am forced to go on writing in order to keep you with me even though I only wanted to write a short letter, must I not curse this country which my father curses? But when I think that even if I had a number, I might just be one of the thousand others your father said would suit you, must I not curse my father who has made me a fugitive on earth? That is politics, Filia, and maybe you don't understand it.

You asked me what I was going to be, and I didn't understand that question (for I was a child, you said). I thought it was sufficient to be myself. But one has to be something else in order to be at all. The world is closed to me, Filia, and my father has not come back with a number, even though he left three days ago. I am not weeping, Filia, and you must not weep either. I don't care to think about all the thousand or ten thousand men your father spoke of, but I know that you are des-

tined to become a mother and I am not destined to become anything other than a son. In the olden days (I have read), when people were believed to belong together in pairs, one of them used to enter a monastery or a nunnery when he (or she) couldn't be united with the other one, but you don't know what a nunnery is, and so I cannot say 'Get thee to a nunnery, Filia,' which I might otherwise have said.

Filia, you said that you would so much like to have a Filius, but you could probably have one in any case, for one is allowed to determine names for oneself—names aren't important, it's numbers that count. But you mustn't tell anybody about me, it would sound too unlikely and may also be illegal. My life was forbidden, Filia, and yet I have lived just the same—together with you, Filia, and so you must try to remember

YOUR FILIUS

When Filius had finished the letter he kissed the envelope before sealing it and went down to post it before shooting himself. When he came up again he turned the pistol towards his heart and spoke aloud to himself: "If I want to be myself I cannot live. But if I take my life, am I not then master of it?" And he became filled with freedom—a freedom that tingled in his stomach and heaved in his breast and beat in his heart and gasped in his throat and behaved quite differently from what he had imagined. The whole of his life flowed into that one moment of freedom. And at that very moment the doorbell rang. Maybe it was his father coming home with a number. Filius opened the door, pistol in hand.

But it was a woman who wanted to speak to Philip Rosc.

"What do you want with my father?" asked Filius.

"To thank him," said the woman. "To thank him for what he has done for my son."

"For *your* son?" shouted Filius. "Do you want a bullet through your heart?"

"Oh, no," said the woman. "Yesterday it would have been in its place, but today I have no place for it. Haven't you heard your father's speech, which he has been making for the past three days? Perhaps you would understand better if I were to say I was the President's wife."

Filius understood no better. Was the President not his

father's enemy? Then could he not do his father a service by shooting this woman? But he himself was his father's enemy, so wasn't it better to join hands with her and shoot his father? But the woman had come to thank his father, who had done something for her son. Then couldn't she, the President's wife, do something for him and find him a number that fitted Filia's?

Filius raised and lowered the pistol.

"Stop waving that ridiculous pistol about! You're too big for that. You're not a child any longer."

"No," said Filius, putting the pistol in his pocket.

"That's my boy! Now come and sit down beside me, you look terribly tired."

Filius sat down:

"I haven't slept for three days, not even at night. I have been waiting for my father. He said he would go to the President and ask him for a number. Was that what he wanted to speak to you about?"

"Alas," thought the President's wife, "those who have sons don't always treat them as well as those who have no sons would like to." Had he forgotten his own son for the sake of hers?

She stroked Filius's hair. Filius thrust his head back towards the wall, looking at her with eyes more terrifying than the muzzle of the toy pistol. Were they his father's eyes?

"You have a good father after all," she said uncertainly.

"What is there between you and my father?" repeated Filius. "Have you been up to something together?"

"Now then, people of your age are always imagining things. I have never seen your father."

"What have you to thank him for? I have nothing to thank him for, and I have seen him often."

"Perhaps we can both thank him for the same thing. If I get my son back you will get a good number—or perhaps you don't even need a number. Names sound better. What is your name?"

"Filius," said Filius once again.

"And my name is Asta. I am so old that I haven't got a number either. It feels like freedom, doesn't it—being free of having a number!"

"Asta!" exclaimed Filius, astonished. "You speak just like my father."

"There's no reason why we shouldn't get on, then. You are your father's son."

"Unfortunately," said Filius.

"You are making a mistake about your father. My husband is a tyrant—you can see that I trust you. When I bore him a son he took it away from me for fear people would suspect he was setting the child up to be his successor. It was really your father who created the suspicion."

"He's a monster," exclaimed Filius, "a tyrant!"

"I too thought that once, and that's why I understand you so well. But now he has got the people to demand my son as future president."

"He's a traitor," shouted Filius. "So he sides with the President."

"No," said Asta, "he sides with me."

"Does that make any difference?"

"The President is the monster. He sacrificed his child for the sake of his own power. But your father foresaw that people would not be able to overthrow him before they could proclaim his rightful successor."

Filius shook his head.

"That is politics, Filius, maybe you don't understand."

"Certainly I understand politics," snapped Filius. "Am I not my father's son? But why does he speak to the people about your son, as you say, and leave me in the lurch? When you rang the bell I was about to shoot myself."

"What a shame," said Asta, like Filia. "But why should such a handsome young man want to shoot himself?"

"I haven't got a number," said Filius, red in the face. "And if one hasn't a number, one is not allowed to love. And when one cannot love one cannot properly live."

"How clever you are," she said, like Filia. "But why do you imagine that love has anything to do with numbers? Nowadays they want parents to be exactly the same age and their numbers to be as similar as possible, so that the children don't come into conflict with themselves but become obedient children. But love is a question of two different people becoming one, so that their child will acquire a complex soul. Oh, Filius, I cannot stand seeing anyone unhappy now that I myself am starting to feel happy again. For I haven't been happy since I last clasped my child to my breast . . ."

. . . and with these words she suddenly clasped Filius to her breast. Filius tried to withdraw his own, but she had two against his one and they were much too soft to push away, even though he pushed with his entire body. And freedom welled up in him again, just as it had before when he was about to die—tingling in his stomach and beating in his heart and heaving in his breast and gasping in his throat . . .

"My dear child," gasped the woman too, and Filius did his level best to smother her words, even before they left her mouth: he didn't want to be a child any longer and was stronger than she, so in the end he managed to come out on top. Then, feeling tender all over her body, she tenderly drew him to her, whispering:

"But Filius, my pet," so that Filius grew even more excited and made the woman forget her son completely. Moreover, he suddenly came to remind her of her husband many years ago; and when the present become one with the past she couldn't help uttering a loud scream, both for one reason—and the other. So they didn't hear Philip Rose until he was standing inside the door—indeed, not before he fell to the floor with a crash. There they lay, all three, gasping for breath. But as two of them got to their feet Philip Rose remained lying where he was, gasping more and more violently, but in vain. He didn't hear Filius start to shout "Father!"

Suddenly the room was full of strange people shouting "Long live Philip Rose!" though they grew silent when they saw him lying there dead. So instead they began bowing to Filius, saying:

"Stop shouting 'Father,' for Philip Rose was only your foster father. You have the honor to be the son of the President. Long live the President's son!"

And then they shouted so loudly that no one heard the

most terrible female scream they would ever have heard. While Filius was being led away in triumph, Asta remained behind alone, sobbing "Woe is me, woe is me!"

FATHER AND SON

The President had foreseen that he would be informed of Philip Rose's sudden death. He was also informed that the deceased had managed to proclaim his son as his successor, to the people's great delight. The President appeared not to be so interested in knowing Philip Rose was dead as in learning what he died of. People imagined he had died of heart failure or possibly of excitement, but the President screwed up his eyes and thought: "If they knew the son had killed him, they wouldn't tell me anyway. For how could I choose a father-murderer as my successor!"

The President would very much like to have felt great relief about Philip Rose's death. After all, he had always constituted a threat, especially in his last days when the sympathy of the people had been directed upon him. This would be redirected when he and the son met officially in public. But that meeting could only take place if the son had murdered his previous father.

The President ordered a careful postmortem examination of Philip Rose. He waited just as restlessly for the verdict as he waited for his wife. His unrest surpassed all previous limits when it came to light that Philip Rose had died of heart failure following three days' exhaustion, and possibly as a result of too much excitement. The President clutched his breast.

On the great morning itself, when he was to celebrate his jubilee, he had not slept all night. At daybreak some gloomy-looking men brought him the unhappy tidings that the bodies of two women had been found, one in each of the rivers. One was only a watchmaker's daughter, but the other was the President's wife, though this was kept secret from everyone else but the President.

He felt faint. The son had already once been separated from his mother—though not from the right one . . .

"I can't see anyone today," said the proper father. "I am indisposed."

The men departed looking gloomy. Teresius himself came to persuade him.

"People must understand that I am grieving over my wife's sudden death. Am I too not a human being?"

Teresius regarded the President with amazement:

"The people have never thought of the President as such. And what will they think of him if they learn that his wife has thrown herself in the river?"

"Teresius, you know that he will murder me. You have yourself prophesied it."

"Not I."

"No, if it were only you, I wouldn't have to believe it, for who puts his trust in human beings. But the Soothsayer . . ."

"Whatever the Soothsayer predicts either comes true or doesn't come true, but its job is to predict. Besides, it wasn't as experienced sixteen years ago. It intimated that his father—and now I mean Philip Rose—would die when the son reached the dangerous age. He died of excitement and a heart attack when he was about to stop being the father of—your son."

"Prophecies are usually taken more literally," said the President. "One even bases death sentences on them."

"As the President commands. But if the President doesn't show himself to the people they might become a little impatient with the President, now that they have found a new one."

"Teresius, you know better than anyone else that it would be my death if I were to meet this badly brought up fellow who has not killed his father. You know that, and yet you still want me to receive him with open arms."

"The President must have patience. Even if the President is to be murdered it doesn't necessarily have to be today. Even inexperienced murderers do not usually kill people with a crowd watching. The first meeting will be entirely devoid of danger, and as soon as we have a chance we will be able to talk him into sense. Now the President must be prepared to sacrifice himself for the people."

"Sacrifice myself? Have I not sacrificed all my happiness for this country I was destined to rule over? My wife's maternal joy I had to sacrifice for the sake of the prophetic truth. My child I had to sacrifice even though it was itself the cruel truth. Must I then end up by dying for the truth I have been living for, even though it was not worth the trouble? For what is truth, Teresius, if it does not lead to human happiness?"

"The people are happy, Mr. President. Just listen!"

The people came nearer, shouting: "Long live Filius, our predestined ruler!" and when the President stepped forward to receive him, they shouted: "Long live the President, our predestined President!" Had he been able to, the President would have rejoiced to hear that, so many years later, the people still had no doubts as far as predestination was concerned.

The first thing Filius said with trembling voice to his trembling father was:

"Where is my mother?"

The President was obliged to answer:

"Your mother is dead."

And it was as if the people had heard their words even though they had found it difficult to utter them, for suddenly they all shouted in chorus:

"The mother—the mother of the President's son!"

Had they got wind of it? Father and son stood looking at each other feeling equally guilty, which neither of them could know, until Teresius whispered to the President that he must calm the people down. So the President spoke:

"My dear people, accept my heartfelt thanks for your acclamation and widespread participation. You see, I have had the great misfortune to lose my life partner. She was looking forward to this day with such great emotion that it broke her mother's heart. In me you see a sorrowful man—and a happy father."

There stood the people—not knowing whether to laugh or cry.

The President survived the day of the jubilee and commenced the twenty-sixth year of his rule. Throughout the entire year he lived in great fear of his life and dared not see his son. Filius was kept busy all day long in learning how the system functioned, and Teresius was able to inform the President that Filius did not appear to have any doubts about its correctness.

"But of course the President foresaw that he who had felt the old-fashioned freedom in his own body would be especially well qualified for realizing its true necessity."

The President's fear of death slowly abated the older Filius became, and in the twenty-seventh year of his rule he plucked up the courage to send for his son:

"Filius," he said, "you know that you are destined to become my successor. Not because you are my son, for monarchy belongs to the past. Not because the people wish it either, for democracy belongs to the past. But because it was predicted at your birth."

"But I," said Filius, "am the only one of my generation who has not been birth-investigated."

"You *have* been birth-investigated, but what you were destined to be is known only by the prophets and me. Your subsequent stepfather, Philip Rose, who was at that time my opponent, realized that you were destined to become President and proclaimed to the people that there must have been something fishy about it. For fear that the people would turn against you, I had to surrender you, Filius—you who were your mother's and my greatest joy. I told Philip Rose to bring you up so that you would not become President, but he brought you up to become President just the same, for what can a mere man achieve against predestination. You know that before his death Philip Rose realized he had been wrong. You are the living justification of the system. You are the truth."

"Yes," said Filius. "But if I was predestined to become President, why was it so necessary to entrust me to Philip Rose—so that my mother came to lose me, and I her? Didn't you yourself believe in predestination? Were you afraid of losing your power if the people believed Philip Rose?"

"Filius," said the President.

"Answer," shouted Filius, standing there with an old pistol suddenly in his hand although he was forbidden to carry arms. The President's legs started shaking, and he fell on his knees:

"Filius, remember that I am your father. It was predicted that you would be separated from your mother."

"That was all very well for you," shouted Filius. "Perhaps it was also predicted that I am now going to put a bullet through your heart?"

"Yes," gasped the President, "that too was predicted. But . . ."

He was about to explain that Filius was originally to shoot his father when he was much younger than he was now, but couldn't get the words out. Filius, on the other hand, shouted:

"Father! And you believed I would murder you!"

The President couldn't even keep erect on his knees, but he was held up by his son and thought for a moment that the murder was now going to be committed. But what he imagined to be the start of the murder turned out to be a filial embrace. Tears were streaming down Filius's cheeks, although he was almost a grown man and hardly any longer at the dangerous age.

"I knew that Philip Rose meant well, though he was possibly mistaken. That was why I couldn't murder him when I realized he was wrong and had therefore also done me wrong. I know how terrible it is to be free, and think it is best for weak people to have their future secured. But I learned from my father—my first father—that it is an advantage for those who rule to lay down those futures so that no one is left in any doubt. I did not know whether you believed in predestination, or whether you were only thinking of your own advantage. But why would you be so afraid of my killing you that you sent me away—from you and my mother—if you didn't believe in it. So now I believe you!"

The President got to his feet with his son's aid:

"Filius!" exclaimed the joyful father, "then you are not going to murder me. So the truth was not as cruel as I had thought."

And he was about to give Filius a fatherly hug. But Filius stood there stiffly, and suddenly pushed his father away.

"But then predestination is a lie!" he shouted, drawing the old pistol out of his pocket. "It is only true if I murder you. If I murder you, you are innocent of my mother's death—and of the death and strange disappearance of the other women. But if I don't murder you, then predestination doesn't exist, and so it's all your fault and you deserve to die, for then you are a murderer. Am I right?"

The President had fallen on his knees again:

"You are right," he said, "I was wrong."

"And it is I myself who decides whether you should live or die?"

"Yes, it is you who decides."

"But then I am master over predestination. And I am free, then!"

"Filius, you shall be rid of me so long as you don't murder me. Let me resign from the presidency instead of resigning this life."

"Resign!" said Filius.

The next day it was reported that the President had abdicated in favor of his son. The news spread all over the country, and even in the mental hospitals the portraits of the old president were replaced by portraits of the new. An old patient, who was just known as Philippa, said to anyone who would listen that it was her Filius who had got the job as president and that he would come and fetch her home. When she had said that long enough, she was transferred to a ward for excitable patients, where there was no portrait of the President to be torn to pieces, and there she became more and more excited until Filius came and fetched her home.

THE FINAL SPURT

The new president's first enforcement was to make birth investigations voluntary. Since he foresaw that schools might be needed for those children whose future was not laid down, he set going a large-scale school building project. He laid down a law that everyone should be allowed to fall in love with whomever they chose provided they could agree about it in pairs. The older people whispered that the President was too young, but dared not say so openly. The young President decreed that everyone should be allowed to say what they liked and even to write it down. A free press sprang up, which attacked the President for not thinking as much as he should about the interests of society and the coming generations. The President ordered presidential elections to be held every five years. The free press wrote that a president who was willing to give up his responsible position was not fit for his position.

The press also wrote a great deal about sports, especially as the Olympic Games were approaching. This time the Games were to be held in their country, and so for more than eleven years they had been very well prepared for. On each day the games were played the nation's heroes lined up as favorites and on the following day were acclaimed as victors in the newspapers, which at the same time attacked the president because he never showed up at the Olympic Stadium, where even a presidential grandstand had been erected.

Perhaps that was why the President appeared on the stand the day the long Marathon race was to finish. Most of the audience cheered the first runner to run into the stadium, because they thought him to be one of their countrymen. When yet another runner entered the stadium they thought that he too was their countryman and the cheering knew no bounds; it came to an abrupt end, though, when they saw that the leader was not their countryman but a foreigner. In their great disappointment over No. 2, who had after all been predestined to win, they became so quiet that they suddenly heard the President himself shouting "Feidippedes!" And Feidippedes evidently heard it too, for he put on a spurt the like of which no one had ever seen before. No sooner had Feidippedes won than he collapsed on the ground, while his beaten opponent stubbornly continued to run around and around and finally had to be stopped by force.

The victor was crowned with laurel leaves and was carried before the President to receive the presidential handshake, while all the people cheered and took snaps. Everyone was standing so high on tiptoe that only those at the very front could see that the marathon runner did not return the President's handshake—he had already died for his country. And when the rumor spread over the stadium, all the flags were lowered to half-mast and the cheering knew no bounds.

Even the free press published enthusiastic pictures of the President and the dead marathon runner. Shortly afterwards the President was re-elected for another five-year term.

Sources

The History of a Guardianship

Das Memorandenbuch Friedrichs III

Joseph Grünpeck, *Historia Friderici et Maximiliani*

Aeneas Silvius Piccolomini, *Historia Friderici III Imperatoris*

Aeneas Silvius Piccolomini, *Pentalogus*

Aeneas Silvius Piccolomini, Letters 99 & 104 (*Fontes Rerum Austriacarum. Diplomataria et Acta* LXI)

Documents and letters in:
Joseph Chmel, *Geschichte Kaiser Friedrichs IV*, 1840–43
E. M. Lichnowsky, *Geschichte des Hauses Habsburg VI*, 1857
A. Jäger, *Der Streit der Tiroler Landschaft mit Kaiser Friedrich*, 1873

Three Legends

Von dem bösen Judas

Von Sankt Paulus, dem Apostel

Von den heiligen Ehleuten Sankt Adrian und Natalia in *Der Heiligen Leben und Leiden, anders genannt das Passional*, 1513

The New Testament

The Gospel according to St. Thomas

The Dead Sea Scriptures, ed. T. H. Gaster, New York, 1956

Lactantius, *Von den Todesarten der Verfolger*, ed. A. Hartle, Munich 1919

Seneca, *De clementia*

Sveton, *Nero Claudius Caesar*

Afterword

SVEN H. ROSSEL

"If Danish were a global language," wrote a reviewer for the leading Danish newspaper *Politiken* (November 17, 1964), "I believe *Tutelary Tales* would rapidly gain a world-wide audience." This evaluation of Villy Sørensen's third volume of short stories both summed up the warm reception the book had among critics and reconfirmed the leading position Sørensen (1929–   ) had gained in Danish literary circles since the publication in 1953 of his debut collection, *Sære historier* (*Strange Stories;* English trans. *Tiger in the Kitchen and Other Strange Stories,* Abelard-Schuman, 1957). The Danish Academy awarded him its Literature Prize in 1962 and made him a member of the organization in 1965. Other organizations have continued to honor his literary accomplishments: the Nordic Council awarded him its Literature Prize in 1974; the University of Copenhagen bestowed an honorary doctorate upon him in 1979 (ironically, the same university where he had studied philosophy and literature, and from which he had dropped out in 1951 as a kind of protest against the uninspirational and uninspired academic milieu); the readers of the weekly newspaper *Weekendavisen* (*Weekend News*) gave him their 1983 Literature Prize for his broadly popular and brilliant personal adaptation of the Old Norse myth of the doom of the gods, *Ragnarok* (1982); and the Swedish Academy in 1986 made him the first recipient of its newly instituted "Little Nobel Prize." That prize, next to the Nobel Prize the most prestigious offered in Scandinavia, is restricted to Scandinavian authors and is considered an indication of where the Academy might look for a future Nobel Prize winner.

Despite the general popularity of a book such as *Ragnarok,* however, a great deal of Sørensen's work is exclusive and demanding, a fact reflected in sales of *Strange Stories*: the 1,500-copy first run did not sell out until ten years later. Sørensen is one of the most well-read and internationally oriented writers in contemporary Scandinavia, and his insights into the human condition are founded on an expert knowledge of ancient as well as modern European intellectual tradition, as even a cursory reading of *Tutelary Tales* would reveal. They and his other stories are permeated with allusions to the Bible, folk ballads, tales, legends, and mythology. His other intellectual pursuits likewise reflect his international orientation and his influence. For example, when from 1959 to 1963 he edited the literary journal *Vindrosen* (*The Compass*) with Klaus Rifbjerg (1931–), it was instrumental in introducing European modernism to Denmark. A general understanding of his background, then, as well as of the range and depth of his intellectual interests, is necessary to have at hand in order to apprehend fully the artistry and significance of *Tutelary Tales*.

Although Sørensen is truly an individualistic author, he has roots in his native literature. From the beginning of his career, Sørensen demonstrated his affinity with other Danish writers of the 1950s: Leif Panduro (1923–77), Peter Seeberg (1925–), and Ole Sarvig (1921–81). With Panduro he shares the theme of spiritual and psychological schism vs. inner harmony and the theme of repression vs. liberation; with Seeberg he shares a predilection for myth, fairy tale, and the fantastic; and with Sarvig he holds the conviction that only through art can life be fully interpreted. These writers have in common—together with Franz Kafka, their source of inspiration—a view of reality as something external and objective as well as a mirror of the identity crisis and fragmented consciousness of modern man. Sørensen has shown his indebtedness to Danish epic and philosophic tradition as well as an affinity with his contemporaries. He couples the allegory and irony of Karen Blixen (pseudonym Isak Dinesen; 1885–1962) with the apparently naíve tone of tales by his favorite writer, Hans Christian Andersen (1805–75), tales that, like Sørensen's stories, are in fact sophisticated symbolic interpretations of our existence. In addition, he shares with Andersen an ability to discover seemingly paradoxical interrelationships in the trivialities of the external world, even transforming that world into a miraculous "fairy tale" universe. Another Danish source of inspiration for Sørensen is the philosophy of Søren Kierkegaard (1813–55), whose *Begrebet Angest* (*The Concept of Dread,* 1844) Sørensen edited in 1960. Kierkegaard's concept of freedom and liberation particularly interests Sørensen. In his words, liberation becomes a release from that which is still repressed within us and under guardianship.

The European sources of Sørensen's inspiration are many, but for the most part he found his major sources in German literature, predominantly in the works of Franz Kafka (1883–1924), about whom he wrote an in-depth analysis (*Kafkas digtning* [*The Works of Kafka,* 1968]), and of Thomas Mann (1875–1955). Kafka's bizarre allegorical tales of absurdity and repression, forces that threaten our complete self-development and lead to our total incapacitation, and Mann's ironic retelling of biblical myths, characterized by paradox and shocking profanity, become the models for the legends, which together with the fairy tales, are Sørensen's favorite modes of expression. In the works of the Austrian writer Hermann Broch (1886–1951), Sørensen discovered the concept of "the breakdown of values": a system of values capable of bridging today's gap between the life of the instincts and that of the intellect no longer exists. Sørensen scrutinizes the complex of problems posed by this "breakdown" in his collection of essays *Uden mål—og med* (*Without Design—and With,* 1973), but modern psychoanalysis, especially C. G. Jung's formulation and amplification of its theories, offers the point of departure for his discussing this gap on a more personal and existential level.

Sørensen constantly searches for the archetypal structures in life, particularly the transition from the child's secure universe to the adult's insecure one. Puberty becomes our first real confrontation with ourselves and therefore can determine whether we choose to enter life as wards or to take responsibility as warders—guardians—not of others but of ourselves. Sørensen's entire body of work can be interpreted as a unified attempt to analyze this archetypal conflict on psychological, social, and philosophical levels as he tries to reconcile the old and now rejected interpretation of life with a new one. Such a reconciliation can bridge the gap, and integration can replace rejection and repression.

Sørensen's writings span an extremely broad spectrum, ranging from literary criticism and commentaries on the contemporary political scene to philosophical essays and translations (of Seneca, Erasmus of Rotterdam, Kafka, and Hermann Broch). His criticism began with *Digtere og Dæmoner* (*Writers and Demons,* 1959); here he juxtaposes two of his favorite writers, Hans Christian Andersen and Søren Kierkegaard, and analyzes the necessarily close interrelationship between art and philosophy. He deals with the new role of art as a critic of modern society after the so-called breakdown of values, and he devotes chapters to Thomas Mann and Hermann Broch as he deals with the problem of the modern spiritual and psychological schism. The same problem receives its final probing through an analysis of some medieval ballads, an analysis that has had a profound and lasting impact on Danish ballad scholarship.

In contrast to his earlier essays, Sørensen's 1961 collection *Hverken-eller* (*Neither-Nor*) concentrates on psychological liberation rather than on the schism, and Sørensen grounds his discussion in Kierkegaardian philosophy. This change of focus leads him to a political preoccupation that manifests itself both in his work as a regular contributor to the socialist weekly *Politisk Revy* (*Political Review*) during the mid 1960s and in subsequent book-length publications. His political involvement reaches a climax in the controversial bestseller and political program *Oprør fra midten* (*Revolt from the Center,* 1978; English trans. Boyars, 1981), which Sørensen co-authored, as well as in his collection of essays entitled *Den gyldne middelvej* (*The Golden Mean,* 1979). In both works, Sørensen favors a revolt for the sake of all humanity in order to achieve near-democracy, comparable pay, and solidarity. He expresses a utopian and perhaps somewhat naïve belief in human nature that, in the course of a fierce public debate, gave rise to accusations of his totalitarianism, a political view as far removed from Sørensen's as is possible to get. But despite the impact of those two books, it is the earlier volume *Mellem fortid og fremtid* (*Between Past and Future,* 1969) that contains the essays that are particularly important for a thorough understanding of Sørensen's philosophy and thus his work in general. They are concerned with the urgent need for humanity to build a bridge between past and future, between old concepts and new ones. It is precisely when our actions no longer correspond to past ideals that new ones emerge in a dialectical process that by no means necessitates a rejection of all traditions. On the contrary, anything and everything that furthers and preserves humanity must be considered. Such things, such concepts, can indeed be utopian, but they must nevertheless reflect humanity's nature rather than a preconceived and preordained social system. Furthermore, the artist's task is to introduce and give expression to these concepts.

These very issues are likewise treated in Sørensen's monographs *Nietzsche* (1963), *Schopenhauer* (1965), and *Seneca* (1976), each of which constitutes a reevaluation of philosophers who, like Sørensen himself, regard art and philosophy taken together as the only medium capable of bearing the burden of our existence. Society must adapt itself to us, not the other way around. Professing a strong belief in the ethical quality of human nature, Sørensen rejects both the Marxist principles of historical development and the liberalist adherence to the forces of free play; he favors a "revolt from the center" or "the golden mean."

Sørensen's critical, political, and philosophical writings point toward a coherent world view, a view that in some ways finds its most compelling and most elusive embodiment in his short stories. There schism vs. harmony and repression vs. liberation constitute his major themes. People realize that they are not, in fact, in complete harmony with themselves. Sørensen depicts their subsequent attempts to either overcome or repress their spiritual and psychological division, with all the traumatic repercussions that might entail. Our attitude toward these traumas is a common theme in Sørensen's first two collections, *Strange Stories* (1953) and *Ufarlige Historier* (*Safe Stories,* 1955). In the first our supposed instincts are symbolized by tigers in an allegorical tale entitled "Tigrene" ("The Tigers"). Like Ionesco's rhinoceroses, they suddenly invade what has been an ordinary life. One solution to the threat they represent would be to try to liberate them—a solution hinted at when the hero, Fif, upon encountering a tiger in his mother's kitchen, wonders if it might not be an enchanted prince. Rather than explore this possibility, however, Fif lures the tigers to imprisonment in the zoo. Subsequently he, like the Pied Piper of Hamlin, becomes the target of the populace's wrath when they realize that they really do not want to live without tigers, despite the dangers they pose; it is thus in a sense more convenient to live with one's conflicts than to attempt to overcome them. Liberation from trauma does not seem possible within the value system described in the tale itself, and it appears equally impossible in our own society. Fif, who actually represents the figure of the artist, simply *reflects* upon the tigers, falling short of fulfilling his (or any artist's) task by failing to *interpret*—in other words, to liberate.

The fateful consequence of the tension resulting from the division between instinctual and intellectual life is illustrated in "Duo" from *Safe Stories.* "Duo," the name of a pair of Siamese twins, is encountered by the narrator at a conference, where all the intellectuals of the world are gathered to discover truth. Duo is, in fact, Truth itself; but since the conference participants do not want to see the truth from both sides, they promptly operate on the twins and thereby separate them so that only the front part, that part which is most presentable, can be seen. The second half, rejected and thus isolated, is now every bit as dangerous as the tigers. Finally confronted by it, the narrator winds up being literally stabbed by truth in the form of Duo's hidden half.

Many of Sørensen's stories depend on similar techniques to symbolically divide a character, as with the character of Otto (the name itself a palindrome) in "De to tvillinger" ("The Two Twins"), or with the adaptation of the Cain and Abel myth in "Mordsagen" ("The Murder Case"), both from *Strange Stories,* or with the two brothers in "Vidunderbarnet" ("The Wonder Child") also from *Strange Stories.* The technique becomes particularly apparent in *Tutelary Tales,* as in the legends of Judas/Jesus or Nero/Paul and in the science fiction story starring Philip Rose/the President. The three volumes of stories share the same poetic universe as well: Sørensen creates this universe by projecting the present into either the past or the future, leaving us with an abstract, timeless, Kafkaesque mythic, or a distorted historical milieu.

Several of the earlier stories touch upon the theme of guardianship, in particular "Købmanden" ("The Merchant") from *Safe Stories,* whose title character by just looking at his customers can see exactly what they need, and forces that upon them instead of what they ask for. With *Tutelary Tales,* however, a significant shift in emphasis is noticeable, for Sørensen moves from a preoccupation with the problems of repression and trauma to a discourse on the dangers of abusive power. The volume's epigraph hints at the possibility, indeed the necessity, of complete freedom: the liberating process is effected either through direct action or through artistic activity, an obligation that Fif failed to honor.

In *Tutelary Tales,* the role of the guardian, who with the very best of intentions makes decisions for others and thereby deprives them of their freedom to decide for themselves, is given a more general philosophical and visionary perspective in the first and last tales. "A Tale of Glass" parallels Hans Christian Andersen's "The Snow Queen," and in it, Sørensen's skepticism about even the possibility of experiencing truth seems bottomless, as the opening lines indicate: "Listen! Now we are going to begin. When we get to the end of the story we shall know no more than we do now. . . ." But we do know more. We know that the catastrophic influences of the vicious circle he describes are inevitable. The glass through which "anything evil and ugly" looks beautiful (in glaring contrast to what happens in Andersen's tale) ultimately makes everybody blind as their glasses are made increasingly strong in order to preserve the pleasant illusion. "That was the beginning of the end," warns Sørensen on the first page. On the other hand, the volume's concluding tale, "A Tale of the Future," hints at a possible way to break the vicious circle. This tale is a variation on the Oedipus legend. Filius discovers that he is able to defy the prophecies and not kill his father, the country's dictatorial president, and thus realizes that he is actually master over life as well as death. He gains this freedom the very instant he learns both to understand and to interpret his own situation and act accordingly, when he, in a Kierkegaardian sense, chooses himself and becomes his *own* guardian.

In three bewildering, indeed almost surrealistic, "Tales the Guardian has to Tell," Sørensen focuses on the relationship between guardian and ward in a series of episodes not strictly bound to any particular historical period. Here the guardian falls victim to his own unbridled power, turning more or less deliberately into his own ward. The attitudes toward guardianship in these tales all express various value systems on the verge of collapse and in need of replacement by something new, something better. Emperor Frederick III of Hapsburg (1415–93), the narrator of "The History of a Guardianship" as well as "The Guardian's Tale," tends to exhibit extreme perspicacity but seems not fully aware of the impending collapse of his value system. While on the surface the Emperor's account seems to be a documentary text—Sørensen has even included a bibliography—the convoluted and artfully subtle tale reveals itself to be quite an intriguing analysis of the psychology of power, and in the final account a crushing self-judgment. He describes in detail his relationship with his cousin and ward, the young Sigmund, as well as his attempts to govern an empire that can but for a short time be held together. The Emperor, though admittedly with a slight tone of resignation, still holds claim to the rights of his well-intentioned guardianship and the propriety of his "house rules." Nonetheless, he, who had once himself been a ward, has in effect become a veritable prisoner to his own role as guardian.

The same set of problems, though without a similarly direct political perspective, is dealt with in "The Boss," a portrait of a man who is tormented both by his own position as boss and by a mysterious young man whom he finally strikes down. The boss is not merely a victim of harassment, though; like the Emperor, he is a prisoner of his own power. The boss is simultaneously a guardian and a ward, since the young man is nothing less than a representation of the boss's repressed youth. Here the resignation of Emperor Frederick has, to be sure, been replaced by at least an attempt at rebellion. The boss's attempt results, however, only in yet another repression rather than in the hoped-for liberation.

Similarly, the title character of "The Wicked Judas," a legend that is reminiscent of both the Cain and Oedipus myths, is a prisoner of his own fate and of the role that world history has forced upon him as a necessary foil to the figure of Jesus. Adrian and Natalia, too, in the volume's third, rather blasphemous and grotesque legend, are caught in their roles as slaves to Christianity's demand for suffering and sacrifice. Patroclus in "Emperor and Apostle" falls victim to the guardianship of Nero and Paul, because of their lack of agreement on a definition of love. It is the same love that Emperor Frederick, in a quite illusory fashion, maintains that he exercises, without once realizing that one cannot be the guardian both of one's neighbor and of one's kingdom.

With "Emperor and Apostle," Sørensen resumes his discussion of repression and trauma. Paul and Nero are "twins," as are Duo and Jesus and Judas. Like the latter two, Paul and Nero respectively represent the spirit and the flesh. As is the case with Duo, the other pairs must eventually succumb to that fateful schism that in our culture lies between instinct and intellect and that Sørensen has diagnosed as the tragic condition of our civilization. Patroclus must die in "Emperor and Apostle," but even Nero and Paul can only play out their preassigned roles. These were given to them by a certain system of values, as were the roles of Jesus, Judas, Adrian, and the Emperor of those men. None of them is actually the guardian he believes himself to be, but is instead a ward.

The requisite rebellion against a system that has become chronically static, and therefore destructive, fails completely for the young girl in "Bird in Maid's Guise," a virtually demonic version of a medieval Danish ballad. Unable to liberate herself from her own fears, she winds up escaping into a tree as an owl, a prisoner of a trauma from which she cannot break free. Elna in "The Foster Daughter," on the other hand, succeeds in escaping from her particular trauma, a childhood spent in the far-off country she had to leave, or, more specifically, childhood itself. Pessimism prevails once more, however, in the modern legend "The Screamer." While on the surface this appears to be the story of a pop star destroyed by his environment, it in fact represents a political documentation of the killing of a messianic figure. Nor is the protagonist in "In Strange Country" successful in providing us, or himself, with redemption. Originally having entered a country of truly Kafkaesque proportions, at the same time tangible yet unreal, with the professed intent of killing its dictator, the stranger gradually becomes a victim himself. Under grotesque circumstances, he, the herald of freedom, is involuntarily roped into marriage, becoming responsible for a large family. He has been trapped into the very same role as that of the dictator. He too has become a guardian. This stranger could perhaps also be interpreted as symbolic of the modern artist, unable to carry out his great task of liberating mankind through his creativity. His actions are thus rendered impotent, and even language, his only other means of communication, seems to fail him. Though according to his dictionary a hotel is "a hotel," he is nevertheless unable to find lodging, and the people he meets are apparently either deaf and dumb or completely incapable of understanding him. Even the stranger himself seems to choose to not understand the language he attempts to acquire.

Villy Sørensen thus offers no guarantees that the vicious circle of guardianship can be broken. At times it can lead to destruction (as with Patroclus, Judas, and Adrian); at others it is repressed and becomes traumatic (as in "Bird in Maid's Guise" and "The Boss"). But loyal to his firm grounding in European humanistic tradition, which is not content with mere interpretation but is eager to act and to point out new avenues of future exploration, Sørensen manages to strike a note of hopefulness in the last tale of the volume. For what the protagonist of "In Strange Country" cannot achieve, Filius in "A Tale of the Future" can. He does *not* kill his father, but in breaking the law reorganizes the country for the better. Some doubt does, nevertheless, make itself known when Sørensen concludes the story rather ambiguously: "Shortly afterwards the President was re-elected for another five-year term." Might the son perhaps follow in his father's footsteps? Might he become a new guardian? As Sørensen has demonstrated in "The History of a Guardianship," power inevitably corrupts, and a definitive interpretation or judgment of these tales' meaning is impossible to achieve.

Tutelary Tales, a difficult and compelling book whose techniques range from stream of consciousness to allegory to symbolism, summarizes Villy Sørensen's literary as well as philosophical authorship. Consequently, although the stories sometimes seem only tenuously connected, they should be read and understood as a carefully constructed unity, a unity that Sørensen himself has outlined thus:

The book is not just a collection of stories, but chapters in the history of the European psyche. The first half is a regression, a recoiling from unsolved problems, ranging from today's society without a central value, through centralized medieval society in the process of dissolution, all the way back to ancient times and the roots of evil, the spiritual schism that "Duo" was all about. The twins Jesus/Judas are here projected into Paul/Nero, and so the world falls apart. This division is then followed through to the present, and so on to the future, which still suffers from the fixations of Antiquity. (Clausen, 30)

While the journey through the ages that is the *Tutelary Tales* may not entirely liberate us from those fixations, it can help us realize that they exist. That, in itself, is a kind of liberation.

BIBLIOGRAPHY

Baggesen, Søren. "Villy Sørensen." In *Modernismen i dansk litteratur* ("Modernism in Danish Literature"), ed. Jørn Vosmar, 125–36. Copenhagen: Fremad, 1967.

Brandt, Jørgen Gustava. *Præsentation* ("Presentation"), 154–58. Copenhagen: Gyldendal, 1964.

Clausen, Claus. *Digtere i forhør 1966* ("Writers Interrogated"), 11–34. Copenhagen: Gyldendal, 1966.

Franzén, Lars-Olof. *Danska bilder. Punktnedslag i dansk litteratur 1880–1970* ("Danish Pictures: Spot Checks in Danish Literature, 1880–1970"), 117–26. Stockholm: Wahlström & Widstrand, 1971.

Jensen, Jørgen Bonde. *Litterær arkæologi. Studier i Villy Sørensens Formynderfortællinger* ("Literary Archaeology: Studies in Villy Sørensen's *Tutelary Tales*"). Copenhagen: Gyldendal, 1978.

Krarup, Søren. Filosoffen ("The Philosopher"). In *Demokratisme. En kritik* ("Democratism: A Critique"), 67–101. Copenhagen: Gyldendal, 1968.

Lundkvist, Artur. "Motsatsernas diktare" ("A Writer of Contrasts"). In *Utflykter med utländska forfattare.* ("Excursions with Foreign Writers"), 42–52. Stockholm: Aldus/Bonnier, 1969.

Øhrgaard, Per. "Villy Sørensen." In *Danske Digtere i det 20. århundrede* ("Danish Writers of the Twentieth Century"), ed. Torben Brostrøm and Mette Winge, vol. 4, 43–64. Copenhagen: Gad, 1982.

Petersen, Ulrich Horst. "Om (nogle af) Villy Sørensens historier" ("About [some of] Villy Sørensen's Stories"). In *Frihed og Tabu* ("Freedom and Taboo"), 108–66. Copenhagen: Gyldendal, 1971.

Sønderiis, Ebbe. *Villy Sørensen. En ideologikritisk analyse* ("Villy Sørensen: An Ideological-critical Analysis"). Grenå: GMT, 1972.

Other volumes in the series
Modern Scandinavian Literature
in Translation include:

Knut Faldbakken, *Adam's Diary*.
Translated by Sverre Lyngstad.

P. C. Jersild, *Children's Island*.
Translated by Joan Tate.

P. C. Jersild, *House of Babel*.
Translated by Joan Tate.

Dea Trier Mørch, *Evening Star*.
Translated by Joan Tate.

Dea Trier Mørch, *Winter's Child*.
Translated by Joan Tate.

August Strindberg, *The Roofing Ceremony* and *The Silver Lake*.
Translated by David Mel Paul and Margareta Paul.

Henrik Tikkanen, *The Thirty Years' War*. Translated by George Blecher and Lone Thygesen Blecher.